THE WREN

A KING SISTERS NOVEL

THE LAS VEGAS LOVE DUET
BOOK 1

PENELOPE BLACK

*for the girls who feel like they
always have to be strong*

AUTHOR'S NOTE

Please note that The Wren is a dark mafia romance and has some darker themes some readers may find triggering.

Please message me if you have any questions: author.penelope. black@gmail.com
Happy reading!

PLAYLIST

"Exit Music (For a Film)" by Radiohead
"The Beach" by The Neighborhood
"In The Kitchen" by Renée Rapp
"Killer + The Sound" by Phoebe Bridgers, Noah Gundersen,
Abby Gundersen
"Shut Up Kiss Me" by Angel Olsen
"Bird" by Billie Marten
"Don't You Wait" by CLOVES
"Deep End" by Holly Humberstone
"Two of Us on the Run" by Lucius
"Flume" by Lotte Kestner
"Possibility" by Lykke Li
"Wait" by M83
"Cold" by Jorge Méndez
"Fragile N.4" by Dustin O'Halloran
"Skinny Love" by Birdy
"Wings" by Birdy

PROLOGUE

MAEVE, 12 years old

"C'MON, MAE. I'M HUNGRY."

I press my index finger to my lips and give my seven-year-old sister my best impression of Mum's glare.

She pouts at me, her adorable button nose scrunching up and her lips pressing together.

I crouch down and place my lips next to her ear. "Don't you want to win, Rosie?"

She nods, her wild dark-red hair tickling my nose.

"Then we have to get to the front of the store before Mum's done shopping for groceries. Follow my lead, okay?"

She nods again and slips her sticky hand into mine. Ugh, I knew she didn't wash her hands after her popsicle today.

Whatever, I'm not about to let a little red popsicle stain stop me from winning. Mum always gives me the hardest challenges and Rosie's *always* my partner. She calls us her bookends. I'm the oldest of five girls and Rosie's the baby of the family.

The rain makes a different sort of noise as it hits the roof of our local grocery store. Less like the white noise machine my sister still sleeps with and more like a hammering. It reminds me of the summer we spent at my mum's parents' house, working on their farm.

I stop at the end of the aisle, scanning left and right before huffing out a heavy breath. My cheeks puff up like a blowfish, and Rosie giggles, nudging one with her finger. I let the air escape my lips and smile at her.

I let my smile settle into a more neutral expression and look at her. "Alright. There are three people checking out that we have to make it by without being seen. Then we're in the clear. What do we do?"

Her eyebrows scrunch down low over her eyes as she stares ahead. "We sneak down the second aisle. There's no one there, and it's three registers away from someone."

I bob my head in encouragement. "Good job. Let's go."

We follow her plan, making it to the automatic sliding glass door without being seen.

"Yes! We're first!" she squeals.

I tug on her hand still gripping mine, but I don't bother stopping the slow grin from spreading across my face. I knew we would make it before everyone else.

It takes another five minutes before the rest of my sisters reach the vestibule. Mum pushes the cart behind them, stopping in the middle of of us, a smile as wide as the sun stretching across her face.

"You girls did so well today. All of you." Mum makes it a point to give each of us her undivided attention as she talks. Like usual, my sisters and I flock to her, crowding around the cart full of groceries.

"Did you see that, Mum? Did you?" Rosie bounces on her toes.

"I sure did, Rosie." Mum smiles at my youngest sister. Her

favorite pink lipstick is still perfectly in place. It makes her teeth look bright under these halogen lights.

Rosie straightens her shoulders and drops my hand. She tips her chin up and looks around at all of us. "That's because Maeve is teaching me how to be the best, and pretty soon, I'm going to be the best. Even better than all of my sisters."

I bite the inside of my cheek to stifle the laughter that wants to bubble up. I don't want to make her feel bad, but she's only seven and I'm nearly thirteen. There's no way she's gonna be better than me.

Mum calls us her little birds, says we're the best when we work together. She's always coming up with activities and adventures for us to do, like sneaking through an entire grocery store without being seen by anyone.

She says I'm one of the best she's ever seen, even more clever than she was at my age. And she would know too because she's been playing these spy games since *she* was a little girl. She's told us countless stories about her and Aunt Molly and Uncle Oliver playing all kinds of games Grandpa Charlie came up with.

Keira and Ava, my Irish-twin sisters laugh, but neither of them contradict Rosie.

Mum leans over and tucks a lock of Rosie's wild red hair behind her ear. "That's right, my little dove. You can be anything you want. Now, since you all did an amazing job today, I got everyone a treat."

She smiles like it isn't something she does every time we play these games. Personally, I think it's a great idea that everybody wins.

I still remember two years ago when Fiona and Keira got into an argument over a game of spies. Mum declared Keira the winner, but Fiona swore it should've been her. It turned into a fight that lasted a whole week. Da even went to stay with a friend for a few days, claiming there were too many women under one roof.

Now he's barely home, so I guess there are still too many women under one roof for him.

Mum leans over the handle of the cart and reaches into one of the many brown paper bags. "Now, where did he put those?"

She mumbles something too low for me to hear under her breath, but I see the smile curling the corner of her mouth from this angle. She flashes me a wink.

She's totally playing with us. I fold my arms across my chest and watch her.

"Ah ha!" Mum stands abruptly, a box of mini ice cream cones in her hand. She wiggles the colorful box around with a flourish. "Now how does everyone feel about a small treat before we head home?"

"Before dinner?" Keira's eyes are wide and locked onto the box.

Mum tears one flap of the box and gives us all one of her conspiratorial smiles.

I mouth the words at the same time she says, "Don't tell your da." She winks at us. "Besides, it's summertime. Shouldn't I get to spoil my girls when I have them home with me for a whole summer?"

"Chocolate?" Rosie asks.

Mum scoffs, but it's playful. "Of course, there's chocolate. What kind of mother would I be if I didn't get my little flock chocolate ice cream?"

Rosie claps her hands together a few times, keeping her arms close to her chest as she bounces on the toes of her sandals. "I love those, Mum. They're my favorite."

"Well, I don't like chocolate ice cream," Ava says as she shifts her weight onto one foot.

Mum reaches into the box and pulls out a white package. "I know that, lovey, that's why I got the variety box."

Ava raises a brow. "With caramel?"

Mum wiggles the package in front of her face, and Ava snatches it with a quick snap of her wrist. She tears open the package and laughs. I guess it must be the caramel flavor.

I tune out the voices of my sisters debating the best ice cream flavor for the millionth time and let my attention drift to the parking lot. I don't really have a preference, so I usually eat whatever's left.

It's raining like crazy. I don't remember Mum saying anything about a thunderstorm. She's usually pretty good about giving us a heads up because some of my sisters still get afraid.

Not me though. I like thunderstorms. Sometimes when Mum's not home, Da will let me sit in the garage and watch the lightning streak across the sky.

I've always enjoyed the sound of rain. It quiets all the thoughts buzzing in my head like bees.

There's something that sounds different about this rain. It sounds angry, almost like some sort of thundering pulse, like the kind of music that plays in a scary movie.

The box of ice cream in front of my face cuts off my view of the parking lot. My gaze shifts to her smiling face.

"There are two left, lovey. Which one do you want?"

I lift a shoulder. "It doesn't matter to me. I'll take either."

Mum hands me a white package. "You did good today, Maeve."

I take the ice cream cone from her and tear open the package. "Thanks."

She squeezes my shoulder. "I mean it. I'm proud of you."

Her gentle praise isn't uncommon, but still, it fills my chest with warmth. "Thanks, Mum. Rosie almost blew it back in aisle ten, but I saved us."

Mum chuckles. "I'm not surprised. Your sister is a touch wild."

I lift my shoulder and take a bite of ice cream. "She's still young. She'll learn."

She tucks a strand of hair that slipped free from my braid behind my ear. "With you looking out for her? I have no doubt she will. They all will, Maeve. You're turning into a wonderful young lady—and an even better spy than me."

Ha! I knew it, I crow inside my chest. I don't interrupt her though.

"And I know that you'll always be there for your sisters, help them when they need it. I'm so, so proud of you." Her eyes get a little bit glassy like they do whenever she watches those cheesy movies on TV.

Goosebumps scatter down my arms and I pull the ice cream cone away. "Are you okay?"

My hair falls from her fingers as she straightens up. Her smile is a little less sincere than a moment before. "I've got my babies and ice cream, and a great summer storm. What more do I need?"

I nod a slow dip of my chin and watch her out of the corner of my eye as I take another bite of my vanilla cone.

"Okay, girls, I'll run and get the car, so you have until I pull up to finish your ice cream. Your da would have my hide if we dirtied up the car so quickly after he cleaned it."

"It looks really nasty out, Mum. Maybe you should wait with us for a few more minutes," Ava says as she eats half of her cone in one bite.

Mum fishes her keys out of her oversized black purse and flips up the hood of her lightweight gray zip-up sweatshirt. "I'm not going to melt, but the other box of ice cream cones will if we don't get them home and in the freezer." She pauses and looks over her shoulder at me. "Maeve, look after your sisters."

6

"Why's Maeve always in charge?" Fiona's face scrunches up with distaste. "I'm almost eleven. I can be in charge too."

Mum places a kiss on Fiona's forehead with a smile. "You're right. You can help your sister watch the little girls, alright?"

Fiona's eyebrows settle back down and she nods as she finishes her cone.

I crumple up my wrapper and toss it into the nearby garbage can as the automatic doors slide open. Mum dashes into the parking lot.

Wind carries raindrops inside the vestibule, and Rosie squeals. She skips over to me, ice cream dripping down the corner of her mouth. I'm not even a little surprised at the way her palm sticks to mine. Still, I just tighten my fingers around hers.

Thunder rumbles, and a flash of lightning streaks across the sky. It illuminates the entire parking lot in a brilliant yellow light.

Thunder grumbles again, but headlights steal my attention from watching Mum run toward the car. They're bright white, flashing directly into the vestibule and blinding me.

My sisters groan and complain about the light, but I tune them out. I hold my free hand up to shield the light from my eyes in time to see Mum stop right next to the bumper of our car.

She turns to face the car with the headlights shining, and I imagine her giving them directions or something. She's always doing that—helping strangers.

Thunder rips through the air, two quick booms.

My mum drops her purse and clutches her chest.

My heart pounds against my ribcage, a terrified rhythm that screams at me for action.

"Hey, what happened to Mum?" Ava asks, her voice small.

Mum drops to her knees and looks toward us. She's too far away to make out anything she's saying, but I think her lips are moving. I imagine her screaming our names.

"We have to go help her," Fiona shouts. She takes two steps toward the door before I lunge for her.

I curl my fingers around her bicep and pull her back. "No, Fi, no. We have to go. Now."

"Are you crazy? We have to help Mum! She's hurt!" Keira looks at me like I'm crazy.

And maybe I am, because it looks like the car's headlights get bigger and brighter. Like it's getting closer—*too* close.

Something inside my brain switches, and before I fully realize what I'm doing, I'm dragging my sisters behind me as we slink back through the grocery store.

"No, we have to go to one of the places Mum showed us, just like we've practiced. But this time, we all stick together, okay?" My words come out in a harsh whisper.

When I hear a crash from the front of the store, I give up the idea of being unseen and start running, holding tight to Rosie's hand.

My sisters follow behind me as I push open the emergency exit and run into the pouring rain. I look over my shoulder to make sure they're still with me, Mum's last words echoing around my brain with every footfall.

Look after your sisters.

Protect your sisters.

1

NICO

"I'VE FOUND YOUR WIFE."

I pause in front of the wet bar on the sidewall of my office in one of our nightclubs, Violet Oak. I don't bother responding to my father just yet. I need something to settle my nerves. I thought my fucking heart was going to explode out of my chest when my father walked in my club ten minutes ago.

My long-lost sister, Madison, and her men were scattered around the private level of our club and the dance floor. They were here on my assurances that they'd be safe.

But not only that—I'm trying to build a relationship with her, and I'll be damned if Vito Santorini is going to ruin one of the last good things in my life. Again.

Fucking hell—they wouldn't have even been in Las Vegas if I hadn't given my sister's men my word that our father was out of town on business. And then that asshole strolls in like he owns the place, and I looked like a fucking fool.

There's little in this life I despise more than looking like a fool.

Fuck.

I exhale and resist the urge to stretch my neck from side to side to release the tension.

My executive office is on the third floor, and it's a sharp contrast to the dimly-lit levels of the club below. Light gray walls with charcoal gray accents, wrought-iron up-light sconces make the room feel larger with their beams of white light.

My desk sits to the right, and a large dark hard-backed leather chair behind hit. Two safes flank the desk to the right, and black leather plush chairs in front of it.

"Did you hear me, son? I said I've found your new wife."

I nod my head, an acknowledgement that I heard him and nothing more.

"Let's wait until Rome is here." I make sure to keep my voice even. I learned a long time ago it's best not to needle Dad when he's worked up like this. It never ends well for anyone.

I grab four old fashioned glasses from the shelf next to me and line them up. I splash three fingers of my favorite barrel-aged sixty-proof whiskey in all four glasses. Pinching the edges of two glasses between my fingers and thumbs, I turn around and hand my father his drink first as a sign of respect.

I set my brother Tommy's glass in his open palm and leave our youngest brother Rome's drink on the edge of my desk. "Rome should be up here in a minute."

Dad sips his drink, but he's unable to wipe the excitement from his face. I haven't seen him this excited in a long time, so it must be something really good.

"And where is your brother, Romeo?"

Sneaking our sister and her men out of the back door.

"Probably fucking someone in one of the private rooms on the second floor," Tommy drawls.

Dad grins, his mouth stretched too wide. "I bet you make a

killing on those private rooms, eh, son? This is the city of sin, after all."

I catch his innuendo, but I do my best to not think about my father using private rooms all over this city with his many, many mistresses.

"We do alright." I sip my drink and look out of the tinted window to the levels below. To anyone down there who happens to look up, all they see is an iridescent window.

Dad puffs out his chest, his chin tipped high. "So modest, my eldest. It's why you're so successful."

I swipe the droplets of whiskey on my lower lip with my tongue, enjoying the sharp sting of the alcohol in the back of my throat. My gaze narrows on my father as unease churns in my stomach. He's untrustworthy on the best of days, and I can count on one hand the times he's ever given me a compliment.

He's buttering me up for something.

Just as silence begins to stretch between us like a thick fog, the door opens.

"Ah, perfect timing as always, son," Dad says.

Rome closes the door and beelines to my desk, veering toward his drink in one corner. "What did I miss?"

"Now we can begin. I came home early to tell you the great news: I've found Nico's wife." His words slice through the mounting tension like a scalpel, doubling it. He pauses and stares at us with a self-satisfied smirk.

No one speaks.

The heat of our father's rage swells within the room as the silence stretches like taffy.

I genuinely don't know what to say. I lean my hip against the wall and watch the anger play out over my father's reddening face.

Maybe I've been a bit over-served tonight, not that I would

admit that to anyone, because I'm not nearly as concerned with him right now.

Or more likely, Tommy told the bartenders to pour with a heavy hand tonight to celebrate.

"What the fuck does that mean?" Tommy finally asks what the three of us are all thinking.

I'm still stuck on the fact that Dad cut his business trip short by five days. Guilt gnaws at my frayed nerve endings. I would've never forgiven myself if Dad ambushed our sister tonight.

The scorn in Tommy's voice is palpable as Dad turns his piercing gaze on my brother. He burrows one hand into the pocket of his black slacks, the other firmly cradling his drink to his stomach. Dad makes a show of pacing around my office, stopping in front of the window to leer at the revelers dispelling their inhibitions on the dance floor.

It's all an act.

He doesn't care about the people or the club. We own it and manage it ourselves, something that's always offended him. As if we wanted to be stuck under our father's thumb for the rest of our lives.

I don't know what made him angrier: the fact that we didn't buy him into the business or that it's legit.

"It means that I've secured an alliance for us. One that's going to expand our operations tenfold," he says with his back to us, his gaze still out the window.

Now I know that I've had too much to drink, because it takes me longer than it should to connect the dots.

"An arranged marriage. That's what you meant about a wife." It's not a question.

Dad spins on his heel, his face lighting up with genuine glee. About the prospect of *more*—as if we need more money or men or territory or fucking stress in our lives. We have enough wealth to last us several generations over.

But Vito Santorini is a selfish, greedy man. And the boss of the west coast Outfit. It's a deadly combination.

"Yes, son. Think of all we can achieve together once we cement this alliance." His eyes dance with excitement, and I can't recall the last time I saw him this excited. Not even when he recently saw our sister—his daughter—for the first time in fifteen years.

"You've never pushed this before. Why now?" Tommy asks.

Dad clenches his jaw and glares at Tommy before switching his gaze to me. "Arranged marriage isn't uncommon in our life, you know that."

I nod a few times. "Aye, I do. But Tommy's right. Why now? What else is going on?"

His greed and desire to grow the family business? Sure, that I buy. But this sudden arranged marriage proposal that isn't needed to grow? I'm not buying it.

He waves a hand around the air in front of him, batting our questions away like they're gnats. "As I was saying, negotiations went exceptionally well, and in two months' time, our two families will be joined. Then, my son, we'll be one step closer to unstoppable."

Rome leans forward in his chair. "Which family?"

"Is there a contract?" I ask at the same time, my voice low and tight.

My gut churns with growing dread as my dad's plan begins to take shape—one that involves me marrying a woman I've never met. The thought is enough to have me feeling a little murderous. It's an unexpected feeling.

"Of course. But before you ask, no, you don't get to see it."

I tense. "Why?" I can't think of one good reason why he'd keep the contract—the name of my soon-to-be wife—from me.

"Eager to find your bride?" He leers at me, and that earlier feeling of apprehension rises.

So I do what I always do and play along.

I force my expression into something closer to his and lift a shoulder. "You know me, Dad."

He claps me on the shoulder. "All in due time, son."

2

MAEVE

"QUICK, slap me, Ava, because I must be dreaming. There's no way on this gorgeous green earth that our da would actually sell us," my sister Keira says. I'm surprised that she only sounds a touch crazed and not nearly as bad as I imagined.

"Ugh, I'm not slapping you. Besides, Maeve wouldn't lie about that," Ava says.

Keira and Ava are Irish twins in the truest sense: born eleven months apart. Though the age gap between all of us isn't much larger than that. Seems to me like Mum was trying to create her own volleyball team.

I flip the page of the home décor magazine without really looking at anything. "I'm not lying. And he's not selling us."

"Well, what would you call it?" Keira snaps.

"An arranged marriage," I deadpan.

"Hell," Ava says at the same time as me.

I look over at her from underneath my lashes. My nineteen-year-old sister and I share the most characteristics out of all the King women. My hair leans more toward the darkest shades of brown that look nearly black and Ava's is rich like decadent chocolate.

But we have the same eyes. Grey like the sky on an early spring morning.

Mum's eyes.

"Why the hell would Da sign a contract for you to marry some asshole you've never met anyway?" Keira throws her arms out wide before letting them fall to her thighs with a slap.

"I don't know. Power, money, a favor." I flip another page, the color teal jumping out at me.

"He already has power, and we don't need money." Keira folds her arms across her chest tightly.

Ava tilts her head to the side. "What exactly did Da say, Maeve?"

I glance from the article about adding a pop of color to your life to my two sisters in front of me. For being the closest in age out of the five of us, Keira and Ava couldn't look any different.

Except for the rage sparking in their gazes. In that, they are exactly the same.

The famous King temper seeps from their pores, rolling over every available surface like fog.

"Just that I'm the first, and if it goes well, it'll set the precedent for you." I pause and glance between the two of them. "All of you."

A stunned sort of silence sits heavy between the three of us. I cock my head to the side and count down in my head.

Three. Two. One.

Keira shoves to her feet in one violent motion, her muscles coiled tight with unspent anger. Indignation drips from her pores as she storms over to the sideboard china cabinet. One violent twist of her fingers, and the glass door swings open with a small whine.

"Why aren't you mad? What else is going on?" Ava asks me,

drumming her fingers on the island. The light gray speckled quartz countertop absorbs the rapid tap-tap-tapping of her fingers as her eyes narrow.

I lean forward, my grip clenching the magazine pages tight. "I'm livid. But I don't need to throw a tantrum to get my point across."

Keira presses a palm to her chest, fingers splayed wide. Her eyebrows rise in an over-the-top faux innocence. "Oh, I'm sorry, am I acting *like a child?* Maybe it's because my fucking father is selling us off like some child brides."

I scoff and swing my gaze to Keira. "If you really think I'm going to let that happen—"

"I knew it!" Ava snaps her fingers and jumps to her feet. "I knew you had a plan."

"Aye, I have a plan." I sit back in the overstuffed loveseat and open my magazine back up to the article about color theory.

"Good. But in the meantime, I'm going to make sure *Father* knows how we feel about this." Keira pulls out a small, shallow glass bowl Da likes to use for nuts and other small snacks. With a nearly maniacal glee, she raises it up high and launches it against the hardwood floor.

Ava and I flinch at the same time, the noise cracking through the air like a whip.

The three of us stare at each other, our shoulders high, as we listen for the telltale footfalls of our father. My shoulders drop after a few seconds of silence.

It's not that I don't think Da should face our ire, it's more like I already know what I'm going to do, and his agenda doesn't factor into my decision. If he can't be bothered to consult me on this huge life change, then I'll extend him the same courtesy.

He wants to shuffle us off like unwanted cattle, but he forgets who we are.

He raised us in his image, after all.

"Well? Do you feel better now?" Ava asks Keira.

A maniacal sort of smile spreads across my sister's face, her blonde hair wild around her head in big barrel waves. "Not even remotely. Try it."

Keira hands Ava another one of the same small, shallow glass bowls. They're from a six-piece set we gave him for Christmas a few years ago. The man does love a good snack, and he always has one of those little bowls out on his desk.

I turn the page and skim the article about how to use wallpaper to give any room a vintage feel. "Not Mum's wine glasses, yeah?"

Keira makes some clucking noise in the back of her throat. "I would never."

I nod but keep reading the article, doing my best to ignore the harsh words whispered between my sisters. Another crash splits the air, this one louder than the first.

I look toward the ceiling, and sure enough, Da heard that one. I track his thundering footsteps as he walks down the staircase, and I imagine him like a bull with steam snorting through his nose. For a man who's known as The Hammer, he lives up to his name for an entirely different reason here. He's so loud, I bet Mrs. Byrne down the street can hear him.

My sisters launch more breakables against the hardwood floor, the crashes piercing my ears a little. A high-pitched ringing seems to echo around the kitchen, and I tilt my head to the right to dissipate the shrill sound.

"Jesus fucking Christ. Will you knock it off and stop breaking your mother's shit!" Da yells from the hallway.

"Fuck you," Keira and Ava yell in unison.

I roll my lips inward to stop the laugh from slipping out. Most people would gasp in horror at the liberty and case in which we swear in our house. But most people aren't trained with weapons in elementary school, so I don't really take their opinions to heart.

"Maeve," Da hollers. His voice carries from the mouth of the hallway where it opens up into the living room and kitchen.

"You're on your own, old man." I pitch my voice louder but I don't bother looking at him.

I wasn't lying earlier. I am livid with him, but I'm not going to change his mind no matter how many things I smash. Instead, I bottle up that rage and betrayal and bone-deep disappointment that my da isn't the man I thought he was, and I shove it way down low where it can't spring free at any moment.

"Some fucking help you are," he grumbles.

I close the magazine with a thwack and push to my feet. It takes effort to keep my hands hanging loose by my side and not curled up tight in anger. I stalk through the living room toward Da.

"Maybe you should be asking yourself why your children are ruining all your favorite things, *Da*."

His head whips toward Ava as she smashes his favorite cigar ashtray. "What the ever-loving fuck are you doing?"

I look at my sisters as they look at our father. Twin expressions of rage mar their pretty faces, twisting their mouths into scowls and dropping their brows low.

"Oh? Now you want to ask questions, Da?" Keira's eyebrows dance high on her forehead.

He stalks toward them, stopping on the other side of the island. He holds his hands up, palms facing them. "Tell me what's wrong like an adult and stop destroying my things like a fucking toddler."

It's the wrong thing to say, and honestly, he should know better by now. I can't hold in the snicker, letting it fall from my lips and float around the kitchen. My mirth hovers in front of my sisters as they raise their arms higher.

23

Their matching scowls transform into smirks. An eerie synchronized movement that has the hair on my arm standing on end. My laughter tapers off, and there's a pregnant pause.

As if it was choreographed, they both toss the glasses. We all watch their low arc before they hit the dark hardwood floor and shatter.

Da's seething, his chest heaving and straining against the emerald green flannel shirt he's wearing. I imagine him as some sort of cartoon villain with smoke coming out of his ears and his eyes bugging out of his head. Only in this episode, he's bested by his protégés.

"Ooh, are we breaking shit for fun again? Leave me some!" Rosie yells as she runs down the stairs, her footsteps quick thumps on the carpeted runner. "Fiona! You're going to miss the fireworks if you don't stop primping and get your ass down here!"

"I'm not primping, Ro. Some of us can't just toss our hair in a messy bun and look like they walked off the runway," Fiona hollers a second before I hear her jogging down the stairs.

Our youngest sister coasts in the kitchen on quick, light steps and grabs an apple. She takes a huge bite as her gaze ping-pongs between us and Da. When no one says anything, she tilts her head to the side and pitches her voice louder. "Fiona, we have the same hair, you know."

Ava grips a wine decanter by its neck, her brow arching into her hairline.

"Oh shit," Rosie murmurs, eyeing Ava.

"Maeve." Da grits my name through a clenched jaw.

It's a bullshit warning, the kind I stopped listening to a long time ago. Still, I walk around the island with a dramatic sigh, really making sure Da knows how I feel about it. I stop next to Keira and lean back. There's just enough room between two of the eight stools at our island for me to lean back on.

I look at him and jerk my head toward my sisters. "They found out about your little arrangement with Vegas."

"Shots fired," Rosie mumbles around a mouthful of apple.

My brows crash down low over my eyes. I didn't tell her the news yet, so how did she—realization hits me over the head.

"How?" I demand of my youngest sister.

She takes another too-big bite of her red apple and lifts a shoulder. She doesn't answer me, only raises a brow as if to ask *Are you really asking me that?*

I look at her for a moment, and she holds my gaze. She continues to chew her apple but doesn't offer anything else.

That girl's attitude is going to get her in trouble one of these days. She's lucky she's so fucking good at what she does. In fact, it's probably *because* she's so good that she can get away with half the shit she pulls.

I dip my chin in acceptance of her non-answer. She'll tell me later, she always does.

Da tosses his hands up in the air before slamming them on his hips. "*That's* what this is about? Are you fucking kidding me?"

Fiona scoffs, the noise barely above a murmur. She settles next to Rosie at the end of the island. The five of us have made a loose semicircle, unconsciously or not.

And Da stands across from us. The implication is clear.

Fiona leans her shoulder into Rosie and stage-whispers, "What's going on now?"

Rosie tilts her head toward her and mutters around a mouthful of apple, "Keira and Ava are *expressing their emotions* about Da's arrangements."

Da runs his hand down his face, the scratch of his calloused fingers on his beard a familiar sound. "Oh, for fuck's sake, girls."

Rosie blinks her dark-brown eyes wide. "What? That's what we're encouraged to do, right, Da? *Express our emotions.*" She enunciates the last three words, twisting Da's words around on him.

It's an expression we were encouraged to act on since we were little. But I bet he's kicking himself for shoving it down our throats like some twisted mantra for years.

"That's not what this is about, Rosie," Da grumbles.

"You're right. Turns out, your children don't like being auctioned off to the highest bidder, *Father*." I sneer as I use his proper moniker like it's poisonous.

Da tips his head back and squeezes his eyes shut like he's praying or something. But I know he's not. The only thing my father ever believed in was buried seven feet under eleven years ago. He blows out a breath and looks at me. "I didn't auction anyone off. I made an arrangement—"

"Arranged marriages might as well be an auction. You took the highest bid! You—you just promised us away like it's nothing!" Ava shouts.

"I didn't—"

"You did though," Keira interrupts him, her tone measured. "You've been talking about promising us to strangers for the betterment of the Syndicate for years."

Da stares at the five of us. For the first time in a long time, I notice the small things like the deepened crow's feet by his eyes, the way his mouth seems perpetually neutral, like it's been too long since he smiled or laughed for more than five seconds.

He shakes his head, a quick side to side motion, like he's clearing whatever thought sifted through his head. "We need heirs—several of them—and you all know it."

Anger sparks inside my chest. I push off the island and throw my arms out wide, spinning a little to showcase my sisters and me. "You have five of them right here. Contrary to the patriarchal bullshit you and your buddies eat for breakfast, you don't need a dick to be the boss."

Da shakes his head, slower this time. Regret lines his face, and I know whatever he has to say won't be anything we want to hear. "It doesn't work like that."

"I would rather die than be sold to a man," Keira hisses before she storms out of the room.

Ava follows behind her, glaring at Da. "You've gone too far this time."

Fiona and Rosie leave the kitchen without another word, walking side by side and murmuring quietly to each other once they reach the hallway.

Da glances at me, scanning my face. I don't know what he's expecting to find, but I don't think he sees it.

Determination and an overwhelming rage to burn it all down sludges through my veins.

"Mark my words, Da, I'll not be shuffled off like cattle."

I drop my father's gaze and go around the island to the sliding glass patio doors. It's dusk now, and the lengthening shadows welcome me in their warm embrace.

3

NICO

"SO YOU'RE GOING to be Dad's little bitch forever, huh?"

I swirl the whiskey in my glass and ignore the taunt from my little brother.

The moniker might be a stretch considering he is an inch taller than me and never fucking lets me forget it.

I stare into the liquid like it holds my future in its amber depths. If only I were clairvoyant and it was tea leaves and not top shelf sixty-proof whiskey in my glass. Then maybe I'd get longer than a few hours reprieve.

It's one of the only things that's kept me going since my dad dropped his little arranged marriage bomb on me last week.

I think I'd prefer an actual bomb. At least then I'd get to escape the mundane. Every day it's a different shade of the same color: wake up, oversee our businesses and make sure everything is running smoothly—which it never does, clean up whatever fucking mess Dad put us in. Occasionally, I have to make examples out of the dumbasses who think they're more important than they are.

All in a day's work.

I scoff at the word.

Work.

Like it's some nine-to-five office job with shitty coffee and piss-poor PTO.

When it's really methodically dismantling factions of assholes who think they can just take from us. Take from *me.* They mistake my quiet, neutral disposition for weakness.

They fear the elusive Tommaso Santorini for his outward displays of violence. But we can't all be raging psychopaths.

Some of us have to exercise our demons quietly.

I ignore the chatter from my brothers behind me, content to wallow in my ever-present existential crisis.

Or maybe it's more a crisis of conscience.

I tap my index finger against the glass, a quick tempo as I mull over the place inside my chest where I'm certain my soul is supposed to be.

It's impossible for me to imagine that I'll ever have the luxury of keeping someone pure and good. Not in this life. Whatever's left of my soul is tainted, stained permanently black. In the past, I used to wallow in pity, but it never changed anything. So I stopped trying.

I learned to accept my fate in this life.

And if the smallest kernel of my conscience whispers that I deserve happiness, deserve the love of a good, kind woman, then it's a secret I'll take to my grave.

I have my brothers. And that loyalty has to be enough.

Their conversation breaks through the fog I was drowning in.

"He's been staring at his whiskey for two minutes. Maybe he's having a mental break or something," Rome muses.

"Nah, he's probably having an internal debate with himself, listing the pros and cons like usual." Tommy is a classic middle child, always talking shit.

I rotate my wrist again, sending the amber liquid swirling up along the sides of the glass. A speck of blood on the cuff of my white dress shirt catches my eye. Irritation sparks along my skin like hot coals down my spine.

This is why I prefer black.

I tip my favorite rocks glass back and swallow the last two fingers of whiskey in one go.

"Damn, someone's not messing around tonight, huh?"

I ignore Rome's teasing and set my glass down on the matching crystal and wood tray.

"He was at the docks today. I heard Marco's crew needed some reminding of the rules. Maybe that's it. You know he always gets weird after he has to shoot someone," Tommy offers.

Maybe it's the curse of the little brother, because even when he's not trying to piss me off, he somehow does.

With gritted teeth and quick movements, I unbutton my sleeves and start rolling them up. It doesn't erase the blood on my cuff, but at least I can't see it anymore.

Rome scoffs. "Most people get weird when they have to shoot someone, bro."

I hear a creak, like Tommy's leaning back in his chair, balancing on two legs instead of four. "Hey, it's not my fault I'm built of tougher stuff than you." Humor laces around his words, and it eases some of the tension in my shoulders.

He's not wrong, but he's not right either.

"I don't get fucking weird. I get tired of repeating myself and that asshole has used up more than his fair share of goodwill. It was his final warning." I keep my voice low, my back still turned toward them, and pour myself another few fingers of whiskey.

Only in the fucking mafia do you consider getting shot in the shoulder as a last warning. The next time Marco Colombo tries to deal his bullshit product in our club, he won't even see me coming.

"Ah, he speaks!" Tommy crows.

"Fuck off, brother," I snap. "I've had a long day."

"Haven't we all, big brother? Just think—in a few short months, you'll have yourself a nice little wife to come home to—"

"Leave it, Tommy." I whirl around, my fingers gripping the glass too tight, and glare daggers at my brother.

I stare at the two faces so similar to mine, there's no mistaking our shared parentage. Our father's proud nose—at least before Tommy broke his fucking around with some assholes in high school.

The grin on his face only grows wider at my irritation.

Rome clears his throat. Always the fucking diplomat between us.

I pinch the bridge of my nose and let my eyes close for one slow blink. "What, Rome?"

"Well, shouldn't we talk about it? It's been, what, a week since Dad told us—"

"Ten days," Tommy interrupts.

Rome glances sharply at him. "What?"

Tommy lifts a shoulder. "Dad told us the great news ten days ago."

"Okay." Rome stretches out the word. "It's been ten days, which means you have a month and a half. You can't just ignore your engagement, Nic," Rome says.

I swallow roughly at the word engagement. The idea of marrying some fucking random woman just so my father gains something is enough to send me into a rage.

My lids spring open, and I drop my hand. "I'm not ignoring it."

Rome nods and leans back into one of two navy blue leather chairs in front of my desk. They're too plush to be proper office guest chairs, but considering they only get used by the two people currently sitting on them, it's not really an issue.

Tommy snorts from his sprawled-out position in the chair

next to Rome. His black dress shirt is unbuttoned at the top, sleeves rolled up to his elbows. He ditched his suit jacket and traded his dress shoes for sneakers. Black, of course.

He sits with his arms propped up along the curved armrests and legs spread wide, always the vision of casual.

Unlike our youngest brother, he has no desire to wipe any emotions from his face. He's an open book—with us, at least.

To the Outfit, he's the gregarious manic who enjoys extracting information a little too much.

But to us he's just Tommy. Loud, sarcastic, pain in my ass. Loyal to us over everything.

I cross the few feet to my desk and lean my ass against the edge, resting my glass against my leg. "Something to add, Tommy?"

He grins at me, completely unbothered in his relaxed position in front of me. "Other than I think you're a fucking idiot if you agree to marry some chick you've never met before?"

"I have no intentions of doing that. Ever."

"Arranged marriage?" Rome asks.

I shake my head slowly, my chest restricting at the thought. "Any marriage. The life we lead, it's not one for spouses and children, regardless of how the marriage happens. We know that better than most."

I don't let my gaze wander to my brother, but I don't need to. The three of us are all thinking the same thing.

Our father couldn't protect us when he had a fraction of the enemies we have now and love in his heart for his sons.

Tommy shifts forward, his arms dropping to his thighs. "Is it finally time?"

I look at the space between my brothers and let the silence grow. It's heavy and thick with unsaid words. It's not like we haven't talked about it before, but that was more abstract. A *one day* sort of conversation we'd have when we had too many drinks.

And even though the frequency in which we had those conversations increased once our sisters came back into our lives, we still didn't put much stock into it.

Or I didn't at least. But looking at Tommy practically vibrating in the chair, I have to wonder if I was the exception. Still, something feels different now.

I exhale and prepare to breathe life into the words we've been dancing around for years.

"It's time."

I inhale and trap the breath in my lungs. I've never been particularly superstitious, but I would swear on my brothers' lives that the lights dip for a split-second.

Fuck, maybe I have had too much whiskey today.

I smooth out the pulsing point between my eyebrows with the pad of my thumb and glance from Tommy to Rome and back again. "Unless you've had a change of heart."

"Fuck, it's about goddamn time, brother!" Tommy rubs his hands together, practically bouncing in his seat.

"Don't look so fucking happy about the prospect of parricide," Rome grumbles, giving Tommy the side-eye.

Tommy leans forward, rocking the chair with his sudden shift in weight. The front legs of the chair slamming to the ground with a thud. "Oh, I'm sorry. Do I look happy? Because I meant to look fucking ecstatic." He flashes his teeth at Rome and me. It's a crude sort of smile, and not for the first time, I understand why he's the most obvious choice for the intimidation tactics and information extraction.

Rome rubs the back of his neck with his palm. "Look, it's no secret that Dad's the fucking worst. But if we do this, it'll change everything."

I feel my eyebrows crash over my eyes. "I thought you wanted to be out from underneath his thumb?"

It's a question that feels like an accusation as soon as it leaves my mouth. But I won't take it back. I've never coddled either of them, and I'm not about to start now. If they're not all-in, then there's no point to this conversation.

I've never been resentful of either of my brothers. Not for shielding them from Vito when we were younger or removing them from the house as soon as I could.

"Don't be ridiculous. Of course, Rome's in. Aren't ya, brother?" Tommy leans toward Rome and nudges his shoulder with his palm.

"I want him gone as much as you do, but I want to make sure we're smart about this. It doesn't affect just us anymore, remember?" Rome says.

A dark cloud forms over Tommy. "Mom's been in the life long enough. She's made her choices."

Rome tsks. "But our sisters haven't. They're walking around unprotected, and if we succeed, then they'll have targets on their backs."

"Madison is fine with the Rossis. We saw that firsthand. But I agree, we should get a lead on Mary. I know she's not keen to meet us yet."

"She'll come around," Tommy says.

Rome dips his chin and stares at Tommy. His face is alarmingly neutral, like he's already mentally preparing himself for one outcome. "Alright, as long as there's no blowback on our sisters, then I'm all-fucking-in."

"You wound me, brother." Tommy presses his palm to chest and rears back sharply to the side. The entire thing is so dramatic I can't stop the smirk curling up the corner of my mouth.

"You get carried away too easily," Rome says.

"I eat, pray, love the shit out of life. And it just so happens that I'm one hell of a negotiator. I'd hardly call that getting carried away," Tommy says.

"Didn't you play darts with that asshole's face not that long ago?" The words are more of a drawl, and it does nothing to disguise the humor in my voice.

Rome smirks, shifting his weight to stare at Tommy. "Ah, is that what we're calling extracting information these days—*playing darts?*"

Tommy grins at both of us. "What? I had to practice for our darts competition and get information. I was killing two birds with one stone." He pauses. "Or dart, I guess."

Rome and I groan at the same time, and Rome snatches the throw pillow from behind his back and whips it at Tommy's face.

Tommy lifts an arm up to block and the pillow bounces to the floor. "What?" he says around a laugh.

"Man, you need to get some better jokes. That was pitiful," Rome says.

"I don't know, brother. Sure made the both of you laugh. So maybe it's your terrible sense of humor." Tommy shrugs his shoulders and grins.

I push off my desk and stop them before their playful bickering turns into a wrestling match and someone breaks something. "Alright. I love you, but get the fuck out of my office. I have shit to do."

"Yeah, yeah. C'mon, Rome. The boss has shit to do." Tommy smirks as he stands up and rights the chair. He bends over and snatches the throw pillow from the floor before tossing it on the seat.

Rome pushes to stand. "Six weeks, Nic." He scans my face, his gaze skimming over my features several times before he nods to himself.

"Six weeks until we take over Vegas," I agree.

"Until we take out Dad," Tommy says.

4

MAEVE

MY HEELS CLICK on the hardwood in the hallway of the New York City loft apartment I share with my sisters. It's one of the many houses we share around the United States and Europe. Some are used more often, furnished and infused with each of our personalities. And some are straight safe houses, bare of anything that could be tied back to us.

But our NYC loft is one of my favorite places in the entire world. I spend weeks here at a time, sometimes alone, but more often than not with at least one of my sisters. We use it as a hub for anything we're working on in the east coast.

Plus, it makes for a good cover story: just a family spending time in their New York City vacation home. Ironically, it's how we started calling our missions *vacations*. No one pays any attention to a group of girls talking about their upcoming vacation. Not that we talk so openly about our work, but it does offer us another layer of protection. And Rosie handles the rest.

The hallway is just long enough for three doors on either side. Five bedrooms and two bathrooms worthy of any luxurious spa in the five boroughs.

Framed photos of us decorate the space between doors. The five of us in Central Park at a John Lennon demonstration with daisies crowns and wide smiles. Ro and Ava with ice cream dripping down their chins, the sun setting in the background of our old house. A candid shot of Fiona, Keira, and Ava dancing in the living room of our house in California. A family portrait in front of Grandpa Charlie's farm from when we were little, when Mum was alive.

Memories preserved and hung on display for any one of us who needs centering.

I trail my gaze along Mum's face, and longing so fierce rips through my chest. I press my palm over my heart and jerk my head forward and away from her smile.

She would be horrified at what Da's done, bargaining our lives and drowning any chance of happiness we could've had.

Or hell, maybe she wouldn't be. Maybe she knew we were destined for this life and that's why she trained us in her own way when we were young. Before we were old enough to really understand what she was doing.

I guess it doesn't really matter, does it? We can't change the past, no matter how much we want to.

I follow the voices of my sisters and find them in one of our flex rooms toward the end of the hallway.

It's a two-step sunken-in room with an entire wall of floor-to-ceiling windows. It offers the perfect cityscape view of New York City from the twenty-fifth floor. Early morning sunshine lights up the space with a warm glow, rhombus-sized blocks of sunlight stretching across the room.

My four sisters are already seated around our round dining room table. It's custom-built with wood from Grandpa Charlie's old barn before it was taken down. Apparently, that old barn wood is worth a fortune. But since we were his favorite grandchildren, he gave us a ton of it to repurpose.

My heels sink into the round navy shag rug underneath the table in the middle of the room. The intricate bronze and cream light fixture above the desk is one of my favorite things about this place. It gives it a Viking sort of vibe, which is fitting for a place Keira christened as the War Room.

Ava tsks at me. "Where's our coffee, Maeve?"

I set my three-quarters-full iced coffee to-go cup on the table and pull out the last chair between Fiona and Ava. I settle into the buttery leather with a smirk. "Next time get up a little earlier and you can come with me."

"I can't believe you walk eight blocks in this heat just for a cup of coffee," Fiona grumbles.

Rosie rolls her eyes. "Oh, please. It's nearly September, it's barely even hot by New York standards."

"Only you would think sweltering humidity and incessant sunshine is *barely even hot*," Fiona teases.

Rosie preens a little, lifting one shoulder higher than the other. "What can I say? I was made to withstand a warmer climate." The subtext is: *I'm better than you.* I swear my sisters make shit-talking and disagreeing with one another an Olympic sport.

"Yeah, well, I'm still used to Ireland's weather." Fiona tilts her chin up and looks down at our youngest sister.

"Well, get used to it. Aren't you headed to the upper east coast soon?" Ava asks.

Fiona blows out a breath. "Yeah. Orientation starts in two days, so I'm heading up there today. I want to get all unpacked and look around."

"Didn't you get the information packet I sent you?" Rosie tilts her head to the side.

"Aye, but it's not the same as being there, ya know? But thank you. It's definitely proven useful."

Rosie preens under Fiona's praise, and I make a mental note to make sure she knows how valuable she is on our next vacation.

"About that, are you sure you want to do this? You can still get the info you need without enrolling." I take a sip of my iced coffee, letting the caffeine work its magic and eat away at my jet lag.

Fiona nods. "I'm sure. You know I always wanted to finish my degree. I just never imagined it would be at some uppercrust private school with more secrets than the ivy league."

I bite the inside of my cheek and scan her expression for any of her tells. She seems genuine, and at some point, I have to trust that she'll come to me if she gets in over her head. "Alright. But you reach out the moment you need help or run into a jam. One of us can be there in a couple hours."

Fiona tips her chin toward me.

I arch a brow and lean back in my chair, mentally preparing for the pushback I know she's itching to shovel at me. "I mean it, Fi. Bail if you get the smallest hint that your cover is blown."

The side of her lip curls upward. "I'm not afraid."

Keira shakes her head. "It's not about being brave. It's about being smart. We have no idea what's really going on there—"

"That's why I'm enrolling, Keira," Fiona interrupts.

Keira huffs, annoyance flashing across her hardened gaze. "I know that. Don't get swept up is all I'm saying. If we have to find another way, we can."

"I'll be fine," Fiona says, lifting a shoulder.

I nod a few times, an unconscious movement more than anything. "Okay. Keira, what about you? Where are you heading next?"

"Ava and I are in New York for another week, and then we're back in Ireland for a bit. I've got a few interesting things that might be worth our while. I have to look into them first though," Keira says.

"And I'm going to meet up with the boys in Monaco while she snoops around," Ava says, jerking her chin toward Keira.

Rosie starts humming a song I don't recognize under her breath, giving Ava a taunting side-eye.

Ava flicks the cap of her water bottle at Rosie. "Oh hush. We're just friends."

"Uh-huh. That's what they all say before they hook-up and fall in love." Rosie sings the last three words in the way only a younger sister can.

Like it's some choreographed move, smiles spread across our faces, a few chuckles lightening the mood.

"Whatever. What's next for you, besides annoying your older and wiser sister?" Ava folds her arms across her chest and stares at Rosie.

Rosie just grins. "School officially starts for me in two weeks. So I'm available until then."

"You nervous?" Fiona asks.

Rosie barely lets Fiona get her words out before she says, "Are you?"

One side of Fiona's mouth tips upward in a smile. "Nah, but I'm older than you, so."

Rosie rolls her eyes. "Pshh, it's only four years. That's barely anything."

"You can't even legally drink here," Fiona says around a laugh.

"Enough about all that," Keira says, waving her hand in the air like she's wafting away their words and stopping the conversation before it devolves into another argument. "Let's talk about Maeve."

Four pairs of eyes swing toward me. their gazes focused and unwavering. A sense of calm settles around my shoulders, despite their intensity.

"Easy." I take a measured sip of my iced coffee, enjoying the way the caramel syrup at the bottom makes it almost too sweet.

"Care to share with the class?"

I set my coffee back on the table and point at my youngest sister. "You're lucky I love you. Your attitude is unreal sometimes."

"Yeah, yeah. But you *do* love me. *And* you're deflecting, so spill. Let's make a plan," Rosie says.

"I already have a plan." I lean back in my chair, the soft squeak of leather comforting. And while no one has as much attitude as my sister, I've been known to be a smidgen dramatic at times.

This is definitely one of those times.

I let the silence grow for another few seconds before I pop it.

"Easy. I'm going to kill him."

5

MAEVE

"WHO, DA?" Fiona looks at me, eyebrows reaching her hairline.

"Nah, not Da. Though he has some serious groveling to do as far as I'm concerned." My words taper off, my register lowering as the rage surges like it does every time I think of what he did. "But the best way to eliminate the arranged marriage is to eliminate my betrothed."

The word feels foreign on my tongue, like it's too bulky and bitter to fit.

No one says anything for a moment. They just stare at me and then exchange looks with one another.

I'm not worried though. They don't have all the details yet. Once they do, I'm sure they'll understand.

"Don't look so shocked. It's not like we haven't done this before."

"Aye, we have. But that was to men who deserved it," Keira hedges.

"And who's to say this man doesn't?" I counter, holding her gaze.

Her face scrunches up a bit as her brows lower over her eyes. "What aren't you telling us?"

I jerk my chin at my youngest sister while holding Keira's gaze.

A thwack cuts through the air, and all eyes shift to the small stack of papers slowly unfurling on the table. Rosie stabs her index finger to the top page, and with a flick of her wrist, sends them sliding across the table to Keira.

"What's this?" Keira asks, plucking the papers off the table in front of her.

Rosie leans back in her chair. "That is the contract Da signed for Maeve."

"What?" Ava leans forward and flutters her fingers toward Keira. "Let me see."

Keira flicks her fingers away. "You can read it after me."

"What does it say?" Ava shifts forward, leaning her elbows on the table.

Rosie nods, more to herself than anything. "Not a lot, actually. Just that the firstborn daughter of Joseph King will marry the firstborn son of Vito Santorini. And upon their union, the two families will form an alliance. Should that union produce male heirs, the firstborn male will bear the King name and the second male will bear the Santorini name."

I'm not surprised that she has it memorized. She's read it as many times as I have, looking for loopholes and ways to breach without repercussion.

"So Da gets his precious heirs to carry on the King name, after all." Ava sneers.

"Tell them the best part, Maeve." Rosie flashes me a grin.

"There are some clauses in the contract that say—"

"In the event that one or both of the parties involved should become deceased, this contract is considered null and void," Keira interrupts me.

I arch a brow at her. "See? It's a good plan. For all we know, Santorini's son could be plotting the same thing for me. So shouldn't we strike first?"

Rosie clears her throat. "There is another way."

I look at my sister, willing her with my gaze to drop it. I'd rather kill him than fuck him.

"There's another stipulation that's . . . what in the eighteenth century is this?" Keira looks from the second to last page of the contract to me, her head shaking slightly.

"It's a purity stipulation." The words feel thick on my tongue, rough to swallow around.

"Well, that ship sailed with Gregory Ryan back in—"

"Shut it, Fi." I groan out her name, even as my cheeks heat.

I lost my virginity to Gregory Ryan in the back of his older brother's black Charger. He lasted two minutes tops, and I was so disappointed with the whole thing I didn't sleep with anyone else for nearly two years.

I made the mistake of sharing this little fact with my sisters years ago after too much wine, and they never let me forget it.

"Purity is misleading. It's not a virginity stipulation, but rather an isolation one. It says the firstborn son and the firstborn daughter are to remain apart until the day of their union. The two parties are not to see, talk, or touch one another until they are married before the eyes of God." Keira pauses and looks around the room. "What the actual fuck is this?"

The incredulity in her voice is a balm to my frayed nerves. It's exactly how I felt the first two times I read it.

"It means they want to keep us apart," I offer.

"But why?" Ava asks.

I shake my head slowly. I don't have the answers she's looking for. Every possible explanation I can think of feels off, and anything I say is speculation. Is it something left over from the old ways of arranged marriages with virginity stipulations? Is it a mind game? Or maybe it's completely unrelated and doesn't have anything to do with us at all.

Ava snakes the contract from Keira and starts reading where she left off. She cocks her head to the side. "And we're sure this is legitimate? It doesn't have anything about how it benefits Da or Vito Santorini."

Rosie leans forward. "Aye. I'm not entirely convinced Da didn't *want* us to find it, because the contract was put in his favorite safe. The one behind the shelves on his bookcase with the code I cracked almost ten years ago."

"Mum's birthday," we all say at the same time.

"Exactly," Rosie snaps.

"So this could be a decoy then?" Ava asks.

"He had to know we'd look," Keira says.

Rosie lifts a shoulder in a half-shrug. "It was tucked in a folder with a bunch of random documents that had nothing to do with any of this. And it was in the middle of a stack of folders."

I drum my fingers on my leg. "I think it's legit. I don't have any proof, but call it a gut feeling."

Keira's cheeks puff out as she exhales a big breath. "Alright. So you're going to take him out then?"

"Aye."

"Good. What do we know about the *firstborn son of Vito Santorini*?" Fiona mocks.

Rosie rakes her fingers over her scalp, loosening the hair from her messy bun. "Not much. For a family that makes their name in the Las Vegas nightlife, the Santorinis are surprisingly private. They must have someone really good on their payroll."

Keira pushes her chair back and stands. She paces in front of the windows. "So, they're in Las Vegas. What else?"

"Vito Santorini has three sons and they're never

photographed. No social media, no public profiles—nothing," Rosie says.

"He keeps them hidden then," Fiona muses.

"Not exactly. From what I can gather, all three sons are part of the family business."

I take another sip of my iced coffee. "They may rule Vegas. But nobody puts baby in a corner."

There's a collective pause. It's buoyed with disbelief, but they should know better by now. A little movie quote is always a good tension breaker.

All at once, my sisters holler at me, booing and laughing. Ava pushes the papers in my direction, and they go fluttering all over the table.

"What? It was the perfect opening, I had to take it." Laughter coats my words, my smile slipping free.

"Puh-lease. You never need to take those kinds of openings." Rosie rolls her eyes.

"Ha! As if you can even talk," Fiona exclaims, pointing at her.

I need to get them back on track if I want to run through the plan twice more before I have to catch my plane.

I'm not waiting any longer to take care of this.

"Look," I say with a sigh. "I know it sounds like I pulled this plan from my arse, but I didn't. It's all I've thought about since I found out. And I'm not worried, so you shouldn't be either."

"And what exactly is your plan?" Fiona asks.

"With Rosie's help, I'm going to sneak into his apartment on the top floor of Stone Rose Hotel, and then I'll leave him a little present to remember me."

"Should we be alarmed at the ease in which we all chat about killing a man?" Ava taps her index finger against her bottom lip.

I roll my lips inward and think. It's a question I've thought of often. A dilemma of morality. Doing things that people would find bad is bad, but what if it ultimately helps people?

"I'll let you know in a few days. For now, we move forward with business as usual."

6

MAEVE

"COME TO MAMA, YOU GORGEOUS GIRL."

I hold the thirty carat oval-cut pink diamond up to the afternoon sunlight filtering through the gauzy drapes. It's the last thing in Caleb Miller's third safe.

Caleb Miller is the son of oil tycoon Tieran Miller. And like his father, he excels at embezzling funds from his fabricated charity and abusing his power over women.

I whistle under my breath. "Damn, I almost want to keep you for myself."

"Talking to yourself again, Maeve?"

Rosie's voice is dry in my right ear. I cluck my tongue at her and roll the necklace up in a velvet roller bag.

"Please. Like you don't have full conversations with yourself when you're locked up in your *lair*."

It's what we affectionately call her workrooms. She has one in every home we have and they're all set up the same: a half-dozen computer screens, three keyboards, and two towers spread out on custom-built desks. It houses all kinds of tech—stuff she builds and stuff she's tweaking to fit our needs.

The number of times I've walked by her office and heard her mumbling to herself is immeasurable. She claims it's how she works out problems, but I maintain that she spends too much time alone.

But in the middle of a job is not the time or place to dive into that well-worn argument.

"True," she says with a chuckle.

I tuck the necklace in my black slimline crossbody backpack, next to the velvet pouch of diamonds and four flash drives. "How much time?"

"Three minutes." Rosie's voice is low, a soothing timbre in my ear as I slip the backpack over my head and settle the strap between my breasts.

Even if she wasn't an absolute genius with technology, I'd still want her running point for me. Truthfully, I can work seamlessly with each of my sisters, but Rosie and I just click on another level. I think it's because Mum paired us up all the time when we were younger. We developed another layer of awareness between the two of us.

Plus, she's excellent when we get into a bind. It doesn't happen too often, but not even the five of us can account for every variable every time.

"Leaving now," I murmur.

I tug down the excess strap of my backpack, so it's flush against my back. The weight of his most precious possessions sit comfortably against me. We knew about the safes in the office and his bedroom, but the one in the library was just a bonus. He must have put it in after the renovations on the town house or some under-the-counter job, since Rosie couldn't find any trace of it on any of the building permits or blueprints. It didn't have any of the financial documents we were looking for, but it had some of the most gorgeous jewels, which is almost as good.

I'm not entirely sure how we're going to use them for our plan to ruin Miller, but my sisters and I are quite the innovators. I'm sure Keira will have an idea or two before I even get on the plane to leave.

I quickly scan the room to make sure everything is still in its place. Sloppy isn't my style, but I'm not usually caught unaware, either. The only thing out of place is the black tube of lipstick. It's a deep, bold red color from a brand found at every drugstore in every city in the country.

It's the kind of color that a woman wears when she wants to make a statement.

It's a calling card of sorts. It's not something I leave at every scene—only the ones that involve women.

I took the words my mum told me all those years ago and turned them into my mantra. Sure, I took care of my sisters in the eleven years she's been gone, but more than that, I started looking after all my sisters—as in all women.

So we formed a sisterhood, one where we mete out justice to those who've skirted it. To avenge those who are never held accountable. Like men who use their fists and then their wallets to make women disappear.

Unlike the filth in positions of power, we can't be bribed or bought.

There are a couple of small groups of conspiracy theorists that dubbed us the Fairy Godmothers. They've made it their hobby—or obsession, depending on how you look at it—to uncover our identities.

I'm not worried about it though. Rosie is always on top of it. There has only been one time where someone got a little too close to the truth, and she took care of it with six keystrokes and sixty seconds.

Like I said, she's a badass in her own right.

We didn't set out to become some sort of avenging angels or harbingers of justice, but somewhere along the way, we started embracing it. We sharpened our skills and wield them like blades.

I'd be lying if I didn't admit that the fear in which people talk about the flock of women who slip seamlessly in and out of lives, righting the wrongs of the world's untouchable brings me a sense of pride.

We're whispers in the wind, impossible to see but wreaking unimaginable damage when it's least expected.

"Maeve."

Rosie's voice snaps me out of my musings, and I focus back on the task: getting out of this asshole's penthouse apartment unseen.

"I'm here."

"Sixty seconds. Don't cut it too close. I don't like the way this guy in the lobby looks," Rosie says.

"Is it him?" My footsteps quicken as I slip out the front door, closing it behind me. The soft snick of the lock engaging sounds like a gunshot in the quiet.

"It could be nothing, but he seems shifty to me."

My heartrate picks up as adrenaline starts to pump into my bloodstream. This kind of rush is addictive, and if I was the type to get swept up in anything, I might be worried.

"I'm out."

"Good. Right at the end of the hall. I found you another way out, something that keeps you away from the guy currently waiting for the elevator."

"I'm not worried, Rosie. No one knows who we are, remember?"

"Yeah, well, I'd like to keep it that way. The last thing we need is some needle-dick asshole who can't keep his hands to himself getting fresh with you," she mutters, the click-clack of her fingers flying across one of her keyboards punctuating her words.

My youngest sister is the perfect blend of modern and what we lovingly call *vintage*. She lives for old TV sitcoms and says things like "get fresh" with a serious face. But she'll also cuss you out six ways from Sunday for looking at us wrong. She's taller than me, which isn't hard since I'm only five-four on a good day. Thick, wavy dark-red hair and big dark-brown eyes that permanently twinkle with mischief.

All of my sisters are gorgeous, and that's my unbiased opinion. But Rosie has that special spark. She could've been a model. She still could be, but she prefers her computers and tech and numbers to posing in front of cameras.

She's my favorite juxtaposition, and I love her all the more for her unwavering dedication to be exactly who she is.

I turn the corner, push the metal bar in and the door opens to a stairwell. Glancing at the writing on the gray wall, I tell her, "I'm in the north-west stairwell."

"Perfect. Go to the second floor and stay to the right. There should be a wall of windows on your right, follow those until you reach the south-west stairwell in the opposite corner. Take that to the parking garage level. Your ride is parked in section E, row seven."

"Got it." I adjust the backpack again. It's more of a nervous habit than need. I've broken myself of many of my small ticks and nervous tells over the years, but some things are harder to break than others.

"Maeve."

It's the tone of her voice that has me freezing, one foot poised in the air. My heart skips a beat. "What's wrong?"

"No, not that. You're fine. I've still got eyes on him."

My heart drums back to its normal rhythm and I continue down the six flights of stairs, quickening my pace. "What is it then?"

She sighs. "It's just . . . are you really going to Vegas for *a vacation?*"

7

MAEVE

MY BROWS SINK into a vee over my eyes. "You already know I am."

"But this is different. He isn't a mark. He hasn't been chosen by us to take out."

Now it's my turn to sigh. My voice gentles as I pass by the wall of windows. "We've been through this already, Rosie. It's a solid plan."

"It's a halfway decent plan at best, and if it were any other situation, you'd agree with me."

The little growl in her voice makes me smile. "Maybe, maybe not."

"It just doesn't feel right. I can't put my finger on why."

I push the bar open to the next staircase and hustle down the six sets of stairs. "Think of him like every other mark. What kind of self-respecting man agrees to an arranged marriage? He's probably a woman-hating asshole who deserves much more than what I'll give him."

Silence hangs between us, but it's not fraught with tension. I don't rush her, content to let her wrestle with her hesitation. I've made peace with the decision. It's not like I want to go around eliminating people from this earth, not even the ones who deserve it.

I don't crave the violence that comes with a lot of our unique brand of justice. But I always do what must be done.

And in the end, this is the only move we have. If Da intends to make these arrangements for us, then we'll eliminate the intended parties. Over and over again until he and everyone else understands the message: the Kings aren't for sale.

It's simple really.

"What if he doesn't want it though? What if he's in an impossible position like we are?" Rosie asks.

She's not being petulant or even playing devil's advocate like Keira likes to do.

"We've gone through this a hundred times already, Rosie. I thought you were on board." My words come out a little harsher than I intended.

"I am. It's just—" She sighs, cutting herself off.

"It's the only way. Once I take him out, then poof! No more contract. And if I don't, then we leave ourselves vulnerable. For all we know, they're planning the very same thing for me. And what if they get shitty intel and get Ava instead, hm?"

"Fuck." It's a harsh exhale, and I can tell I finally broke through my sister's hesitation.

I bite my lip, my mind spinning over all the different variables. "Let's say they're not plotting my demise as we speak. That still leaves us in the dark. We have no idea what Da promised them for me. And we have no way of stopping him from cashing in on it. All we can infer is that it must be something big, otherwise, it would be outlined in the contract." The words feel like ash on my tongue, bitter and ugly. The fact that I even have to have this conversation with my baby sister is insane.

But I didn't make this game. I'm not even a willing participant.

But if I have to play, then I'm going to win.

"You're right," she says.

"Tell me you've found something else—anything else." If I sound a touch desperate, she's kind enough to not call me out.

She sighs, the noise loud in my ear. "No. They're like ghosts, Maeve."

The tiny seed of trepidation that embedded itself in my gut five days ago when we sat around our table discussing options grows. Not into anything unmanageable, but enough to steal my breath for a moment.

As a rule, we don't move on anything until we have sufficient intel. We always have at least two alternate plans in case circumstances change.

But time is not a luxury we have right now. The sooner it's done, the sooner we can move forward.

"Okay. Run through everything again with me."

"Fine, but first, where are you?" Rosie asks.

"In the parking garage. Nearly to . . . tell me you didn't."

Her laugh echoes in my eardrums and I nearly rip the earpiece out. "Jesus, Rosie. Not so loud."

"Sorry, sorry," she says between quieter chuckles.

"Ava's going to kill you, ya know."

"Nah, she won't, because I promised her the same car when she lands in Monaco." She chuckles, her laughter edged in mischief.

"I don't know how you did it, but thank you. This car is gorgeous," I murmur, ghosting my fingers down the sleek lines of the black Ford GT.

"I have my ways." She says it so matter-of-factly, I can imagine the expression on her face. Her lips curling into a smirk, chin tipped upward, single brow arched over her eye.

I slip my backpack off and slide into the car, the black leather soft beneath my thighs. I pop the middle console and see the key fob resting front and center. Only Rosie would leave a two-hundred-thousand-dollar car unlocked with the keys inside in a public *parking garage*.

I press the button and the engine rumbles to life, it's a quiet purr beneath me. I whistle low under my breath. I don't have a fixation on cars like Ava does, but I feel like I've absorbed some of her fascination by osmosis.

I put it in drive and make my way out of the parking structure. I'm heading to the drop off where Keira is and then hopping on a plane to Las Vegas.

"Okay, I'm driving now. Let's go through it again."

"Right, so Vito Santorini is one scary asshole."

"How scary?" I interrupt.

"Like there are several rumors on the dark web that claim he orchestrated all the attacks on his own family."

"What kind of attacks?"

She clucks her tongue. "Not sure exactly. There isn't a lot of information available, but I did find an old newspaper that talked about the Santorinis a lot before they stopped publishing."

"What did it say?"

"This journalist, Edward Hale, seemed to hate the Santorinis. He wrote about them every couple of weeks, claiming they were a family of criminals. Said they'd be the downfall of Las Vegas."

I cluck my tongue and follow the smooth, curved roads toward the drop-off point. "Well, that's not exactly newsworthy now, is it?"

"No, but there is one article that caught my eye. It was a detailed recording of mass casualties. This Hale guy claimed it was a mafia war spilling into the streets. Twenty-three dead, including a bunch of people from the Pisano family. I'm assuming that's some sort of rival."

"Let me guess: he blamed the Santorinis?"

"Yeah, but here's where it gets interesting. Two of the other victims were Vito's older brothers."

My mind turns over this new development. "So the real question is: is Vito the type of person who betrays his own brothers to get the crown or is he opportunistic?"

"And did he raise his sons in his image?"

We're both quiet for a moment, the only sound is the gentle hum of traffic in the background.

"Remind me again what the Santorinis do."

Even though I've already asked her three times, she doesn't hesitate.

"Drugs, prostitution, gambling, hotels, other entertainment. Basically, all of Las Vegas is their playground."

"Okay, so what does Vito gain from an alliance with us? That's the real question."

"Already ahead of you, babe. Vito has a lot of enemies. I mean this dude makes Quinn Kelly look like a playground bully. So my best guess is protection and expansion. Vegas could be part of a corridor from Mexico to Canada and maybe the west coast."

Cillian Kelly is the head of the original Brotherhood line in Ireland. Not too long ago, he named his nephew Quinn his successor.

The original Brotherhood is technically its own entity, but they work so heavily alongside the Syndicate that I often think of them as one and the same.

Quinn infamously torched twenty houses in one night. Apparently, some assholes were making jokes about his ma in the pub, saying she warmed his uncle Cillian's bed more than her husband's.

I drum my fingers on the steering wheel as I roll over the information for the umpteenth time. "And his sons?"

"Ah, your betrothed. One Nico no-middle-name Santorini, oldest son of Vito Santorini."

I wait a beat, assuming she got distracted by whatever is on one of her nine screens. When she doesn't continue, I expel a breath, my chest tightening. "And?"

"And that's it."

Disbelief inflates my lungs, the emotion sour. "How can that be it? Nothing in those newspaper articles you found?"

"No, the articles stopped fifteen years ago or so, when the paper shut down. There's virtually no record of any of them. I couldn't even find a fucking photo, just some vague comments about him being drop-dead gorgeous. But if he's so hot, then why the hell would he need an arranged marriage? I call bullshit."

My disbelief morphs into annoyance. "You're probably right."

I make the final right turn and steer around the bend and pull into the driveway of the quaint rental house Keira and have been staying in while here. I ease the brakes, letting the car slow to a stop next to the front walkway. I throw the car in park a little too hard and stare out the windshield.

I bite my lip and let my gaze roll out of focus as I tried to think of anything we could've missed.

"Our plan still stands, Rosie. I'll be in and out."

"And I'll be your eyes from here," she assures me.

"Aye, then I'll wait for you in Chicago."

She huffs, and I imagine her rolling her eyes. "I told you that you don't need to go with me, let alone be there before I am."

"And I told you that I'd never let you move into some dorm room in another city without checking it out first. Besides, you know one of us has to pay our respects to the Chicago general. Better me than you."

"Alright," she says on a sigh. "Call me when you're in Las Vegas."

"I will." I end the call but I don't get out yet.

I check the rearview mirror and side mirrors a few more times to make sure I wasn't followed. A glance at the dash lets me know I'm running late, so with a sigh, I push open the door and climb out.

With the backpack in one hand, I nudge the door closed with my hip and stare around at the darkening sky. Brilliant streaks of pink and orange and purple paint the horizon, and my chest squeezes at the sight.

I never relish taking a life, no matter how many sins they've tallied up, but something about this feels . . . off. I can't put my finger on it.

But it doesn't matter. I have to do this. Not just for me but for my sisters.

I just have to keep my morality at bay for twenty-four more hours.

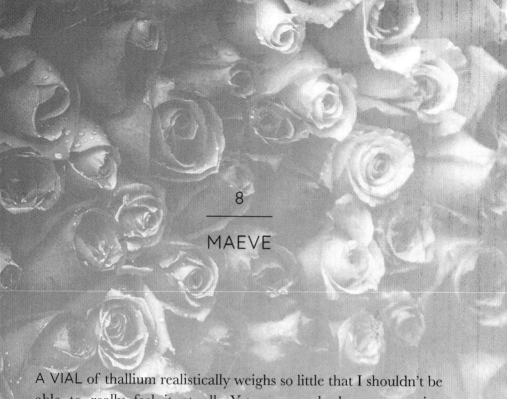

8

MAEVE

A VIAL of thallium realistically weighs so little that I shouldn't be able to really feel it at all. Yet my crossbody purse resting comfortably across my chest feels like it's made of iron and not supple leather.

I didn't have enough time to do my own extensive reconnaissance, so I'm relying heavily on what little information Rosie dug up and my one experience with Las Vegas.

And considering that included exactly three hours on the strip during a layover, it's not saying much.

What I can do, however, is dress the part.

I feel like I was poured into the bodycon dress I'm wearing. Soft black fabric that almost shimmers with every step, spaghetti straps that are more for show than function, a subtle sweetheart neckline, and barely falling to mid-thigh.

It's the perfect outfit to blend in with the crowd.

I ride the elevator up with a group of six women, all wearing short brightly-colored dresses. They're this side of tipsy and still firmly in the hugging and loving stage of drinking. They're pretty and giggly and very clearly having the best time. I imagine they're here on a girls' trip.

It's a foreign concept to me. A girls' trip being an *actual vacation* and not code for slowly dismantling someone's fortune or empire is almost inconceivable.

Sure, I have those moments with my sisters. The times when our bellies ache with laughter and our cheeks hurt from smiling.

But there are no coordinating outfits and nights spent hopping from club to club.

I don't know if I'll ever have that experience.

Did I even want it?

My future hasn't been my own for longer than I can remember. I've grown accustomed to thinking of my future in a sort of abstract way. Something that I occasionally indulge in but never let myself get carried away with.

I'll never be the girl with a husband and two-point-five kids and a dog and a white picket fence.

It's an outdated concept, sure, and I'm not saying these women even want that sort of future. But there's no denying that they look like they're having the best time with each other.

The hot poker of jealousy slips between my ribs and pricks at my soft insides. I exhale a breath and vow to create a similar experience for my sisters and me.

After I get clear of this arranged marriage, of course.

I keep my head angled away from the camera in the corner, but I nod my head a few times to make it look like I'm talking to the girl next to me. She gives me a serious side-eye but then her friend in front of us whirls around in a cloud of perfume and fruity cocktails.

"Oh my god, Tiff. I totally forgot to tell you that super hot guy at the bar was definitely checking you out!"

The girl next to me, Tiff, leans forward, eyes bright, and starts plotting out a way to find him again.

She's already forgotten about me.

The elevator door opens to reveal a typical hotel hallway lit by fluorescent lighting, the chatter of the group of girls already spilling out. I step out of the elevator behind the group of girls as they exit on the fortieth floor. With my head bent so my hair covers my face, I march out behind them, but as they turn left, I turn right. I head toward the long-term rooms used as condos and apartments.

The top floor of Stone Rose was originally built with two presidential suites. But five years ago, Nico Santorini purchased both and hired a company to do an entire remodel. He turned two two-story, five thousand square feet presidential suites into one two-story ten-thousand-square-foot penthouse fit for a king.

Just not this King.

Rosie got the blueprints from the general contractor's server so easily, it's almost embarrassing.

Four bedrooms, each with their own ensuite luxurious bathrooms, three rooms labeled as office, two different dens, a formal living room, theatre room, personal gym and sauna, a ridiculously large kitchen, a small wine cellar, and several more rooms than any one person ever needs.

The curious thing isn't that the eldest Santorini purchased both suites and turned them into his private residence, but that no one owned or ever used either suite for years beforehand. Not on record, at least.

I have my own theories on this, but since this little vacation is already running on assumptions and bravado, I'll keep those theories to myself. It doesn't really matter how long Nico has been living here anyway. It doesn't change anything.

I reach the end of the hall and take the stairs to ten floors above me. Thank god this dress already came with a thigh-high slit, exposing almost my entire left leg with each step. Otherwise,

I would've created my own with my favorite knife currently tucked against my right thigh.

I pause outside the door and check my watch. No messages from Rosie, which means there are no problems.

Despite her begging and her frankly convincing argument, my counter was just as good: she can assist from literally anywhere in the world. There's no reason for her to be in Las Vegas.

Especially not when I'm going to take out my betrothed.

She's safer in our New York apartment until we meet in Chicago.

I tap the wave emoji at her request to signal that I'm in position. I don't understand her very specific emoji selections, but we rotate through them every six months or so.

I exhale a breath and press my palm against my chest to will my heart to slow down. It's doing its best impression of a drumline against my ribs right now.

My watch buzzes on my wrist and after a quick glance, I see the sunflower emoji.

She's ready.

"Here we go," I murmur.

My heart thunders in my ears as I shove the metal handle to release the lock and ease the door open. I slip inside, only hearing the faint snick as it clicks shut behind me.

I know Rosie looped the camera feed in this hallway and the private elevator, but I can't help but feel eyes on me. I do my best to remain alert while appearing like I'm exactly where I belong.

My shoulders lose some of their tension, relaxing into a neutral position and I glance around. It looks like the hotel lobby, but with even more upscale furnishings.

The marble floor is cream, gold, and light brown, arranged in a sort of patchwork pattern. Pale-cream patterned wallpaper lines each wall with pale-cream crown molding. Gold-plated keypads in front of the elevator and each door. Even the elevator door looks like it's made of some sort of gold or distressed bronze.

Extravagant Edison bulb gold chandeliers hang every twenty feet from the domed-recessed ceiling.

Dozens of tall windows line the halls on either side, offering glimpses of a large gym, a swimming pool, a little coffee shop, and darkened conference rooms.

It's surprisingly quiet, but I suppose not many people are using these amenities at this time of night.

Still, I don't want to push my luck.

My heels click quietly on the marble floor as I cross the hallway to the residential elevator.

I place the key fob Rosie had made in front of the scanner. It's the one thing we absolutely needed for this to be successful. There's no other way to get into the residences—not even through emergency exits.

It flashes green, and the vice grip around my heart marginally loosens.

I will my hand to stay steady as I press the single button above the scanner. I take a shuddering breath as the elevator dings and the doors open.

I keep my head straight and step inside the elevator. It's no less extravagant than the hallway. I press the P button and clasp my hands in front of me. The itch to move pounds in my blood-stream, demanding I turn to look at the cameras I know are behind me to the left. But I shove that need down deep and keep looking straight ahead.

A jazzy rendition of a pop song plays quietly on the short ride up. I recognize the tune, but I can't remember the artist. The name is on the tip of my tongue when the elevator dings again.

I'm here.

9

MAEVE

I WAIT.

Thirty seconds. One minute, two. Three minutes.

After three minutes of absolutely no sound, I enter Nico Santorini's house. I don't venture far at first, giving myself a few moments to take everything in.

It's an open floor plan like I would expect to see in a sprawling ranch-style home in the countryside.

It's nothing like I would've imagined considering the hotel he lives in. Where Stone Rose is overstated luxury with gold plated and gold-trimmed everything, this penthouse is understated.

There's no denying the extravagance, but it's more lived-in. Casual even. I've had a lot of time to ponder what kind of man Nico Santorini is. After walking through the lobby downstairs and then seeing his apartment, I'm no closer to figuring him out.

It's a sea of light gray and white and black with modern industrial finishes. Despite its lived-in appearance, it doesn't seem to have many personal touches.

An entire wall of windows with an electronic blind system.

The cream-colored fabric hangs halfway down, letting the twin-kling lights from Las Vegas in all her glory shimmer in.

In another life, I'd slip off my shoes by the door and pad across the shaggy eight-by-ten-foot light gray rug in the living room. I'd pause to kiss my husband on the cheek, but he'd stop me with a hand on my waist and pull me down for a proper kiss hello. Then I'd continue toward the balcony and have a cocktail in one of the blue and white striped loungers and soak up the last rays of sunshine.

I blink and the vision is gone.

I shift forward and balance on the balls of my feet as I walk down the hallway to the left. The blueprints showed a kitchen, dining room, small home gym, and laundry room to the right, bedrooms upstairs, and several rooms labeled office to the left.

I pause in the mouth of the hallway as a tremor skates down my spine. I glance over my shoulder, half-expecting a gun in my face.

But the only thing near me is a wide spiral staircase that leads to the bedroom and loft area on the second floor.

Shaking off my nerves and whatever we're calling my momentary lapse in judgment, I tiptoe down the hallway. I push open the first door on my left with my index finger. It's nearly empty with a desk that looks like it's staged for decoration.

The second door is halfway open, and I quietly push it open further with my fingertips. It looks like a conference room of some kind. An oval table that seats ten in the center of the room with a projector screen covering one wall.

I back out of the room quickly and slink down to the last door.

It's wide open, and I know as soon as I step inside that this is the room I'm looking for. The energy shifts as I cross the thresh-old, and I almost pause, fear of some sort of booby-trap seizing my muscles.

I've clearly been watching too many movies with Rosie lately.

Two tall bay windows take up most of one wall, the vertical fabric blinds pulled nearly closed, letting only a sliver of the twinkling skyline in. An oversized clock hangs between the two windows. It's a mix of black metal and natural wood with large roman numerals and a hollowed out ring around the center to give it the appearance of floating.

A pine built-in shelving unit takes up the wall perpendicular to a large desk. Small metal bars run vertically from the bottom to the top, matching the rest of the penthouse's modern industrial vibe.

Books decorate the shelf, and I scan the spines for any familiar titles. Wood carvings and a few glass awards for something hotel-related serve as bookends, but for the most part, the bookshelf is surprisingly bare.

The desk takes up the back third of the room, all clean lines of pale oak craftsmanship with minor detailing around the trim. A large black leather chair sits behind the desk.

A crystal decanter sits on a mirrored tray on the shelf closest to the desk, a modern diamond-studded texture on the bottom two-thirds of the bottle. Two matching old fashioned glasses sit next to it, turned upside down.

I couldn't have planned it more perfectly if I tried.

I let my heels sink into the plush carpet and cross the room. The navy and cream patterned rug is too big for a room this size, only leaving six inches of hardwood floor showing.

I don't need to look at my watch to know that the clock is ticking. Santorini has been coming home around the same time for the last few days, and it wouldn't serve us well if I got caught in the act.

I grab the decanter by the neck and bring it under my nose for a sniff.

Whiskey.

Smells strong too. If there was ever a time to bend the rules, I think today is that day. I'll never hear the end of it, but fuck it. I deserve a small respite for this.

I pour myself a generous five fingers of whiskey in one of the clean glasses. And because I'm not a total slouch, I dig around in my purse for a small vial of what we've dubbed Hail Mary.

I upend the dropper and watch as a bead of liquid falls into my whiskey. If it turns blue, then poison or drugs are present. If it doesn't change colors, then it's safe. As much as five fingers of whiskey can be safe.

I give it an additional sixty seconds just to be sure, and only when it stays the same amber color do I take a small sip.

I relish the quick burn. It reminds me I'm alive.

I make short work of adding twenty milligrams of thallium saturate to the undoubtedly expensive whiskey in the decanter. It's more than enough to take out Santorini.

The smallest part of me, this tiny scrap of innocence that nestled its way into my heart protests at the idea of poisoning our betrothed. It's the same part that believes in true love and the magic of a kiss too.

It takes one thought to squash that morsel of concern: if I don't stop this, then Da will make arrangements for my sisters as well. And their situations would be so much worse.

In a choice between us or them, I choose us.

Always.

I replace the lid on the decanter and take my drink to Nico's leather chair. I blow out a breath and sit down.

This part of our plan was a point of contention between the five of us. I wanted to stay here, witness his consumption of our poison of choice. It's fast-acting and moves through the blood-stream quickly. It's nearly untraceable, and only those well-versed in poisons would ever suspect it.

To everyone else, it'll look like my betrothed had a heart

attack at the young age of twenty-four. They'll never investigate, and even if they did, they'd never be able to trace it back to me.

I know myself well enough by now that if I didn't witness it with my own eyes, then I'd always be looking over my shoulder. The stress would consume me until I was a bitter, hardened shell of myself.

Which doesn't sound much better than marrying the asshole to begin with.

My sisters didn't see it that way. They argued I should drop the thallium in something he'd be likely to drink soon and leave.

But there was no way to know that he drank it *and* that he was the only one. Casualties are often a byproduct of the Syndicate, and I imagine they're similar for the Italian mafia men.

But my sisters and I are different. We don't play by their boys' club rules. And we sure as hell don't chalk up innocent bystanders as casualties and call it a day.

So I pulled the oldest card and vetoed all of them and their concerns. It was a bullshit move, and I know I'll never hear the end of it. But I'll gladly face their wrath so long as I *get to see them.*

A seedling of guilt threatens to take root inside my heart once again, but I remind myself that my actions aren't selfishly motivated. Not entirely, at least.

If I don't end this, then I'll be trapped in a horrible marriage with someone only using me for their own gain. And worse than that, it'll sign my sisters' lives away.

So I throw more dirt on the seedling, burying it so far deep inside me that it'll never grow.

And I wait.

I'm not leaving here until I see Nico Santorini on his back.

10

MAEVE

AFTER TWENTY MINUTES and he didn't show, I got curious and decided to look around. By the hour mark, the ticking of the clock became unbearably loud, so I turned on the speaker I found while I was snooping. It wasn't hard—the console, the part that controls the entire system, sits proudly in the middle of the bookshelf designed as a piece of art.

It's an extensive system with speakers built in around the room, giving the listener a true surround-sound feel.

I found a satellite radio station that played some indie music I was familiar with, and I haven't changed it.

The Neighbourhood, Arcade Fire, Interpol, and others bore witness to my lackluster snooping skills.

If you need something stolen, I'm your girl. But if you need someone to infiltrate, to spy undetected, to gather intel, then that's all my sister, Fiona.

That's how I found myself singing the lyrics to a Lumineers song under my breath, flipping through an accordion file of papers with one hand and clutching the old fashioned glass in the other.

And then I hear it—the noise I've been waiting for nearly two hours now. Doors creak as they open and then presumably close. Footsteps echo throughout the house, the sharp clack-clack of dress shoes on the marble tile flooring of their hallway.

I tighten my hand into a fist, the paper crinkling with the force of my grip.

Shit.

I drop the file into the drawer and nudge it closed with my hip.

They get quieter as he reaches the long runner rug in the hallway, and I exhale relief that it's only one pair of footfalls I hear.

I didn't think about what I'd do if he had someone with him. Then I'd have two marks on my soul instead of just one.

As soon as I reach the desk, I shove the crumpled-up paper into my small clutch. I skirt the side of the desk and sink back into the plush leather chair.

I don't bother turning off the music. What's the point? He already knows someone is here.

Plus, a really good song just came on. As far as last songs go, it's a good one to usher you to the next life.

The chair creaks as I adjust my weight. I'm feeling particularly brazen, so I kick my heels up on the desk, crossing one ankle over the other. Just to paint the picture of casual, despite the thundering of my heart.

My fingers rest on the rim of the crystal old fashioned glass. I have roughly two fingers of whiskey left. Getting drunk is a rookie mistake, so I've enjoyed it slowly, savored it.

The footsteps slow into a soft thudding as he pads down the hall. If he's anything like the rumors of his father, he'll already have his gun drawn, finger poised above the trigger.

I remind myself of all the terrible things Vito Santorini has done and the likelihood that his son, the man set to inherit the

Santorini kingdom, was made in his image. It's a patch to the cracks in my resolve, stemming the guilt from seeping through.

I close my eyes and imagine Nico strutting into his office and his angry expression when he finds me behind his desk. I bet he's the type of man who never likes anything out of place. I let the vision play out behind my closed lids, his footfalls getting closer and closer. He's nearly here.

Anticipation hums inside my veins, churning the whiskey sour in my gut.

My fingertips tingle and a whispered chill rolls over me. The air stutters in my chest, and I blink my eyes open.

He stands in the doorway looking nothing like I imagined.

Black dress shirt opened at the collar and rolled up halfway along his forearms, exposing black tattoos to his wrists. Hands tucked into the pockets of his black suit pants.

He's tall and broad-shouldered, the fabric of his shirt molded to his traps and biceps in a way that should be criminal.

His dark hair is wild, a few locks curling over the middle of his forehead like he spent the last ten minutes running his hands through it. His sharp jawline is visible through his five o'clock shadow that's a day or two away from a full-fledged beard.

I didn't think I liked men with facial hair, but after seeing him, I might have to change my stance. Full pink lips curl into a smirk at my obvious perusal, and my lower belly tightens at the sight.

"What an unexpected surprise," he murmurs, tilting his head to the side. His voice is low. Amusement falls from his words, and it's almost jarring. I expected anger, wariness, and distrust.

But not pleasantries. Not curious mirth.

His reaction causes me to pause. I had planned on standing up and introducing myself as Scarlet Baldwin, the leader of the Golden Sixers, offering him a drink under the guise of working together. The Golden Sixers is a fictional community we made up from Arizona and looking to make a name for ourselves in the west.

It has just enough possibility to be true, and by the time he realizes it's a bullshit story, he'll already be dead.

But that was before I saw him look at me like that. It's not recognition—thank god—but something else. Intrigue maybe.

His tongue peeks out between his full lips, swiping along his lower lip. "I'm—"

"I know who you are," I quip, taking my time to bring the glass to my lips. I take a small sip and let the whiskey mellow on my tongue before swallowing the harsh burn.

It's a stupid power play, but it makes me feel better and calms my thundering heart to a more manageable racing. This attraction is . . . an unwelcome surprise.

The corner of his lips quirks up briefly. He leans a shoulder against the doorframe, crossing his right ankle over his left. "This is normally the part where you introduce yourself considering you're inside my house."

"You can call me Sandy."

The words are out of my mouth before I even give them conscious thought. I have no idea why I blurted out Sandy, but I'm going to blame Ava. She was singing a song from *Grease* three days ago, and it hasn't left my head since.

He chuckles, this low, throaty noise that has my lower belly clenching again.

What the fuck is going on here?

"Sandy, huh?"

I slide my legs off his desk, letting my feet fall to the floor and leaning forward in one, smooth movement. I brace my arms on the desk, forming a V shape, and stare at him. "Enough pleasantries. I came here to make a deal."

His smirk morphs into a grin. It's a little too sharp around the edges to ever be considered joyful. He pushes off the door and saunters into the room. He reminds me of a panther, all long strides and lethal grace.

It's the kind of energy that speaks to me on a molecular level, something that's hard to describe.

"Perfect. I love making deals." He grasps the back of one of the two chairs in front of the desk and pulls it back a foot. Before he sits down, he pulls a handgun from behind him—tucked into the back of his pants, if I had to guess. He leans over and places it on the desk, halfway between the two of us.

My breath stalls and my gaze laser-focuses on the firearm between us. As far as guns go, it's a standard issue among mafia men: a Smith & Wesson.

I give him my attention without moving a muscle. Hell, I'm barely breathing.

"What's this?" I glance from him to the gun and back to him again.

He sinks into the chair in front of me with a long look, widening his legs and folding his arms across his chest.

"An act of good faith. I'm told it's standard in negotiating."

My muscles twitch with tension. "Is that what we're doing? Negotiating?"

His smile is slow to grow. "You tell me. You're the one in my house."

Sweat beads on the back of my neck. This isn't how it was supposed to go. This feels like a trap.

Rosie's words come back to me. *"What if he doesn't want it though? What if he's in an impossible position like we are?"*

Could it be that simple? Could I cut my own deal with him?

How could I know though? Indecision plagues me, rooting me to the chair as an idea begins to take shape.

How could I be sure though? How could I ever trust someone who'd willingly agree to such an arrangement anyway?

Five questions, I tell myself. *I'll give him five questions for me to decide.*

Mum always said I was the best judge of character she'd ever met. I took that praise and ran with it, channeling it into what my sisters and I do now.

"Tell me, Santorini, if you had one day left on this earth, how would you spend it?"

He stills, his muscles contracting and freezing in an instant. His eyes darken to nearly black as his brows sink low over them. "Do I have one day left, *piccola seduttrice?*"

My heart jumps at the Italian words rolling off his tongue. I swallow down the lust swelling around me like a fog.

He clocks it anyways, tilting his head to the side. "I thought you said you knew who I was?"

"I didn't know about the Italian though."

He grins. "My grandfather taught my brothers and me when we were younger, but I don't get enough opportunities to practice."

My pulse speeds up at the mere idea of him whispering in my ear in Italian. I need to redirect the conversation back to neutral territory.

I nod a couple of times. "Is that where you would go for your last day—Italy?"

"What is this? An interview?"

I arch my brow and twist my lips to the side in a smirk. "Humor me."

He tilts his chin up. "There's a give and take. I'll answer your question but I want something in return."

"What?"

He rakes his front teeth over his bottom lip. "Nothing much. A small thing really." The corner of his mouth tips up into a grin that can only be described as predatory. "A kiss."

11

MAEVE

MY EYES WIDEN before they narrow on him. What's his angle?

"You're not at all how I thought you'd be," I murmur.

"Ah so you did think of me."

"Aye, a time or two."

"Uncharitable thoughts, no doubt."

His grin is forced, too wide like an ill-fitting sweater. He's trying to keep it flirty but there's a wound there. And not for the first time since I walked into this apartment, I wonder who Nico Santorini really is.

"An answer for a kiss?"

"I, for one, think this is a fair trade," he says, his grin smoothing out into something more natural.

I told myself I'd give him five questions, but perhaps I could find the answer I needed in a simple kiss. I've heard Fiona and Keira talk at length about all the ways a man can kiss you and how it's indicative of broader things.

Now I wish I'd stayed to hear the whole conversation.

I haven't had many experiences with men—I'm no prude. But I've always had other, more important things to deal with.

"I can practically hear you thinking, you know."

I scoff, but he's not wrong. I *am* overthinking.

It's one kiss.

"Fine." I stand up and stride around the desk.

The shag rug practically swallows my red-soled black pumps. He pushes to his feet and eliminates the space between us in one stride.

I knew he was tall, but standing in front of him like this only amplifies the height difference. I tilt my head to hold his gaze, and for the first time all night, I see an emotion I wasn't expecting on his face: lust.

He looks at me with a hunger so intense it makes my knees weak.

I swallow roughly, clenching my hands into fists at my side. "Well, Santorini? Here I am—"

He palms the back of my neck and dips down to claim my mouth. For a second, I freeze. His lips are softer than I expected. His five o'clock shadow scratches against my skin as he drags his lips over mine in soft, sweeping kisses.

My eyelids drift closed and little pinpricks of starlight flash in the corner of my vision. Tingles race across my skin. They have nothing to do with whiskey and everything to do with him.

I never thought kissing anyone would feel like this. And I definitely never expected it to be the man I have to kill.

I pull back when reality slaps me in the face. His gaze pingpongs between my eyes for a moment before he lets his hand fall from the back of my neck. He steps back but he doesn't sit down. And I don't either.

The task of ending his life presses against my breastbone, making it difficult to breathe. I can't explain it. I don't know what makes him different from any of the other lives we've taken or ruined except that it *is* different.

Plan B it is. Or is it plan C now?

This whole night has gone every way *except* the way I thought it would.

I clear my throat and lean my ass against the front of the desk. "I have another question."

He slides his hands in his pants pockets. "But I didn't answer your first one."

I waft a hand in the air as if to wave his words away. "Forget about that one. This is the only question that counts."

He scans my face for a moment. The need to ask what he's looking for pounds against my teeth, but I don't.

"Alright."

I grip the desk behind me, curling my fingers over the lip. "How far would you go for the people you love?"

"To the end." There's no faltering in his answer, as if he's been asked this question many times. I imagine in his life, it's quite possible.

My chest expands, filling my lungs with more than breath.

"Your father's going to bring you a contract, and I need you to terminate it."

Stillness wraps around him like a blanket, and he holds my stare. "A contract?"

I wet my lips and forge forward. "A *marriage* contract."

He blinks once, a slow sweep of his dark lashes. I didn't realize how expressive his face was until every inch of it was smoothed into an unfeeling mask.

He cocks his head toward me. "Why?"

My pulse whooshes in my ears and I fight to remain calm. I didn't think this part through. I have to play this very carefully, otherwise, it's going to blow up in my face.

"My cousin." I purse my lips, unwilling to offer any more information.

It's the most realistic explanation I can think of right now. I blame him and that kiss for scrambling my wits.

His face relaxes into a small grin, like he's remembered something amusing. Or hell, maybe this whole conversation is entertaining to him.

I subtly shift my body in front of where I know the gun is. I won't be able to reach it from this angle, but at least I can block his access to it. Though I seriously doubt that's the only weapon he has on him.

Luckily for me, I'm still armed.

He swipes his thumb across his bottom lip, his eyes raking over me from head to toe. "And what do I get?"

My nipples tighten in response to his hungry gaze, my fingers curling tighter around the desk. The low rasp of his voice is playing tricks on my nervous system.

"What do you want?"

"You," he breathes without hesitation.

I scan his face but all I find is raw truth.

Fucking Nico Santorini would hardly be a hardship. And if it buys me my freedom without ending his? How could I refuse?

My sisters are going to kill me but that's a problem for tomorrow.

"Okay."

The last letter is barely past my lips before he's on me, hands tunneling in my hair and tipping my face toward his to devour my mouth.

Gone is the gentle brush of his lips and in its place is a man starved. He flicks his tongue out and everything changes. I sigh, parting my lips, and he takes advantage of it immediately.

I lose track of time as our tongues war with one another.

At one point, he growls, this low noise in the back of his throat. His hands drop to the backs of my upper thighs and without stopping our kiss, he lifts me into the air and sets me on the edge of the desk. I wrap my legs around his waist and tug him to me tightly.

My brain shorts at the feeling of his cock pressed against my pussy through the thin fabric of my thong. He's long and thick and hard, and I realize with a start that I'm looking forward to fucking him.

You can learn a lot about someone by the way they treat a lover, and I hope for his sake, he lives up to my mounting expectations.

I rip my mouth away from his, tipping my chin up and gulping in air. His palms leave my neck to slip the straps of my dress over my shoulders with deft fingers.

His lips carve a path down my neck and along my collar bone. I tip my head to the side to give him better access, sinking my fingers into his hair in a vain attempt to hold his lips to my skin longer.

The neckline of my dress sags, exposing my tits almost to my nipples. Lust has taken over my body, piloting my limbs. My pulse drums a frantic rhythm, echoing lust's demands for him to give me *more, more, more*.

I use my grip on his hair to tug his head down further. I don't need to spell it out—he knows exactly what I want.

He uses his nose to nudge down the fabric, my breasts now on full display.

"Goddamn," he groans before he gives them the attention I crave.

He alternates from one to the other, sweeping his tongue around and nipping just hard enough to feel the tug directly in my clit.

My hips wiggle against his. I don't get the friction I crave from this angle. It's just enough for the tip of his cock to tease me. And I've had enough teasing.

I push at his shoulders, and he lifts his head. His eyes glassy and lips shiny and swollen.

"Fuck me, Santorini."

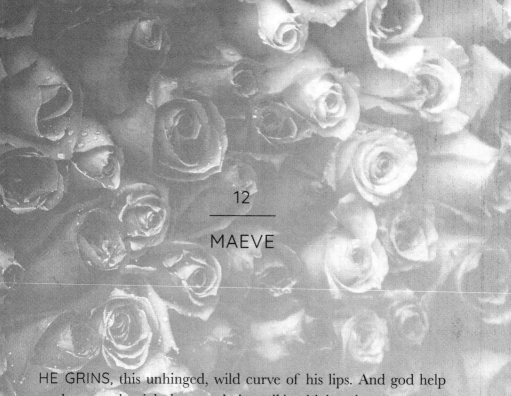

12

MAEVE

HE GRINS, this unhinged, wild curve of his lips. And god help me because the sight has my desire spiking higher than ever.

I nudge his shoulder to get him to step back, but he surprises me by wrapping his arms around my torso and pulling me closer. He carries me around the desk and sinks into the leather chair. It's barely wide enough for my legs on either side of his.

My heart pounding in my chest, I slowly push myself up and hold his gaze. I don't waver as I reach for the button on his jeans. It releases and the metal teeth of the zipper part, the sound somehow loud in the charged atmosphere. I slide the zipper down, my breath catching at the sight.

I'm not surprised that there's nothing but skin underneath his trousers. He doesn't strike me as the kind of man who bothers with boxer briefs.

A hiss slithers from his lips when I wrap my hand around his cock. And *goddamn* is it a big cock.

"Fuck. Just like that," he groans.

His rasped words layer over me, empowering me in a way I

could see becoming addictive. I tighten my fist and slowly bring it up and down, reveling in the way his face pinches with pleasure.

"Tell me, *piccola seduttrice*, are you already wet for me?" he murmurs, his fingers gripping the end of the armrests tightly.

I don't answer him with words. Instead, I grab his right hand with my left and drag it up my thigh to cover my pussy. He doesn't need any further encouragement.

He hooks a finger around the scrap of material in his way and wrenches it to the side. The pads of his fingers brush against me softly, my lust soaking his fingertips in a second.

"So wet already," he murmurs, his fingertips fluttering over me.

He drags my arousal up to circle around my clit. The pressure is too light, I need more. I lower my hips, my mind focused on chasing the feeling of him.

He tsks and grabs my hip with his free hand, applying just enough pressure to let me know he doesn't want me to move. I hover over him, twisting and jerking his cock in my fist and imagining him inside of me.

"I wonder, do you taste as sweet?" He trails two fingers through my slick folds and brings them to his lips. I hold his gaze as he wraps his tongue around his fingers and sucks them into his mouth.

Holy hell, why is that so attractive?

He slides his fingers from his mouth and whispers, "*Dolce.*"

My breath hitches at the sight, and I decide I'm done playing. If I don't have his cock inside of me in the next thirty seconds, I'm going to do something stupid like say fuck it and marry the bastard just to be able to have this every night.

I lean forward and crush my mouth to his, swallowing his groan, distracting him. I position myself, using my grip on his cock to line us up. I rock my hips forward, the head of his dick bumping my clit and easing just the barest centimeter inside of me on each pass.

"You're driving me crazy," he groans against my mouth.

"Good." I sink lower, stopping when he's just barely inside of me. My muscles quiver with anticipation, my lust a tangible form, pushing at my skin, begging me to take all of him.

But I can't yet. Not until I've made sure he understands how serious I am about our terms.

I slam my lips against his and pull the thin blade from my thigh at the same time. It's awkward and the angle hurts my wrist, but I position it so the tip gently prods the base of his cock.

I drag it across his groin, pressing hard enough to scratch but not hard enough to draw blood. It takes him longer than I thought it would to notice.

He rears back, his eyes slow to blink open. He stares at me for a beat, then drags his gaze between us. One of my hands squeezes his cock and the other squeezes the handle of the blade.

He looks at me from underneath his lashes, his lips parted and swollen. "If you wanted to bring blades into this, *dolcezza*, all you had to do was ask."

His eyes brighten and his grin grows wider. And so does his cock.

My hair tickles my shoulders as I lean forward, adjusting my grip on the blade. My tits are inches from his face, but his gaze stays on mine.

"It'd be a shame, you know." I drag my blade around the base of his cock.

"Hmm?" He lifts a brow.

"For you to have to lose such a pretty cock."

His hands find my hips, his grip oddly possessive. "If you're trying to turn me on, it's working."

I slowly stroke his cock. "If I don't see a terminated contract within twenty-four hours, then I'll assume you broke our agreement. And I'll come to collect my revenge. Starting with your cock."

I swear his dick swells in my hand, growing impossibly harder.

"Consider it already done."

I look into his eyes as I flick my wrist, slashing a small line in the place where his hips and pelvis meet. And not for the first time, I'm rewarded with an expression I never would've guessed: hunger.

"Something to remember me by," I murmur as I tuck my blade back in my thigh holster.

He sucks his teeth. "Ah, *piccola seduttrice.* I'll never forget—"

I lower myself on his cock, delighting in the stretch and slight burn as I accommodate his size.

There's dead air for a split second. In the time it takes for one song to roll into another, a weighted bubble of surprise and wonder engulfs us.

Then we're reaching for each other, our mouths crashing together. His hands fly to my hips, encouraging my fast rhythm. It's not going to take me long. I can already feel the tingles starting in my toes, slowly growing and spreading up my legs.

"Tell me your real name," he begs between panting breaths.

The edge of my lip curls up in a smirk, and I roll my hips. "Where's the fun in that?"

"Goddamn it." He slides his palms underneath my thighs, his fingertips pressing tight enough that I know I'll be wearing his prints for days. He pushes to his feet without another word— without untangling us.

I throw my arm around his neck with a pitiful squeak, clenching around his cock without thinking.

"Fuck me," he groans out, walking us the two steps to the desk behind me.

"Isn't that what we're doing?" I nip at his earlobe, biting down hard enough to draw another groan from his perfect lips.

He sweeps his arm across the top of the desk, sending all the contents flying to the floor before he sets me on the edge. The angle changes, deepens. My toes curl inside my heels, and my fingers dig into his shoulders.

He's broad and muscular, and I've never felt more desirable in my life. He handled me like it was nothing, like he does this sort of thing all the time.

I stop that thought in its tracks as the first spikes of jealousy creep into my lusty fog. I cut them off at the knees. I don't have any right to be jealous. He's not mine, and he never will be.

Tonight has to be enough.

I pull back and crush my mouth to his with a renewed passion. Our tongues fight for dominance as his hands slide to my inner knees, pushing them wider. He rolls his hips then, these long, drawn-out slides of his cock that are a form of torture.

Nothing should feel this good—*nothing*.

I pull back and pant for air, tipping my head back to look at the ceiling. One hand leaves my thigh to slide up my neck. He pauses with his palm just over my collar bone, his fingers light and loose. With a gentle nudge, he pushes me back.

The desk feels cool against my exposed back. My dress is a tangled heap of fabric that barely covers anything, but I already know I won't take the time to take it off. No matter how much I want to feel his skin against mine.

Once I'm flush against the desk, he picks up his pace—not faster but *harder*.

"Holy fuck." He sounds tortured.

Pleasure dances along every nerve ending. "Don't stop."

I buck my hips, and the motion rubs my clit against his pelvis. More sparks of pleasure fire, and I'm getting close to coming. My chest heaves with labored breaths as the two of us find a new rhythm. For a split second, I imagine this as my life.

My husband coming home and fucking me like it was our last night on earth. Every single night.

He brushes my clit with the barest pressure, and I tilt my hips toward him, chasing his hand.

"Tell me your name, *piccola seduttrice*. Tell me and you'll come harder than you ever have."

He brushes his thumb over my clit again, more pressure this time, and it short-circuits my brain.

"M—"

My eyes slam shut, stealing my words as I race toward that peak of pleasure.

He mistakes my grunt for my name. "Em. It's perfect, just like this pussy. That's right, squeeze my cock."

He thrusts a final time, stilling as he comes with a shout.

We're wrapped around each other, way more familiar than either of us have any right to be considering we just met an hour ago. Still, I don't shove him off of me, and he takes his time catching his breath.

Eventually, we part.

I keep waiting for the shame to hit, the guilt to ransack me and hold my emotional stability hostage. But as I watch him slip out of me, his face surprisingly boyish and open, it doesn't come.

"I'm going to go take a shower. Come with me?" He holds out his hand, a direct invitation.

A shiver rolls down my back. "I'll be right there."

It's a lie. One I hope he believes long enough for me to slip away. I'm not foolish enough to mistake the post-orgasmic bliss for anything other than what it is.

If he breaks the agreement and I have to pay him another visit, then that's a problem for another day. But showering after sex feels like the kind of thing couples do.

He trails his fingers over my bare shoulder. "Upstairs and to the left."

After one last lingering look that promises more orgasms, he turns around and leaves the office. He whistles as he walks down the hallway, unbuttoning his shirt and pulling it from his trousers.

I slip my straps up my shoulders, tuck my tits beneath the stretched-out fabric, and hop off the desk. He pauses at the end of the hallway to turn around and flash me a grin.

I return it and shimmy my dress down over my hips. The slit lost a stitch or two, but it's hardly noticeable. I grab my clutch and wait, listening to his whistling get quieter the further away he gets. Eventually, a door above me closes and the whistling muffled.

I cross the room, desperation to leave this place quickening my steps. But then I remember the poison and it stops me instantly. I can't leave it here. But it's not like I can take it with me and smashing the bottle makes too much noise.

So I do the next best thing.

I take the crystal stopper from the bottle and place the decanter on its side. The whiskey sloshes against the sides for a moment before pouring out of the open top and splashing against the rug.

"Sorry about the mess, Santorini," I murmur.

I shift my weight from foot to foot as the last dredges of the bottle fall to the floor, but just to make sure, I upend the entire thing and leave it face-down on the rug.

And then I get the hell out of there.

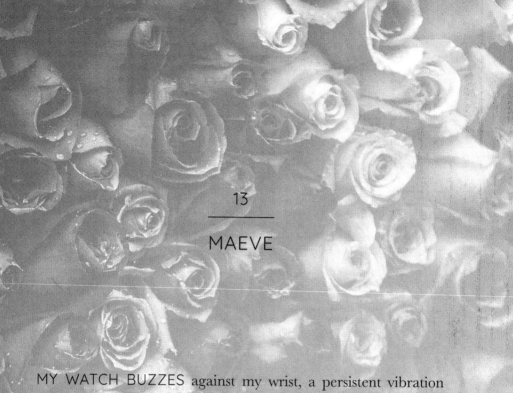

13

MAEVE

MY WATCH BUZZES against my wrist, a persistent vibration that I do my best to ignore. I already know who it is.

I missed check-in with her. I didn't signal any distress, but it's not like me to miss a call like that. Unfortunately, she's going to have to wait a little longer for that call.

I send her a sunflower emoji from the shortcut on my watch. It's a quick way for her to know I'm alright. Though knowing her, she's probably watching me right now and cursing my name.

I blow out a breath and finger-comb my hair a little.

It's fine. Everything is fine.

Maybe if I repeat it enough I'll just start believing it.

My legs quiver, a tangible reminder that I was seeing stars ten minutes ago. A quick peek into the light gold reflective walls of the elevator surrounding me confirms my suspicions.

Pink cheeks, hair wild and kinked, dress askew.

I look freshly fucked.

Instead of eliminating my target, I fucked him. Worse, I *enjoyed* it. I really fucking enjoyed it. I couldn't have deviated from the plan further if I tried. But I might've solved our problem without having to stain my soul any further.

What would Da say if he saw me now? If he knew I sabotaged his contract and made my own deal?

Shame lies heavy on my tongue, thick and hard to swallow. Twenty-three years old and the idea of disappointing my father still makes me queasy.

I've bent Da's rules before, pushed boundaries, and skirted the truth on more than one occasion.

But I've never gone this far before.

Anger burns away the shame, leaving ashes of guilt in its wake. If he didn't sign a contract to give me away like a fucking party favor, then I wouldn't even *be* in this situation.

Though I can't bring myself to regret him—or what we did. And if he wasn't who he is and I wasn't who I am, I might even consider doing something reckless like coming back for round two.

I skim my palms down my sides, a vain attempt to smooth out any wrinkles from my dress as the elevator descends straight into the residential parking garage underneath the hotel.

At least I'm still on track for this part of the plan.

My watch buzzes again. The elevator dings with arrival to the garage level, and it's like a lightbulb flashes in my mind.

Oh shit.

The blood drains from my face as I connect the dots.

Rosie stopped the cameras from recording and looped the footage for the hallways and Santorini's apartment, but she still had to monitor the live feed in case I ran into trouble.

Which means my baby sister just saw me *renegotiate* with our enemy.

The air pouring in from the vents above does nothing to cool the embarrassment settling in against my skin. I hope for both of our sakes she didn't actually watch. And thank god, there was no sound.

I glance at my watch as the elevator doors open. Messages populate one after the other, moving too fast on the little screen that I only catch a glimpse of a few of them.

> Rosie: What is going on? Why are you talking so much?
>
> Rosie: Pls tell me you're not going to hook up with him
>
> Rosie: Don't make me call Keira!
>
> Rosie: What the fuck, Maeve! You better call me as soon as you're in the car!

Guilt and shame twist together into a macabre knot, wrapping around my throat and sinking into my stomach like a lead weight.

What will my sisters think of me now?

I honestly don't know what came over me or how I went from poisoning to fucking, but here we are.

My emotions are condensing down into a sticky, tarred ball, rolling around inside my gut and growing bigger and bigger.

Shit.

Take a deep breath. It's just sex. It's not that big of a deal, and they're totally going to be fine with it. And if they aren't, well . . . I'll figure something out. I always do.

I find the black SUV exactly where Ava said she dropped it off yesterday. Originally, I was going to be the one to plant it, but she insisted on it. Claimed it was on her way to meet some friends before heading to Monaco.

As casually as possible, I snag the magnetic hidden key holder inside the driver's side wheel well. I make quick work of sliding the top open and snagging the universal key fob Rosie and Ava made together last year. As far as inventions go, it's one of our most used ones. I place the key fob next to the handle and wait five seconds for it to calibrate to this car's signature. At least, that's how they described it to me.

I'm not much for cars. I leave all of that stuff to Ava.

I allow a few extra seconds, pretending to rummage inside my bag like I'm looking for something. I try the handle and exhale as it opens without any trouble.

Zipping my purse up, I slide into the cool leather interior and pull the seat forward a couple inches. Being the shortest gets old sometimes.

Keira has a whole half-inch on me, a high point on her biography, no doubt.

I dig around my purse for my earpod headphones and place the right one just inside my ear. I pull out of the parking garage and follow the Ava-approved exit strategy to get the fuck out of here.

I press the right earpod and hold it for two seconds until I hear the beep. "Call Rosie."

She answers on the first ring. "Maeve Tallulah King. You have some serious explaining to do."

I drum my fingers on the steering wheel and nod like she can see me. Apparently, my point-five-second pause is too long because her dramatic sigh thunders in my ear. I wince and take the right corner a little too quickly.

Even though I'm not fleeing a poisoning, I still don't want a record of me being in this city.

"I couldn't do it, Rosie." Resignation coats those five words like honey.

"You don't say." Her voice deadpans, and I'd bet the pink diamond necklace she's doing that upper lip half-snarl thing she does when she's unimpressed.

"Yeah, uh, how much did you uh . . . see?"

"Enough to know that Nico Santorini's big dick energy is totally warranted. God damn, Maeve." She cuts herself off with a low whistle.

"Jesus, Rosie. I don't know how I feel about you getting front-row seats to . . . that."

"Oh, relax. As soon as he started tongue-fucking your mouth, I turned it off. I checked it ten minutes later, but Nico isn't a two-pump chump." I can hear the smirk in her voice, she's awfully proud of her dirty innuendos.

At the thought of Santorini and his cock, a flush rolls down my body with the speed of a box turtle.

I clear my throat and shift in the seat. The soft leather crinkles with my movement but I'm too busy mentally chastising myself. "Yeah, well."

She waits a beat before she says, "Someone has to say it, okay?"

I flick my blinker on and turn left. I'm almost to the small airport. "Say what?"

"You didn't kill him."

"I know."

"Not only did you not kill him, but you *slept with him*." She drags her words out like I'm being obtuse.

"I *know*."

"So . . . maybe you want to reconsider breaking the marriage arrangement."

My mouth falls open and I shake my head. "Are you serious? I'm not going through with a fucking *arranged marriage*, Rosie."

"All I'm saying is a lot of people marry for a lot less than sexual chemistry."

"Yeah, well, he's probably an anomaly. Most of the men on the other side of these Syndicate *arrangements* aren't really marriage material."

"And they don't look like Nico Santorini." She whistles under her breath.

"No kidding," I say with a snort before I shake my head to clear his image from my brain. "But it doesn't matter. It's not like Da's vetting these men before he's signing our lives to them."

She sighs. "Okay, so how are you getting out of it if he's still breathing?"

She doesn't comment further on marriage contracts. What else is there to say right now?

Here comes the tricky part. I have to convince my sisters that Santorini will keep his word and reject the contract. Hell, I have to convince *myself* that he'll follow through.

"He told me he'd reject the contract within twenty-four hours' time."

"And you believe him?" Rosie sputters.

I sigh. "Yes. No. I don't know. Look, I don't know how else to explain it other than saying I believe him. Plus, I told him that if he didn't, he wouldn't see next week."

"So you threatened him, and he *still fucked you*? Man, Nico Santorini is a total trip. It's too bad he had to be arranged to marry you. He could've been legit for you, Maeve."

I brush off her sentiment before I let myself get tangled up in the what-ifs. It's a dangerous game that never ends well. I stopped playing it eleven years ago, and I don't intend to start now.

I pull into the private airport and throw the car in park. "I'm at the airstrip, so I gotta go. I'll see you in Chicago tomorrow, okay?"

"Looking forward to it, sister. Then we can pick up this conversation."

She hangs up on me, her penchant to always have the last word can grate on my nerves most of the time. But I'm more relieved to be done with this conversation. And if I have it my way, we won't be revisiting it.

14

MAEVE

THE SOUTHSIDE of Chicago welcomes me as it always does: with smog and danger in the air.

Blaring horns, squealing brakes, shrieking sirens, and yelled arguments form a chorus around me. I've always liked the noise of a big city. You can tell a lot by the voice of a city, a neighborhood.

Like the one I'm currently in. Men and women grabbing a pint and a burger during their lunch breaks. Soldiers dipping in and out of connected businesses, legitimate and fronts.

There are a lot of eyes on me right now. Even if I can't see them all, I can feel them. It's such a stark contrast to how I usually work that it always takes some adjusting. Somewhere along the way, it became easier for me to slink around various towns and buildings than walking down the street in broad daylight.

I'm in Emmett O'Boyle's neighborhood, so I know it's safe.

Well, as safe as you can be when you're the daughter of one of the most notorious members of the Irish Syndicate and you and your sisters run an underground ring of vengeance.

But I'll be fine in O'Boyle's territory. He's a general in the Syndicate, and he and Da used to run some jobs together when they were both coming up. But then Da met Mum, and their paths diverged.

Until two years ago when O'Boyle's niece ended up on our radar.

Rosie found a way into the network she'd been working on for a few months on the dark web. She discovered a trafficking ring was happening in Chicago, and this slimy Wall Street wannabe was responsible for at least half of the disappearances himself.

Rosie sent two encrypted messages. One to the guy with an address for the meet-up and one to the people he was supposed to be meeting.

We intercepted the Wall Street wannabe and tipped off the FBI for his buddies.

I can count on one hand the times we've ever brought in government officials, but some things are outside of our skill set. And short of killing all the men waiting on the docks that day—a plan Keira voted for—we had little other options. We didn't have the relationships with the cleaning crew that we have now.

And we didn't know how involved O'Boyle was. Was he turning a blind eye? Was it happening behind his back? Or was he orchestrating it?

We found our answer among the women: Darla O'Boyle. Emmett's niece was kidnapped by the Wall Street asshole and she was on her way to be auctioned off.

And since that day, we've had a sort of arrangement. We give him a head's up if we're in the area, and in return, he looks the other way if a few men in his city face our vengeance.

I've got twenty minutes to kill before heading into The Underground to meet O'Boyle. I requested a proper meeting with him to confirm his stance on Rosie staying in the city.

I don't expect her to wander into the thick of O'Boyle's neighborhood, but his reach extends to the entire city. Including Harrington University.

A bead of sweat rolls down the back of my neck, sinking into the collar of my black linen racerback tank top. It's hot as hell here this time of year. The humidity swells, and each step feels a little more like wading through soup.

I'm glad I wore jean shorts, even if I usually prefer to do business in my black faux leather pants. They offer amazing flexibility for anything, but they're too form-fitting for nineties in Chicago.

I stroll down the block, peeking in the storefront windows as I go. In some ways, this neighborhood feels stuck in time. Several delis, a couple bakeries, a chocolate shoppe, and lots of pubs.

I pause in front of the window of Ruby's Confectionary. She's packing squares of chocolate fudge into small cellophane bags. Damn, that looks good. I'm going to have to stop here on my way out. I bet they have those jelly candies Rosie loves too. The strawberry and orange hard candies are her favorite flavors.

My phone vibrates against my ass. I slip it out of my back pocket without taking my eye from the methodical way Ruby alternates peanut butter and chocolate squares. I blink at the preview on my screen.

> Unknown Number: You forgot something.

It's NOT a number I recognize, but that's not surprising. Only a few people have this number, and all of them are saved in my contacts.

I slide my thumb across the screen to reply.

Me: Wrong number.

Unknown Number: I don't think so.

I DON'T HAVE time to correct some random person texting me. I tap the power button on the side of my phone and the screen goes black. Before I can slip it in my back pocket, it buzzes again.

I pull it out and see another preview notification for a text from the same number. Irritation straightens my spine, and I open up the message again.

This time he sends a photo.

It's a tube of lipstick on a glass side table. Caleb Miller's side table to be exact. It's the last mark I had since my life flipped around into whatever this bundle of chaos it is now.

Shit.

Did I actually leave something behind? Something traceable?

Fuck. *Did Miller find me?*

I wipe that thought clear as soon as it forms. Miller is a pompous idiot who lacks the intelligence required to track who broke into his safes. But that asshole has money, and money can buy a lot of things—including the temporary allegiance from someone who does have the intellect to start connecting some dots.

But that still doesn't explain how they found my phone number. I thought I read once that if you had the patience, you could conceivably try every number combination, and eventually, you'd reach the right person.

I'm out of my depth with this, but thankfully, this is Rosie's bread and butter.

I pull out my other phone from the hidden pocket inside my crossbody purse. We all have a burner that we only ever use to call one another. They're as untraceable as possible, thanks to Rosie's genius.

My youngest sister answers on the first ring. "I know, I know. I'm running a little late, but you can blame Keira for that. I'm still in New York because Keira—"

"I don't care about that right now. I need you to track something."

"What's wrong?"

I bite my bottom lip, hard enough to sting. "Besides the obvious mess that I've made?" Anxiety coats my throat, making it hard to form words. "I think I fucked up, Rosie," I whisper.

Rustling comes down the line as she moves stuff around. "Shit. Okay. Tell me what happened."

I lick my lips and glance over my shoulder again. No one is behind me, despite the feeling of eyes on me. I scoot to the side of Ruby's window, leaning my shoulder against the side of her building.

"Where is Caleb Miller?"

"That asshole is licking his wounds somewhere in the Caribbean on mommy and daddy's dime."

I exhale a slow breath. "You sure?"

"Hang on." I hear the clicking of her keyboard, and I imagine her fingers flying across the numbers and letters as she works her magic. "Yep. He's still there. Why?"

"You found him fast," I murmur.

"You know I always keep tabs on our friends we vacation with."

"Aye, I know." I pull my bottom lip into my mouth, letting my mind wander.

"What's going on?"

I shift to stare out into the street, looking up and down the blocks. I don't see anyone that looks shady. "I got a text from an unknown number."

"Which phone?"

"My newer one. Not the emergency burner or this one, but the one I've been using for the last few months."

"Maybe it's time to change them?"

"Yeah, maybe. But first I want to see if you can track them. Here, let me forward their contact information."

I pull up the information from the unknown number and forward it to Rosie before tucking it back in my pocket.

"Got it. Give me like ten minutes. Thirty if he's covering his tracks, yeah?"

"Okay. Thanks."

"Always, Maeve. What did they say, anyway?"

"It was a photo of the lipstick I left at the last job."

The line is quiet, but I know she didn't hang up.

"Fuck."

I nod a few times. "My thoughts exactly."

"Okay, give me a little time. I'll call you back soon. Oh, and Maeve? Don't go to my dorm, okay? Go somewhere public."

The wariness in her voice is so unlike her, my feet stop without conscious thought. I make sure to gentle my tone, bleaching the worry out. "Hey, I'll be fine, yeah? I'm going to meet O'Boyle soon, and afterward, I'll kill time at a pub before I head to your dorm room."

She blows out a breath, the noise loud in my ear. "Yeah, alright. I'll be there late tonight. Keira found me a red-eye."

We murmur our goodbyes and hang up. I tap my bottom lip with the corner of the phone, trying to remember every step of that job. I don't think I left any trace of us, but I was definitely distracted.

Shit.

Okay, let's see if I can't get a little information out of this person before Rosie finds them. Any advantage is good, no matter how small.

> Me: Who is this?

He replies in an instant.

> Unknown Number: Romeo.

> Me: I suppose that makes me Juliet, then?

> Unknown Number: You look more like a Wren to me.

My heart seizes in my chest before it pumps double-time. My brows crash into a low V over my eyes. I whip my head from side to side, eyeing everyone on the street. No one has their eyes buried in their phone. I tip my head back and look at the windows of the second-floor apartments above the shops and pubs across the street.

Fuck.

Anyone could be watching me from any one of those windows. I don't like the way it makes me feel. Vulnerable and exposed.

My phone vibrates in my hand, and my shoulders flinch toward my ears.

But it's not the unknown number or even my sister. In some ways it's much worse. It's Da.

My fingertips tingle, anticipation sweet on my tongue. Did Santorini live up to his end of the bargain? It hasn't even been twenty-four hours yet.

I never knew my freedom was the cost of living as a King. But Da should've realized it was too high of a price. He could've found another way.

But he chose not to. So I did.

And I'll bear the weight of that decision and the fallout.

I stretch my neck from side to side, loosening some of the

gathered tension and send him to voicemail. As much as I want to pick up his call and get my answer, I don't have time for the emotional warfare, not when I'm walking into a meeting with O'Boyle.

I exhale, send Da to voicemail, and walk to The Underground.

15

MAEVE

I HAVE to blink a few times to get my eyes to adjust to the dimly-lit pub. Smoke curls in the air from the two old-timers half-heartedly playing pool in the corner. Some hair band from the eighties blares from the speakers, no doubt selected by the table of six men near the jukebox. Their beards are long, gray, and splashing in their pint glasses with each bob of their head to the beat.

I lean against the short backrest of the stool, the metal bar digging into my lower back. The Underground is a mashup of modern and vintage. Modern light fixtures with white lights and hardwood floors. A jukebox and cracked red vinyl benches. I can't tell if O'Boyle stopped updates halfway through a renovation project or he inherited the place like this. It's been his for at least ten years though, so I figure he must like it, or he would've changed it by now.

I let my gaze roll over everyone scattered throughout the room. I recognize some faces, but there are just as many unfamiliar ones too. I'm not surprised. Turnover is inevitable in this neighborhood. For every man that moves up the ladder, another one falls off of it, by choice or force.

O'Boyle catches my eye and lifts his right hand with a little finger wave. It's my cue to approach him.

I slide off the stool with a nod at the bartender and weave around the square four-top tables until I reach the booth in the corner. It's a wide C-shape with black leather bench seats and a matching backrest. Sitting in the exact center with a view of the entire bar is Emmett O'Boyle. His right hand man, Neil Doherty, sits on his left. The space to his right is noticeably void of his other number two: Callahan Hayes. I file that away to have my sister do a little digging tonight. I've never seen O'Boyle without both of his captains.

I pause in front of the table and force myself to stand still. We regard one another for a moment, as we always do. It'd be an insult to ask me to leave my weapons with Doherty before we had a chat. But he'd be a fool to underestimate me. He's in a tough position, but an easily navigated one.

Dark auburn hair cut short with gray at his temples and a close-cropped beard. His navy blue suit jacket parted to reveal his light blue shirt unbuttoned at his throat.

Power oozes from O'Boyle, billowing out in a soft wave that has the hair on my arms standing on edge. I've talked to him long enough to know he's not trying to intimidate me. It's just his way.

He's unpredictable in the way all Syndicate men are. It's a common trait all of the men in the higher positions share. If they didn't exude power and authority, they would be dead. There are no usurped men walking around in this life. They're on the top until they're in the ground.

The corner of my mouth tilts up on one side when I remember that I've been told countless times that I give off an air of intimidation. Ava swears it's why men don't approach me as freely as they do my sisters.

I think it's because men are weak.

I stopped making myself appear docile and handing out

smiles to every man with a shitty pick-up line like candy on Halloween. And poof, they scattered like leaves in autumn. My sisters are no less intimidating than me, they just hide it better for their own reasons.

An image of Santorini's cock flexing inside of me flashes across my consciousness.

Most men are weak, I amend myself. There was nothing weak about Santorini that night.

O'Boyle smirks and jerks his head to the side. Doherty pushes up from the table and slides out of the booth with a small nod in my direction.

"King."

"O'Boyle," I reply with the same amused tone as he greeted me with.

"Sit, sit." He gestures to the space next to him with his left hand.

I sit on the bench to his left, close enough to the edge to be able to hop up at the drop of a hat. I trust O'Boyle as much as I'd trust a stranger off the street.

I have trust issues, obviously.

"How's business?" It's a throwaway question, and we both know it. He's not going to tell me anything of importance, which is fine because I don't care for those finer details.

He lifts his modern-cut old fashioned glass to his lips for a sip of amber liquid. Scotch, if I had to guess. "Can't complain. How're things for you and your sisters?"

It's a subtle nod to our last venture in Chicago. Part of our arrangement means that we stop by for a courtesy hello whenever we're passing through his town. That's going to change soon though.

"Roisin's starting college next week. Moving into her dorms soon." I keep my expression blank, trying my best to gauge his reaction.

This isn't new information, but leaving my sister alone in O'Boyle's city has never sat right with me.

He grins. "Ah, the computer prodigy. She's going to be running the classrooms before she even graduates."

I chuckle, letting his mirth ease my nerves a little. "Most likely. But it means we'll be here more often."

He swings his right arm out slowly, his palm up. "The Kings are always welcome in my city."

I incline my head toward him in gratitude. "Thank you. We'll still honor the agreement for anything unrelated to college visits."

"But of course you will. A King always keeps his word." He flashes me a cunning smile that's all teeth.

I let the old phrase roll off of my back like raindrops on a summer afternoon. It's no secret that the Kings have been part of the Syndicate since its conception. A son taking over for his father for tens of generations.

Until now.

Until my father had five girls instead of boys.

But the saying doesn't bother me. I've made my peace with the Syndicate's rules more befitting the dark ages. Mostly, at least.

"And Darla? How is she? And the baby?"

O'Boyle's niece settled down with the son of one of his captains last year and had their first child three months ago. Sometimes it pays to listen to Keira prattle on about the Syndicate gossip like we have any stake in it.

"Paul is the apple of his mum's eye."

Warmth settles around my heart at the news. Keira enjoys checking-in on those who have benefitted from our special brand of justice. It never fails to fill my soul with joy to hear of someone thriving after a situation like Darla's.

"I'm glad to hear it. Please give her my best."

He nods and takes another leisurely sip of his drink. "Anything I need to know about?"

I lay my palms flat on the table, pausing before I push to stand. "Nothing in your city. I'll let you know when there is something noteworthy."

We both know it's a matter of when and not an if. But he doesn't need a reminder, and it's not really my place to offer it in the first place.

"Enjoy your time in my city, King. We'll be seeing each other."

"Until next time, O'Boyle." I stand up and grab my mostly untouched drink with my fingertips.

I make my way out of the bar much the way I came in, pausing only at the bar to deposit my drink. I slip a twenty under the glass and rap my knuckles on the bar top twice.

"Later," I call to the bartender.

He waves, but I don't stay to chat. My phone vibrates in my pocket, the weight growing exponentially with the secrets Rosie has no doubt sniffed out.

And Da's unanswered call.

I can feel O'Boyle's assessing gaze on my back. It's not something entirely foreign, but in all my years of being questioned and sized up, it never got easier to shoulder.

I got better at ignoring it.

16

MAEVE

THE STEEL DOOR of The Underground slams shut behind me, the resounding clank swallowed up by the night's revelry. Damn, I love this town, second only to New York City.

It's a beating heart, a unique pulse that can't be replicated anywhere else. And when the sun goes down, the atmosphere changes. It serpentines along the belly of the town, enticing you to let your hair down and enjoy yourself.

In New York City, I can shed Maeve King like an ill-fitting dress, leaving only me behind. It's the rare glimpses of who I might've been if I didn't fill my days with plans of vengeance and vacations and traveling.

I can just *be*.

But it's not as easy here. Not in a city where one of the Syndicate's top captain reigns, even if his fist is less iron and more copper.

Still, it offers me some anonymity. Which is exactly what I need after this past week. I can still slip into a crowd and lose myself a little to music and the infectious air of people shedding inhibitions.

I love our family home in Belvin. The towering trees that we used to try to climb, the old stone well that Da boarded up when Rosie almost fell in, the planter boxes we painted with Mum one summer.

But it doesn't call to me. Not the charming downtown or the sunny days of our short-lived summer.

My fondness is rooted in nostalgia and love for my family. Not a desire to plant my own roots and let them take hold.

But there's no escaping this identity that Da's given me. It weighs heavily on my shoulders like the swollen gray clouds that always seem pasted above our town.

My phone feels like a brick in my back pocket, swelling in size with each minute that I don't acknowledge the unanswered calls and texts.

Cowardice isn't one of my flaws, so there's no point in delaying the inevitable. The thick swath of worry wrapped around my shoulders is unpleasant.

I turn the corner and subtly glance over my shoulder. I'm just outside of O'Boyle's immediate neighborhood, which means the eyes should've lessened. I'm cautious every day, but after Da's marriage announcement, my attentiveness has morphed into a little bit of paranoia.

It's too soon to go to Rosie's dorm, but I still head that way. I have plans to waste some time and grab a drink in a pub I find on the way.

I slip my phone out of my back pocket and unlock it with a quick passcode. The number three on the text icon is what steals my attention. I open my sister's text first.

> Roisin: Whoever this Romeo is, he's good. His location is an encrypted trail all across the world.

> Roisin: I reached out to Rush, but he's not in the country right now. So I called in a favor from a friend to help me.

Rush Fitzgerald is the next boss of the Brotherhood, a branch underneath the Syndicate. We grew up with him and his brothers, seeing them at least twice a year at the Syndicate *family* gatherings. We've all gone our own ways for a few years now, but we continue to remain on good terms with all three brothers.

When Rosie was eleven, she took a liking to computers and Rush started mentoring her. She likes to boast that she's surpassed his skill set now, and I don't know enough about it to say either way. But if she's reaching out to him, then I need to heed her unspoken warning.

My unknown number could very well be more dangerous than we realize. Speak of the devil, I see a new text from him.

> Unknown Number: You don't have to worry. Your secret is safe with me.

The hair on the back of me neck stands up, and a shiver of foreboding trickles down my spine. I cast another look over my shoulder, but I don't see anything or anyone.

> Me: I don't know what you're talking about. You have the wrong number.

> Unknown Number: A candidate?

Another text comes through instantly. It's a link, and the preview title says *Hal Kristofferson's Third Wife Declared Missing*. I don't click on it even though the curiosity feels like a fly buzzing around my head.

But whoever this guy really is, he seems to have some familiarity with the tech. Add in the fact that Rosie is still working on tracking him? I'd be willing to bet that this link is a ruse, spyware designed to find me.

> **Me:** I'm not opening a random link from a random man.

> **Unknown Number:** You're right. The Wren would never slip up like that.

Live music filters through the air, brightening the atmosphere further. I clutch my phone in my fist and cross the street toward the bar. I sigh, mentally drained from the job and the day and a preemptive exhaustion from settling my baby sister into her new home for the next four years.

> **Me:** I don't like playing games.

> **Unknown Number:** Don't you though? You dismantle empires, sometimes systematically and slowly. That sounds like a game.

> **Me:** What do you want from me, Romeo?

I stare at the phone, waiting for the dancing dots to flash. But they never come and neither does his reply. After two minutes, I'm almost to the pub with the live band playing. A group of drunk college-age guys stumbles out of the pub, spilling onto the sidewalk in a ball of sloppy laughter.

Pass. It's not really the vibe I'm looking for tonight, so I choose a quieter pub across the street. The Red Lion has an emerald green awning with a shamrock on the side. Shamrocks have become so synonymous with Irish heritage, it's hard to tell if it's an actual Irish pub or just a gimmick. Luckily for me, I've been here before.

I check my phone again, but only the number one by the

phone icon taunts me. Da's voicemail. It's been twenty-four hours, time to see if I need to visit Las Vegas again.

I blow out a breath, press the play button, and put my phone to my ear. The silence stretches for a few seconds, and I pull my phone away to make sure I actually hit the right button. I did.

Da's sigh fills the line then, this noisy exhale that elicits a Pavlovian response from me. It's the sound of him trying to bury his anger, leashing his temper so we don't see the full force of The Hammer. I wipe my palm on my jean shorts absentmindedly, mentally fortifying my walls just like I've done since I was a kid.

"Was it you? Or were you foolish enough to let your sisters meddle in this? I don't know what you've done, but you've gone too far this time, Maeve. This isn't one of your little projects that you think I don't know about. You talk about stepping into the head of the family and yet you disrespect my order like a child. I expect you home in thirty-six hours. A moment less and you won't like who I send for you *and* your sisters."

I pull my phone from my ear and stare at the screen, my jaw slack.

The relief that Santorini kept his word is overshadowed by my father's judgment. It sticks to my skin like sludge, wet and thick and hard to dislodge. Emotions swirl inside my gut, churning and twirling.

He won't ever let me lead our family, no matter how many *vacations* my sisters and I plan. He sees all the good we do as *pet projects* like we're still in primary school.

I'm a tool, a bargaining chip he can use in his favor. Something to secure his foothold in the Syndicate.

Not an equal.

He'll never see me as equal.

The cloud of emotion grows with every uncharitable thought

that enters my brain until it's a dark mass, rattling against my bones, crying to be released.

I clench my phone in my hand, my cheeks pink with shame and anger. It wars within me, but it's all overshadowed by a hopelessness so acute, I can feel the sharp pain of it beneath my ribs.

I tip my head back, exposing my throat to the moon and the stars and tap my phone against my thigh. Anger blazes a path through my body, the kind that sparks reckless and dangerous ideas.

Like saying fuck it. Fuck all the strict rules I've governed myself with for most of my life. For one night, I'm going to act like a normal twenty-three year old woman. I'm going to drink too much and flirt with attractive men and dance to my favorite songs.

A glimpse into what my life could've been like if I were born into any other family.

For a few hours, I'm going to pretend.

I inhale deeply and open my eyes, bringing my gaze to the pub in front of me.

The door is propped open with a metal doorstop, letting the din of the pub join the chorus of all the pub-goers on this little block. I cross the threshold, blinking a few times at the light change. I've been inside The Red Lion a few times before but always with one of my sisters.

It's a big rectangular pub with the bar taking up half of the wall to my left. Shamrocks of all sizes and material cluster in little shelves around the pub. It's quiet but not overly so. Two large TVs play a baseball game, but I've never been much of a sports fan.

The dance floor is nonexistent, barely bigger than my favorite eight-by-ten area rug in our NYC apartment. But it's big enough for me to dance on, I just need the right song.

A handful of two-top and four-top tables take up space

between the bar and the opposite wall. A couple dart boards, some vintage arcade games, and an old-fashioned jukebox are against the wall.

With only ten people in here, it's much quieter than the bars across the street. It's not exactly the place I had in mind when I decided to stop pretending for a night, but it'll do.

The bartender ambles over with a dirty towel thrown over his brown and cream flannel shirt. His name is Eddie and he's been tending bar at The Red Lion Pub for longer than I've been walking this earth. And somehow, he doesn't look a day over forty. If you ever ask him, he claims it's his dedication to drinking two glasses of red wine every night and a whiskey sour on Sundays.

I try not to get pulled into any conversations with Eddie if I can help it. The man loves to talk. He's chatting with the couple seated at the bar, and then he throws his head back with a laugh.

Yeah, The Red Lion will do just fine.

17

MAEVE

THE ATMOSPHERE PICKS up inside the pub. It doesn't take long for the tables to fill in. It's not packed, but it's much livelier than it was an hour ago when I came in.

Eddie saunters over to me. "Another?"

"Aye," I murmur, pushing the empty highball glass across the bar top toward him.

He snags the glass and sets it next to the stack of dirty glasses on the counter behind the bar. I've seen a couple waitresses floating around, and one of them loaded a bunch of dirty glasses into the dishwasher on the opposite end from where I'm sitting.

He plucks a clean highball glass and fixes me a strong-handed Long Island iced tea. They aren't my number one choice, but they have their perks. Namely, propelling me toward that delightful drunken buzz while tasting like delicious black tea.

A minute later, he slides me a fresh drink and moves toward the next customer. I take a sip and spin around in my chair, brazenly checking out everyone in the pub. People really are fascinating creatures if you give yourself time to properly observe.

A couple on the edge of the small dance floor are wrapped up in one another, hands roaming and making out like they're in the privacy of their own home and not in the middle of a crowded space. I know some people who have a serious exhibition kink, so maybe the fact that they're in public is what's firing them up? I've never tried it before, but I'm feeling adventurous lately. And I have this persistent itch to flirt and dance with someone tonight.

It's so unlike me that if I weren't pretending tonight, I might be alarmed.

I'm blaming the dark-eyed Las Vegas stranger anyway. Though it feels hard to think of him as a stranger considering he was inside of me twenty-four hours ago. I shift on the hard seat of the barstool, my thighs protesting a little. There's a delectable soreness there that I've never felt before.

The stool to my right screeches against the wood floor as someone pulls it out and sits down. I see a flash of dark hair in my peripheral and glance over my shoulder for a better look. A man around my age sits with his hands clasped on the bar top, alternating his gaze between Eddie and the TV behind him.

Even from his profile, he's easily the most attractive man in this place.

I can't help myself, thoughts of flirting and dancing and kissing—*and fucking*—fill my head. Something else to blame Santorini for. That asshole broke me, and not in the fun kind of big dick energy way. More like now that I started thinking about dick, I can't *stop* thinking about dick sort of way. It's honestly inconvenient.

It doesn't help that the couple has progressed from kissing to practically fucking on the table in the back. The alcohol warms my blood and my eyelids, and if I squint my eyes just right, I can see the fog of lust hovering underneath the ceiling, billowing through the air like a monstrous beast. It's writhing and contorting to the beat of a silent rhythm of desire, content to feed from everyone in the room.

The man next to me shifts in his seat, widening his legs and bracing his forearms on the bar. Looking at him from the corner of my eye is starting to give me a headache. Since I have nothing but time to kill for the next ninety minutes, I give up the pretense and swivel my stool to face him completely.

His hair is probably two shades lighter than the dark brown it looks in the darkened atmosphere of The Red Lion Pub. He wears it slightly combed back, the sides shaved short. His cheekbones are sharp but his jawline could cut glass. It's the kind of profile men would trade their souls to have. Dark lashes frame darker eyes and dark scruff covers his jaw. He doesn't radiate danger, at least not more than most of the people inside this pub already.

If he's annoyed by my attention, he doesn't show it. And I'm just reckless and buzzed enough to not care either way.

Hesitant tendrils of attraction unfurl inside of me the longer I stare at him.

I'm starting to wonder if I have a type. If Santorini has ruined my appetite for men. The tall, dark, gorgeous, and a little dangerous vibe is suddenly the only thing working for me.

The thought alone makes me want to fly back to Las Vegas and correct my mistake. I know I won't, though. He held up his end of the deal. And so I'll honor mine.

He raises two fingers in the air to signal the bartender, and my gaze zeroes in on the veins on the back of his hand. I don't know what Eddie put in my Long Island iced tea, but I can't get the image of him wrapping his big hands around my hips, veins popping, out of my head.

"Whiskey neat, please, top shelf." The stranger's voice shatters the image, bringing me back to the present.

"Sure thing, kid," Eddie says, snatching a clean glass and getting to work on his drink.

I watch in fascination as a muscle in the stranger's jaw tics at the word *kid*. I roll my lips inward, before releasing them with a slow shake of my head. "You're not from around here, are you?"

He keeps his gaze on whatever sport is on the too-small TV in the corner. "What gave it away?"

I jerk my chin toward Eddie. "He calls everyone kid, regardless of age or gender. He always has."

Eddie slides his fresh drink down the weathered bar top, and the guy next to me grabs it with his index finger and thumb. He tips his head in thanks, and Eddie mumbles something about rich pricks being in his pub and wanders down to the other end of the bar.

He chuckles but it lacks any real humor and finally gives me his attention. "So what you're saying is I'm not special?"

I tilt my head to the side and scan him from head to toe. Again. Eddie's not wrong. This guy stands out in his tailored charcoal-colored suit, the coat unbuttoned to reveal a deep black button-up shirt. I twist my lips to the side as I study his face. He's pretty in the sort of way male models are. And I was right—he's definitely the most attractive man I've all day.

"That depends."

He runs his index finger along the rim of the glass, circling it slowly. "On what?"

"Do you care what Eddie thinks about you?"

He angles his body toward mine further. "I don't care what anyone thinks of me."

The corner of my mouth kicks up into a sly smile. "Then you'll fit in just fine here."

We hold each other's gaze for a moment, and I wonder what he sees when he looks at me. He breaks first, turning to focus on the TV.

I swivel my bar stool around to survey the pub-goers once more. A handful of people have trickled in from the street, beelining to the open table by the jukebox. A girl squeals in delight and feeds the machine some money. Her friend joins her, their heads bent together, and they make their selections.

A moment later, I hear a familiar song. I smile around my straw as I drink the rest of my cocktail in one sip. The stranger next to me groans, stealing my attention from the bubbly friends at the jukebox.

I spin toward him once more. "Not a Swiftie?"

"She's alright," he answers. "But I prefer something a little . . . harder."

I love this song, and if I were alone, I'd be belting out the lyrics. But I haven't had enough alcohol for *that kind* of wild abandon, so I settle for humming it.

The song doesn't even end when the first notes of Nirvana's "Come As You Are" sink into the air. Like he willed it from the jukebox.

I glance at the lust-monster smudges on the ceiling out of the corner of my eye. Maybe there *is* a bit of witchcraft happening here tonight. I side-eye the man next to me with renewed interest. I know I've been binge-watching too much TV when I start to wonder if perhaps he has magical powers, like he changed the song by simply *thinking* it.

Or maybe it's divine intervention. A sign from the universe to squeeze every last drop of anonymity and freedom from this night.

And he's going to help me.

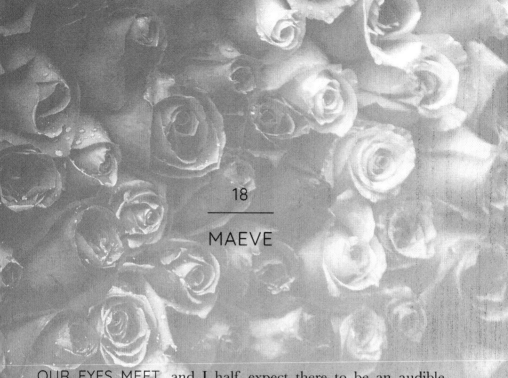

18

MAEVE

OUR EYES MEET, and I half expect there to be an audible smacking sound for the way his intensity beats at my skin. Two feet of space separates us. It's less than it should be but it's more than I want.

"What's the last song you'd listen to before you die?"

He pauses, his icy intensity slowly fading into a simmer. His eyes narrow even as a hint of a smirk dances across his lips, like he's finally taking notice. Of me. There's a subtle shift in the air as he angles his chest toward me.

"Why? Am I going to die?" he asks, his voice dropping into a low rumble. I can't tell if I've had too many drinks or if there's a touch of mockery in his tone.

I lift a shoulder and hold his gaze. "We all die eventually."

"We do. Which is why I like to live each day like it's my last."

I can't keep the snort in if I tried. "I'm sorry but that sounds like a line from a bad commercial. You don't actually believe it, do you?"

He sips his amber-colored drink from a plain rocks glass with a lift of his shoulder.

"And if I did?" There's a challenge in his question and judgment in his gaze.

"Then I'd be disappointed. You're in the wrong neighborhood to believe in such cliches."

He raises a brow. "Oh? Is there a right neighborhood for such thoughts then?"

"Aye. Somewhere out of the South Side of Chicago."

The conversation stutters into silence, both of us facing forward. Eddie swaps out my empty glass for a fresh cocktail, and I wink at him in gratitude.

"So, you come here often?"

Annoyance drips from my fingertips at the overused line. Disappointment lands heavily in my belly. "Are you really going to use such a tired line on me? I thought we were becoming friends."

The side of his mouth hooks into a slow grin. "Is that what you're doing—trying to make a friend?"

I lean forward and capture the straw with my lips, pulling a long drink and letting him sweat out my silence. I lean against the backrest and look him over. "You look like you could use a friend."

The pad of his index finger circles the rim of the glass as he shakes his head slowly. "I have plenty of friends."

"Liar," I murmur.

He laughs, and the sight and sound stun me for a moment. I blink, my lashes fluttering a few times. His face transforms from its previous serious expression to one of unbridled delight. His laugh is low, throaty, and full of mirth. But what takes me out is the goddamn dimple winking at me from the side of his cheek.

It feels cruel to everyone else in this pub for him to have so many of my boxes checked.

He angles his barstool toward me, his smile never dropping. "So, you're from around here then."

It's a statement this time, like he's got me figured out already. I raise a dark brow at him and let the full weight of my Irish accent spill out. "Do you think I'm from around here?"

I was raised on American television, and I've spent the last ten years exploring the world. My original accent is hardly recognizable at this point, and mostly, it sounds like a twisted American accent.

His smile only grows wider. Ah, so I've surprised him. Good. *And he likes it.* Even better.

"A transplant then?"

"Nope." I pop the p and stare at him as I use my red straw to swirl around the drink.

He rubs his fingers across the edge of his jaw. "I have a hard time believing that you're here on vacation and came to this bar."

I roll my lips inward to stifle the smile. "And what's wrong with this pub?"

His lips flatten together. "Nothing. But it's a hole-in-the-wall and not the kind of place I'd imagine you visiting."

I look at him from underneath my lashes. "And yet here I am. And here you are."

"So we are." His voice is lower than it was a moment ago and he holds my gaze.

I know I've been reading into the horoscope predictions that Ava's been shoving down all of our throats recently, because the thought in my head sounds like it was plucked from one of her many adages.

Don't be afraid to take a chance when opportunity presents itself.

Or maybe I just want to fuck him.

Maybe this is the way I get Santorini out of my head. By replacing his touch with another's.

AN HOUR and a drink and a half later, lust competes with alcohol buzzing in my veins. The vibe in the pub has devolved into something more debauched. People grind on one another as song after song with slow, deep bass lines play and couples inch closer and closer to one another.

My sexy stranger's lips look more inviting with each word that falls from his mouth. I'm not paying attention to what he's saying, distracted by the way my skin feels hot, my chest flushed.

He stops talking, slanting me a wry grin. "Are you still with me?"

"No," I murmur, looking at him from underneath my lashes. "Your mouth is distracting."

His bottom lip is slightly bigger than his top lip, pouty and plush. He twists his lips to the side for a moment, like he's suppressing another grin. He leans in close, only leaving a minuscule amount of space between us. "Is that so?"

My chest rises with deeper breaths, my lids lowering. I'm a step past tipsy, but not so much that I'm going to forget what I'm about to do. I tilt my head and eliminate the space between us. He inhales sharply, like maybe I surprised him again.

His hesitation lasts for one second before he slams his mouth to mine and tangles his hand in my hair at the back of my neck.

I groan into his mouth and arch into his kiss without even thinking about it. My nerve endings feel like they're on fire, sparking with pleasure and chanting for more. He kisses me like a man with something to prove, like the fate of the universe depends on a single kiss.

Not at all how a first kiss should go. I expected wavering, indecisiveness, and too much tongue. A man so good-looking surely has to have one major flaw. Something to balance the scales.

Whatever it is, it's not his mouth. The man can *kiss*. He tilts my head and deepens the kiss further, his other hand snaking out to grasp my waist.

He kisses me how I imagine he fucks: passionately, possessively, and unapologetically. And I don't even know his name.

I pull back and gulp in some air. My head spins with lust and my clit throbs with desire. At some point in our kiss, I grabbed his shirt in a fist. I relax my hold and let my hand linger on his chest for a moment.

"That was . . ."

He swipes his thumb across his bottom lip, his eyes dark in the low light as they scan my face. "An amazing kiss."

I push my barstool back and slide down the front, letting my body rub against his. He's hard in all the right places, and I bet he's got an incredible body underneath that suit. There's only one way to find out.

"I'm going to, uh . . ." I trail off, holding his stare for a beat longer than necessary before I jerk my head to the back left, toward the restrooms.

It's an invitation, and I only hope he picks up on what I'm offering. I've never done this sort of thing before, so I don't know if I'm showing my inexperience right now. But I'm honestly too worked up to care too much.

And I can't deny the wild need that thumps against my ribcage for a moment longer. It demands I step outside of my comfort zone and embrace my fantasies. To start living with abandon.

While I still can.

His teeth rake across his bottom lip as he gives me a slow nod. It's as much an understanding as I'm going to get.

I wind around the busy tables until I reach the small hallway at the back of the bar. There's an emergency exit, a door with "Employees Only" scrawled across the wood in black permanent marker, and two doors with the classic restroom signs.

I press my shoulder into the door furthest away, nudging it open. The room is just as well-loved as the rest of the bar, and while clean, it could definitely use some TLC. The walls are painted a bland beige color, and it smells like a combination of bleach and lavender.

There's a wider, larger stall in the corner with two smaller stalls closer to the door. A wide mirror hangs across from them, stretched across almost the entire wall with a little shelf at the bottom. Two sinks are centered beneath the mirror and a black domed trash can sits in the corner. Wadded-up brown paper towels litter the floor around the trash can like someone played a game of basketball, missed, and walked out anyway.

I don't know if it's the sight of the trash on the ground or the fact that the fog of lust has cleared now that I've moved out of his orbit, but hesitation sprinkles in. And with it comes the crushing weight of second-guessing.

What the hell am I doing?

I don't sleep with anyone in years and all of the sudden, I'm fucking two men in the same weekend. Tacky strings of doubt and unease stick to my skin, dousing my good feelings with a wave of nervousness.

Do I really want to do this or am I trying to wrangle the reins of my life back into my own hands?

I brace my hands on either side of the single porcelain sink and stare at my reflection. My hair is wild from humidity, and my cheeks are flushed. My black linen tee slips down my right shoulder, exposing my thin black bra strap.

My lashes are the darkest black, coated in mascara and curled slightly upward. The whites of my eyes lean pink from lack of sleep, smoke irritation, or alcohol. I'm not sure which, but I don't think it really matters either. My lips are swollen from *his* mouth, parted with realization.

I look different.

Uninhibited. Alive. *Free.*

I press my fingertips to my lips and marvel at the concept of being free. Will I ever be truly free or will I settle for stolen moments with strangers in a pub?

Or a penthouse?

Thoughts of my time with Santorini revive the lust cooling inside my veins, burning away the doubt. It heats me up when I remember the way he let me sink down on his cock, the way he let me take my pleasure from him.

I pull my bottom lip into my mouth, dragging my teeth into the tender flesh.

I've never felt so reckless as I have in the last forty-eight hours. My father's expectations and ideas of grandeur lay in ruins beneath my feet.

But I don't think it's some teenage angst-fueled revenge scheme to get back at my father.

It's the aftermath of a woman's shattered rose-colored glasses. It's the moment she tastes freedom.

And it tastes fucking delicious.

I walk past the three stalls, applying the lightest pressure with my index finger to each stall door. All three of them swing open easily. Empty.

Now I wait and see if he joins me.

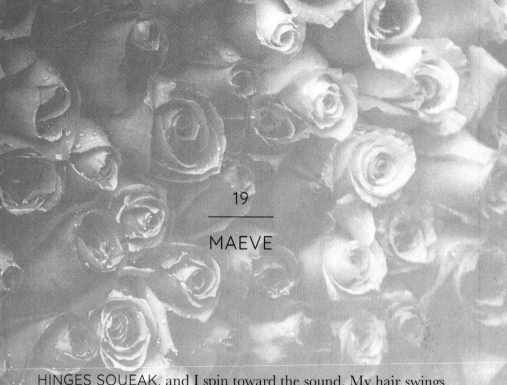

19

MAEVE

HINGES SQUEAK, and I spin toward the sound. My hair swings around with my jerky movement, settling around my face as I stare at him.

He stands in the doorway, backlit by the hazy yellow light from the hallway. His broad shoulders nearly taking up the entire space. I don't remember him being so big, but I suppose I haven't properly seen him yet. It's cliché as hell, but I can't stop my gaze from trailing over the rest of him and wondering what else is big.

I'm going to be so disappointed if his fatal flaw is his performance.

He braces himself with hands on either side of the doorway and pauses. His face is shrouded by deep shadows, but I can almost sense his smirk. It's the deadly kind of expression that says *I've got a secret* and I'm about do wicked, dirty things to you.

He looks over his left shoulder and practically growls, "Bathroom's out of order. Use the men's room."

Holy hell.

I can't believe I'm going to fuck him. In the bathroom of a pub.

And why does that growly thing he did with his voice make my pussy clench?

He turns toward me and stalks into the bathroom, kicking the door closed with his heel. The bathroom plunges into dusk once more, and I have to blink several times to clear the bright yellow spots from my vision.

He prowls toward me like a man on a mission. The lethal grace of his stride reminds me of the last man who approached me the same way.

He stops a few inches in front of me, close enough that the tips of his black dress shoes skim the tips of my boots.

"Are you sure?"

His breath feathers over my lips, and my head swims with lust. "Aye, I'm sure."

I see the flash of a smile before he lunges for me. He claims my mouth in a brutal kiss. There's no warm up, no curious exploration of my mouth. It's a dominant kiss that takes and takes.

And fuck me because I give it to him.

I push onto my toes and wrap my arm around his neck, pulling him toward me. Our height difference makes it difficult for me to feel all the hard lines of his body. But I desperately want to because he is, without a doubt, jacked underneath that posh suit of his. He has to be.

I almost wish I had a hotel room here, because then I could see him in his entirety. I'll have to settle for mapping him with my hands.

I run my free hand over the top of his shoulders, down his biceps, and over his chest. His body heat warms my palms as I trace his hard lines. It's like being under the sun, basking in the warmth. He feels like he could pick me up and pin me against the wall with ease.

All the while, his mouth ravages mine, nipping and sucking

and biting. I can't catch my breath. I don't know if I'm breathing or if I'm drowning in him.

He threads his hand into the hair at the nape of my neck, tilting my head back and to the right. He deepens the kiss with a groan, and I feel myself getting lost.

Lost in him and in the way my body is waking up. It's like I didn't realize I was hungry until I had Santorini in Las Vegas. And now I realize I'm fucking famished.

I let him lead us away from the last stall and toward the sinks. I've never messed around in a bathroom before, let alone somewhere so public, but I've got freedom on my tongue and lust in my blood.

He breaks away from me but keeps his grip on my neck. His burning eyes lock onto mine as he arches my head back further. I can feel the strength quivering in his muscles, and it excites me. "Last chance to back out. No hard feelings."

I appreciate his warning, I do. But I'm not backing out now. I'm too keyed up, and I'm so turned on I'm practically salivating. I arch a single brow and deliver a gauntlet, hoping he takes the challenge. "Afraid you won't be able to make me come before someone walks in?"

My heart races as I wait for his reaction. His eyes become slits and that muscle in his jaw flutters. He stares at me for what feels like an eternity before I get the reaction I was hoping for.

He slams his lips to mine in a kiss so brutal and demanding. It says more than any words ever could. I moan into his mouth, and he devours it with a low growl on his own.

He pulls away quickly, leaving me panting for breath and desperate for more.

"Turn around," he commands in a low voice.

I spin around slowly and watch him in the mirror. He uses his grip on my hair to sweep the strands off of my neck. My shirt dips low in the front, offering an impressive view of my tits pushed together in my favorite black lacy bra.

He stands behind me with his gaze locked on mine. His hands ghost along my back, close enough for me to feel the heat of them. "I won't insult you by asking if you're sure again."

"Good." I arch my back, my ass just brushing against the front of his pants.

He flattens his right hand along my back, dragging it down my spine and curving it over my right hip. His gaze stays glued to my back as he murmurs, "I wouldn't have pegged you as the type of woman who takes a man in the back of the bar."

"Fuck you," I snap through gritted teeth. There's heat in my words, but not much. Maybe a quick and dirty one-night-stand is exactly the type of girl I am. At least for tonight.

His hands clamp down on the curve of my waist, stilling my movement. He leans over my back, his head close to mine as he murmurs, "Oh, I plan to. But first."

His fingers trail the collar of my shirt, tugging it down to expose more of my shoulder and back. He makes this low, throaty noise a second before I feel his lips on the top of my spine.

My eyes flash to the top of his head over my shoulder in the mirror. In a move so perfectly timed it feels coordinated, he lifts his head and holds my gaze. His eyes darken to pools of black, reminding me of that show about demons Rosie made me watch last month.

Lust coils tight in my lower belly, and I fight the shiver that wants to roll down my spine. Our gazes are locked together, my quick exhales the punctuation to our silent conversation.

His hands sweep down my sides, pausing at the waistband of my jean shorts. I know I can look down, but it feels like I shouldn't. Something about keeping my eyes on his through the mirror heightens everything else.

His right hand slides across my stomach, flicks open the button on my shorts, and drags the zipper down in the next breath. My chest constricts, adrenaline fueling my lust. Anyone could walk in the bathroom right now, and we could walk away relatively unscathed. But as soon as my shorts are off, it gets trickier—*messier*.

The idea of getting caught fucking in the bathroom of a pub is only heightening my desire. It's a new experience for me, and I don't know if I'll have it again.

I banish all thoughts of anything other than the way his fingertips feel as they curl around the waistband of my shorts and drag them over my ass and down my thighs. I expect him to do the same thing to my thong, but he surprises me. Again.

It seems to be a running theme with me and men this weekend. I'm not sure if I like it. But the orgasms sure do help.

Our connection breaks when he sinks to his knees behind me, stealing my view of his face.

His breath warms my pussy from behind, his big hands palming my ass cheeks and spreading them, opening me up.

Holy *fuck*.

It's the last coherent thought I have before he starts tonguing me *through* the thin cotton mesh of my red thong. There's nothing soft or hesitant about the way he just dives in, licking and sucking and groaning against my flesh.

"Oh my god," I moan under my breath.

One hand leaves my ass to press firmly against my back. I follow his wordless command and bend over the sink further. I brace my forearms on either side of the sink, widening my legs shamelessly.

"Good girl." He groans his approval, and I feel the rumble more than hear it. He hooks a finger around the thin piece of fabric and pulls it to the side. "Goddamn, this pussy is delicious."

I don't get a chance to respond before he eats me out like a man starved. His nose bumps my asshole, and my muscles tense. I've never even explored that part of myself with anyone before, no matter how curious I am.

He nudges my legs wider still, giving him more access to my pussy. I flatten myself over the sink just as his fingers start to play. The hard porcelain sides dig into my hip bones as his fingertips dance around my clit, close enough to tease but not enough pressure to make me come yet.

One quick yank and a pinch of pain later, my thong is free from my hips. I want to be indignant, but he's currently tongue-fucking me like it'll solve all the world's problems.

My orgasm unfurls slowly like a cat stretching out in a patch of sunlight. It starts in my toes and leisurely climbs up my calves and over my knees. It curls around my thighs and pulses in my clit before it races up my arms and sets me free of this world.

Dots dance behind my eyes as my breath leaves my lungs. I'm floating above the ground, hovering in between planes.

Surely this feeling is too big to exist on Earth's axis. It has to be from some magical world. And my stranger its ambassador.

Aye, black magic, indeed.

It's the only logical explanation.

20

MAEVE

I GLIDE BACK to earth on a cloud of contentment. "Holy shit," I breathe out, my eyes still screwed up tight.

I feel him move to stand up behind me, his large palms gripping my hips in a decidedly possessive way. I don't hate it. I don't hate it at all.

The almost greedy way he manipulated my body. The way his fingers are *still* working me, tenderly running through my arousal.

I had thought this kind of hookup with a stranger might feel cheap or dirty—and not the fun kind, but it doesn't feel anything like that. If anything, it feels too good.

"You good, Lemon?" His voice is low and deep, stirring things low in my belly that just started to settle down.

I lift my head and blink at him over my shoulder. His face is cut from stone, the shadows of the bathroom playing along his face. His jaw looks sharp enough to cut and his eyes still the endless black depths.

"Lemon?" I raise both brows. We didn't exactly exchange

names before he dove headfirst into my pussy, but that doesn't mean I want to be called by some other girl's name.

He steps into me, his hard cock pressing against my bare ass through his pants. I imagine my cunt leaving a mess all over the front of his perfect suit, and the image brings a smirk to my face. He's going to be wearing me all over his face and his pants.

He leans down and inhales, brushing his lips against that sensitive spot behind my ear. "You smell like sugared lemons."

His soft-spoken words are tortured reverence. It edges close to sweet, too close to whispered words between lovers.

My reaction is visceral. The familiarity pierces at the part of my soul I thought I buried under duty years ago. It's insane and ridiculous, and I need to steer the conversation in another direction immediately. I squash the wispy feelings until they disintegrate like cotton candy on my palm.

I let a satisfied smirk tip up the corners of my mouth, not that he's even paying attention to me. His head stays buried against my skin, breathing me in. It's not the move I expected from some suit I picked up at a bar in the South Side.

I wanted something wild and dirty, a little exploration into exhibitionism.

Not sweet nothings whispered in my ear. Not to kick off the whole experience with him on his knees for me, delivering a world-shattering orgasm.

Maybe I'm overthinking it. Maybe that orgasm scrambled my senses. And by that logic, I'll need another to reset my thoughts.

"Are you going to fuck me or wax poetic about fruit all night?"

He nips at my skin, scraping his teeth along the tendon in my neck. "Impatient little thing, hm?"

"I'm not," I lie, grinding against his erection.

His right hand slides off my hip to palm my ass with a low

groan. "I might believe you if you weren't grinding this perfect ass against my cock."

Thick blankets of lust drape over my shoulders, making my limbs feel warm and heavy.

The muffled thumping from the bass inside the pub changes. It's louder and slower than it was a minute before. Loud enough that I glance toward the door, half-expecting it to be open.

"Anyone could walk in here right now——"

"And you fucking love it."

He's observant, so I don't bother denying it. I groan when I hear the snick of a zipper. The fabric against my bare ass shifts away, but not so far that I can't feel the heat of him.

I rub my thighs together, desperate for friction. Impatience pokes at me. "I don't like to be teased," I murmur.

"Baby girl, I'm still wearing your cum on my lips like frosting from my favorite cake."

I wiggle my hips back against him. "I guess I'm greedy then."

The head of his cock bumps against me, a measured tease dragging against the length of my pussy. He nudges my clit, spiking sparks of pleasure. "Perfect, greedy pussy."

I angle my hips back and breathe out, "More."

"Hands on the sink, baby girl. Hold on."

I roll my eyes a little and curl my fingers over the edge of the sink. He's talking a big game. His mouth is incredible, which gives me hope for his cock and the way he uses it.

He lines himself up, and with one thrust, he's inside of me. I groan at the fullness, delighting in the twinge of soreness.

"God damn," he says on a groan. "You feel incredible."

I drop my head forward, letting my hair obscure my face. He's being gentle, these slow, shallow thrusts. But I don't want soft and gentle. I want him to fuck me hard enough that I feel him for days.

"Harder," I beg.

He follows my command, fucking me into the sink with long, hard strokes. I arch my back and meet him thrust for thrust, the sound of my ass cheeks hitting his thighs competing with the baseline from music at the bar. His movements are controlled passion, pushing me closer to the edge until he surrounds my senses.

My orgasm takes me by surprise. One moment I'm aching for more, and then I blink, and I'm careening over that blissful peak. My toes curl, and my muscles tighten as he fucks me through my orgasm.

Before I finish floating back into my body, his rhythm picks up. I lift my head to watch his face in the mirror, determined to catch his expression when he finally comes.

And I'm so glad I did. He looks possessed, staring at the places our bodies are connected with fierce concentration. A pained grimace flashes across his face before his thrusts stutter. He's almost *too* deep at this angle.

He comes with a drawn-out moan, panting nonsensical words that I can't make out over the thundering of my heart. I feel boneless and on edge. It's a strange combination of toe-curling orgasms and exhibitionism.

He drops his head to my shoulder, and we stay like that for a moment.

"That was incredible." He places a chaste kiss against my shoulder blade. "This motherfucking pussy was incredible."

I chuckle, inadvertently squeezing him with my inner muscles.

"Fuck me, I'm getting hard again already." He drags his lips across my back and cups my pussy from the front. "It's this magical pussy."

I smirk at him. It seems we both had thoughts of witchcraft tonight, even if I like the way those words fall from his lips.

He pulls out of me, and we both groan at the sensation. "Ten minutes. Give me ten minutes to rally."

My smirk falls. I wasn't planning on a repeat, no matter how good it was. Best to slip out before it gets awkward. "Aye, I better freshen up then."

He's slow to step away, his lips last to leave my skin. I straighten up as he steps into the middle stall behind us with a little hum under his breath.

I reach over and grab a couple of paper towels. They're the cheap dark brown kind, but unless I want to walk around the South Side with cum sliding down my leg, it's my only choice. I gingerly wipe my thighs and clean myself up as quickly and delicately as possible. It's not perfect, but it's good enough to get me back to Rosie's dorm. I'm sticky and sweaty and in desperate need of a shower.

I toss the paper towel into the garbage can in the corner, the loose ball sinking in easily. Then, I step into my jean shorts, tugging them up my legs and wiggling a little to get them buttoned properly. I glance around the floor for my ruined thong, but I don't see it. I don't remember if he tossed it over his shoulder, and I'm not about to knock on the stall door and ask him.

I don't know if this is his attempt at being a gentleman or if he really had to pee. I don't know if he was serious about round two or it was one of those platitudes like "let's do this again sometime."

But this was a one-time thing for me, so either way, I'll take it as an opportunity to slip out.

I scoop my crossbody purse off the counter, grabbing the side to double-check my phones are still there. I finger-comb my hair as I cross the room with quick, quiet steps. I wrench the door open by the brassy handle, but it doesn't budge.

My brows crash together as I pull it once more. My gaze snags on the deadbolt, the thumb turned in the locked position.

My face smooths into a small smile, warmth unfurling inside my chest that has nothing to do with the fantastic orgasms.

I glance over my shoulder, half expecting him to be there. But he's still in the stall.

That's fine. It makes this all so much easier.

I flip the lock and tug the handle. The door opens easily, the noise of the bar smacking me in the face. It's a stark difference to the cocooned bubble of the bathroom.

Shoulders high and head back, I strut through the crowded pub until I reach the street.

After all, I'm still a King.

21

ROMEO

MY HEADPHONES FLY off my head, and I turn around and jump out of my chair swinging. I hear my brother's chuckle before I see his smug, smiling face.

"The fuck, Tommy?" I growl, reaching for my favorite headphones.

They're noise-cancelling, over-the-ear, expensive-as-fuck headphones. They give you the surround sound feel without blaring noise. And my brother's dangling them from his index finger just to piss me off.

I stretch for them again, but he dances back a few paces, the blonde oak floorboards of the reformed yoga studio creaking under his quick movements.

I renovated one of the two yoga studios in our building years ago. I have a good work setup in our apartment, but I needed a bigger, more secure location, and this space was free.

I left the entire wall of windows but added UV blocking film, so I can have the blinds open and never have to worry about even the highest powered telephoto lens. It houses two of our servers, several workstations, various computers and parts, plus a small kitchenette and bathroom.

I suppose I could've made any area of the building I wanted into a work space for me, but unlike my brother, I care about disrupting other people. In this situation at least.

I never shy away from a little chaos if the circumstances are right.

Tommy skips backward until his knees hit the couch on the other side of the room. It's an overstuffed dark gray module style that doubles as a single bed. It's pushed in one corner with a small blonde oak TV stand and TV across from it.

All courtesy of my mother-hen of an older brother Nic. He came in here last month and called me a dumbass for staring at a screen all day, told me I'm going to go blind if I don't step away once in a while.

Naturally, I told him to fuck off. I was knee-deep in my favorite puzzle: unraveling the mystery that is the Fairy Godmothers.

The Fairy Godmothers is a fan-given name to a group of people—allegedly women—by the conspiracy theorists and amateur sleuths.

The message boards and dark forums lose their collective minds for the Fairy Godmothers and their style of justice. These people really are amateurs. Good at internet snooping, but they're no match for me. They speculate for fun, something to pass the time in their mundane lives.

But it's more than that for me.

The Fairy Godmothers piqued my interest a couple years ago, but it wasn't until later when they really caught my eye.

It's a little too vigilante justice for me, but I'm more of a *dismantle life as you knew it kind from the comfort of my massage chair* kind of justice server.

And the night Nic wandered into my office and spouted some

bullshit about takings breaks, I was up to my neck in theories. The only thing I was missing was a rolling cork board with red yard, photos, a map, and push-pins.

I'd found a previously-unseen thread buried under some conspiracy theories on a dark forum I keep an eye on, and nothing was going to tear me away.

Truthfully, I've crossed into the obsessive territory a while ago, but that's a little fact I'm keeping to myself for now. And Nic wasn't wrong, I do need to step away more often.

The next day, the couch, TV, and TV stand showed up. It was a nice gesture, so I didn't give him too much shit about mothering me.

Instead, I let myself fall further down the rabbit hole, untangling the puzzle that is the Fairy Godmothers.

But I have an ulterior motive for looking into the Fairy Godmothers.

One I haven't shared with my brothers yet.

I want to feed them information.

I'm not a fucking idiot. I'm behind screens *by choice*, not because I don't possess the same skills as my brothers.

Well, not *all* the skills. I don't have the same affinity for creative psychological torture as Tommy or the same ability to view everyone as squares on a chess board and anticipate possible outcomes based on probabilities.

But I am absurdly good at puzzles. Finding patterns, connecting them in a way that others miss, and solving them.

My working theory is that the Fairy Godmothers are a group of women enacting vigilante justice. But I've had my eye on one in particular.

The Wren.

From what I can tell, she's a modern-day Robin Hood. A ruiner of men.

The Wren is an unexplained puzzle that I intend on solving.

But first, I'm going to hand-deliver her some men. Evil men that I can't personally take out without making waves that I can't weather. Not until my father's gone, at least.

"Oi." Tommy snaps his fingers in front of me. "Are you listening to me?"

I glare at my brother for pulling me from thoughts of her. Of the Wren. "I hear you. And you know I hate being snuck up on like that." I snatch my headphones back and toss them on my desk behind me. I straighten my black tee to distract my hands from wringing Tommy's neck.

"I called your name like ten times," he says on a laugh. He collapses into the couch, spreading his arms wide across the back.

"Yeah, well, I was busy."

"Chatting up your online obsession?" He waggles his eyebrows, his smile inching higher on his face.

"Fuck off, Tommy. I'm not obsessed." I fold my arms across my chest and widen my stance.

He laughs, this full belly laugh like I just told a real knee-slapper of a joke. His mirth grates on my fucking nerves. Mostly because he's kind of right.

Only I prefer to think less obsession and more curiosity. A persistent, enthusiastic fascination.

"Aw, c'mon, man. You gotta get outta here. Come out with me tonight. We'll hit up Carnival and find you some real women to obsess over."

"She is a real woman." As soon as I say it, I wish I could stuff the words back in my mouth.

He leans forward, letting his hands slide from the back of the couch to the cushion on either side of his hips. "She? *She?* Since when do you know it's a *she?*"

An uncomfortable itch prickles the back of my neck. "I just know."

The internet sleuths got that much right. Besides, if you look objectively, it just makes sense. All of their victims, at least the ones we know about, are men. Most of them try to cover everything up, the pound of flesh the Fairy Godmothers carved from them. But people should know better than to think that sort of paper trail would disappear. The internet holds your secrets long after you've forgotten them.

He doesn't reply, so I walk back to my desk. It's a custom-built desk big enough to be classified as a dining room table with monitors along the back and both left and right sides.

I rarely actively use all the monitors at the same time. I have some background programs that always run, but those screens often remain blank. If I have too many going at once, it's easy for me to get distracted and overwhelmed by the scrolling code and images.

I don't bother sitting down, just lean over my desk and start shutting down the programs I won't need. I check my watch. Damn, I lost a few hours of time researching and hunting the Wren today.

"Holy shit." He drags the words out slowly. "You know her. This Wren chick you're obsessed with."

I clear my throat and ignore him. "Nic should be here soon. He was checking the docks again, hoping to catch them in the act."

We've been having some issues, small kinks that need to be ironed out. It was Nic's idea to drop by unexpectedly.

"Don't change the subject, brother," he muses.

I bristle at his perceptiveness. "I'm not. I don't know her, and I'm not obsessed."

Unless you call creating a program with the sole intention of using existing patterns to predict future movements and then using that information to triangulate the local cell towers and pull data from all the nonlocal numbers using a specific type of phone obsessed.

Then, yeah, okay. I'm definitely obsessed.

I've been working on this program for nearly six months, fine-tuning it after several rounds of beta testing and finding huge flaws. Technically, it's still in its beta phase, but I decided it was time to test it for real.

I added all of the suspected locations of The Wren's *justice*, correlating them to any public and private names mentioned *and* the alleged damage. And a pattern began to form.

And then I found the lipstick. A bold red-blue color in an embossed black tube with a gold filigree stamped on the front.

I created profiles of each of her targets, using the conspiracies on the dark forum to fill in any blanks. The program generates similarities and predictions for her next targets.

Including cities.

And then, then I fucking found her. I've been riding the incredible high of discovery ever since.

It took my program nearly thirty-six hours to find her, but I did it. I texted fourteen different numbers with fourteen different burner phones, just to be safe.

Despite her replying wrong number, I know it in my gut, I'm not wrong. The numbers don't lie.

"Bullshit. You've been talking about the Wren for fucking months." The couch groans as Tommy pushes to his feet. "God, you're a terrible liar."

My shoulders hitch without my permission, and I curse myself out inside my head.

"Ha!" He stops next to me, wagging his finger in my face. "I knew it!"

I bat his finger away with a scowl and focus back on my computer. I'm not ready to share this with my brothers.

To share *her*.

I have an idea, and inkling of the type of woman she is. And if I'm right, she will be exquisite.

And I'm feeling fucking selfish. Possessive of her.

A woman I know only by rumors and alleged reputation. A woman I find myself thinking of far too often.

My phone sits like lead weight in my pocket, taunting me with its silence.

"You don't know shit."

Tommy spins around and hops up on the desk next to my keyboard. He swings his legs a little, reminding me of a kid. "C'mon, gimme all the details. I know you're dying to tell someone."

I don't bother answering him. If I give him an inch, he'll take a mile. I focus on scanning the programs I have running some of the betting odds in our casinos. I still hear my father's voice demanding I understand that the house cannot lose.

"Don't you want to give me all the boring details about your little message boards and the newest conspiracy from the hive of computer geeks you talk to?"

His mirth beats at my skin like a buzzing fly, landing on me over and over again. Time to kill it.

"Why are you so happy? Get someone to extract information from today?"

He grips the edge of the table and grins. "Nah. I had an errand that kept me out of Vegas for a bit."

I arch a brow and close out the next few windows. "Were you with Nic? That kind of *errand?*"

Father insists on making Nic do *house calls*. Sometimes they're for our own soldiers and sometimes they take him out of state. Tommy usually accompanies him, but not always.

"Nah, I went solo on this one."

I straighten up and look at my brother, I mean, really look at him. My gut clenches at what our father has him doing. He always says he doesn't mind, but I've never believed him. No one is immune to that kind of violence and psychological warfare. Not even him.

"What did Dad have you doing?"

He shrugs. "A little of this, a little of that. Nothing big."

My gaze narrows on him, sweeping from head to toe. He looks okay, actually, more than okay. I'm pretty sure I heard him whistling a song from Hamilton earlier.

"You sure?"

He claps me on the shoulder. "Don't worry about me, baby bro. Worry about your internet girlfriend."

I shove his hand off of me and nudge him off my desk. He curls his shoulders inward and lets me push him, laughing the entire time.

I drag my palm across my mouth, my patience running thin. "Jesus, fuck. I don't have a fucking *internet girlfriend*. I'm not twelve."

"Oh yeah? Then what would you call your little infatuation with *The Wren*?" He waggles his eyebrows at me.

My jaw feels stiff from clenching it so hard. I don't like the intimate way he says her name. He arches a brow, taunting me for my silence. His eyes a shade too bright. My heart thumps against my ribs the longer I look at him.

"What's going on with you? Why are you so fucking happy?"

Tommy dances back on the balls of his feet, shaking his shoulders out like a boxer does before a fight. "Who, me? I'm living the dream, bro."

"No," I say, pointing at him. "Hell no. Last time we shadow-boxed, you *accidentally* forgot to pull your punch and broke my fucking nose."

"And you nailed me in the kidney right after. I was pissing blood for a week." He moves closer, practically dancing on his feet. He throws a faux punch and hops from foot to foot.

174

"That's because I taught him how to fight," Nic says from the doorway.

I glance toward him, surprised I didn't hear him come in. It's the distraction Tommy was looking for. He charges me and wraps an arm around my neck. I anchor my hands on his forearm and twist violently to the side, dislodging him.

"Are we fucking around, or are we planning a murder?" Nic snaps, but there's no heat in his voice. He flicks the double locks on the door and crosses the studio to the small refrigerator.

Tommy releases his hold, and I stumble back. I shove his shoulder and mumble, "Asshole."

"I think the word you're looking for is brother," Tommy says with a smug grin. He saunters back to the couch, dropping into the seat closest to the door.

It isn't until later that night that I realize he never told me why he's so fucking happy.

22

ROMEO

I PICK at the label of my beer bottle in a poor attempt at distracting me from the five unanswered texts. I've sent her five carefully chosen candidates in the last thirty-six hours. All five of them fit their bill: men who abuse their power.

None of them are the real targets.

I'd planned on earning her trust slowly, one suitable candidate at a time. But I find my patience growing thin. She should've texted me back by now.

I narrow my gaze, biting the inside of my cheek as I let my focus drift. The only reason she wouldn't reply is . . . if she's on a job.

Unless it's not her. Unless you got the wrong information. The intrusive counterargument flaps across my mind before I slap it away.

No. I know it's her. It has to be. Everything else matches up. But she's taking too long to take the bait, and as much as I'm trying to be patient, I feel like I've been waiting months to get to this point. Annoyance tightens my shoulder blades every time I think about how she left me on read.

Or maybe I'm fucking annoyed with myself and my disappointment over someone I don't know.

It doesn't feel like I don't know her though. I've spent hours and hours looking over her work, trailing her movements around the globe, learning her patterns. Too many times, day turned to night and then dawn broke across the sky. And still, I was hunched over my screens looking like Golumn. She was *my precious*. All I needed was the missing pieces of the puzzle that made up the Wren and the rest of her Fairy Godmothers.

I've built her up in my mind, unwittingly placed her on a pedestal, and I can't knock her off.

I don't want to.

I drum a beat with my index finger on my bottle, letting my mind spin out with ideas. One starts to take shape. It's risky—but no riskier than anything else I've done.

Without a word, I grab my specialized laptop from the bag at my feet and leave my brother on the couch. The conversation around the room halts as I cross the expanse of the office Nic uses at Violet Oak and slip into his chair behind his desk.

I disregard their weighted silence. I can't give them my attention now, not when I need every bit of concentration to hold onto the first steps of the new plan formulating in my head.

Nic crosses the room and sinks into the left chair in front of the desk. "What's wrong with him?"

I ignore him and open my laptop, excitement thrumming in my veins like a kid on Christmas morning.

I can use the program I created to actually figure out her identity. I wanted her to willingly come to me, but I'm running out of time. I didn't want it to go down this way, but she'll understand. She's pragmatic and logical. I know I'll get her to see reason. Eventually.

Tommy pushes off the couch and joins Nic across from me.

"He's probably pissed because he was catfished." Humor laces his words, but I let it slide off of me.

I can remotely access my servers and programs from my laptop easily enough. My system at home would be better, but this works in a pinch.

"No shit?" Nic shifts forward, bracing his elbows on the desk across from me.

I use all the data I've mined plus the phone number. Assuming it's a burner phone, it'll take some time to find her through geo-tagging. I'm sure she has someone in the Fairy Godmothers covering her tracks. Whoever she is, she's good.

But I'm better.

"I've got twenty-k on it being a middle-aged dude living in his momma's basement with a Princess Leia fetish," Tommy says with a laugh.

It's just absurd enough to break through my concentration. I lift my head and scowl at my brother before shifting my glare to my other brother.

Nic stares at me for a moment, and just when I think he's going to get us back on the topic at hand, the corner of his mouth twitches. "My money's on a woman in her fifties with five cats who's bored and lonely."

I pinch some paper clips between my fingers from a little bowl next to me and launch them at their grinning faces. They duck to the sides, letting the little bits of metal fall to the floor with a dull thud.

"You're both assholes."

"Yeah, yeah. Tell us something we don't know." Tommy grins and rolls his eyes.

I took a chance—a risk—earlier in texting the Wren without telling either of my brothers, but it's not the first secret I've kept. And I'm sure it won't be the last.

Better to ask forgiveness and all that.

Besides, I physically couldn't stop myself. There's a burning need inside of me, fueling me forward until I figure it out.

Figure *her* out.

I'll tell them if it pans out.

Probably.

Maybe.

My fingers still on the keys, and I shift my gaze to look at my brothers.

I trust them, but I don't want to give them the gift of the Wren. Because that's what she is—a motherfucking gift. Someone who reaps that specialized brand of justice *has* to be extraordinary, right?

I love my brothers, and I'd do anything for them. But would they treat her with the proper reverence she deserves?

Better not to chance it.

I clench my jaw and look back at my screen, concentrating on the proper commands I need to enter.

We've shared nearly everything for our entire lives. Our bond is something closer than brothers, forged in violence and cemented with loyalty.

Our mother left when I was a toddler, fucked off to the other side of the country. Despite her still coming back to Las Vegas every few months, it's never to see us. It's always to see him. Our father.

Though calling him a *father* feels like a slap in the face to all the men who actually love and care for their children.

Vito Santorini is a selfish, covetous, vindictive motherfucker who would burn the city down rather than hand it over to us.

All the more reason we need to ruthlessly dismantle his hold on the city. Some might argue that we'd be cutting off the head of a snake only for another to slither in its place. And they're not wrong.

Separately, my brothers are fine. But together?

They're leashed chaos.

It's why my role in our little trio is vital, even if they like to treat me like their dumbass kid brother. Without me tempering them, they'd burn to the ground.

My phone vibrates in my pocket, and I slide it out to read the preview notification on my home screen. It's not her. But the news is almost as good.

I slip my phone back into my pocket and jerk my chin toward Nic. "When were you going to tell us?"

He leans back into the chair, his arms resting on the armrests. "I've been talking to you for ten minutes. You haven't been listening."

I shake my head a few times and tilt my head to assess him. "How'd you do it?"

"Do what?" Nic asks, the mirth sliding off his face like mud in a flash flood.

"What're you two talking about?" Tommy asks.

"Dad," I say, watching Nic's expression carefully. He doesn't give anything away, the asshole.

Tommy shifts to look at Nic. "Oh shit. Did you kill Dad already?"

"Nah, I don't go rogue, Tommy. That's your thing," Nic drawls, looks between us.

"Fucking harsh, man," Tommy rumbles.

Nic lifts his shoulders. "I didn't kill him. But our path just became easier."

"Will one of you stop talking in riddles and just tell me what the fuck you're talking about," Tommy snaps.

My gaze stays on Nic as I answer Tommy. "Nic is the proud owner of a canceled marriage contract."

There's a beat of silence before Tommy barks out a quick laugh. "Why the fuck are you acting like this isn't great news? Now Nic isn't saddled to some random woman for the rest of his

181

life. We should be celebrating." He pauses and looks at our brother, his eyes narrowing into slits. "Unless you wanted to be Dad's puppet and marry the woman he negotiated for you?"

"Don't be ridiculous," Nic says with a scoff, reaching for his espresso cup on the edge of the desk.

"Then what's the problem?" Tommy presses.

There's something he's not telling us. Secrets are only fun when I hold them, not when they're being withheld from me. "How'd you get out of the arranged marriage Vito wanted, Nic? And what sort of punishment should we expect from him?"

Nic pauses with his midnight blue espresso cup halfway to his mouth. His eyes narrow over the rim of his cup at me but it doesn't bother me. I stopped being intimidated by my brothers when I found them watching show tunes and humming the songs ten years ago. So I flash him my most charming smile and raise my brows.

"It doesn't matter. It's done and now we can move on."

Tommy leans forward, forearms on the tops of his thighs. "Move on how? Operation Dad Dies?"

Nic sets his cup down without taking a sip and pinches the bridge of his nose with his thumb and index finger. "Jesus, Tommy."

Tommy tsks and sits back in his chair, holding his arms out to the side. "Okay, I admit it's not the best name, but you two vetoed Operation Kill Vito, Vito Must Die, or my personal favorite, Alexander Hamilton."

"That last one doesn't even make sense," I say with a groan.

"Exactly," Tommy snaps his fingers.

Nic side-eyes him. "You have to stop watching Broadway shows so much."

Tommy nods a few times, a platitude at best. "Sure, sure. Right after you stop eating ice cream every night."

Nic's face scrunches up with confusion. "That's not even remotely the same."

Tommy holds his index finger up. "I beg to differ."

"Can we focus? I've got shit to do, yeah?" It's a bullshit attempt to pull rank on my brothers, but they let me get away with it. If I don't wade it, they'll go in circles with one another. I don't have that kind of time to waste today.

They both shift their annoyed faces toward me, and I smile.

"The way I see it, we can adjust our timeline to take out Dad. We don't need to wait the five weeks we'd originally planned," Tommy says.

"And what do you propose?" Nic asks.

Tommy flashes us a grin as he taps a few things on his phone. "I'm free next week."

23

MAEVE

I ARCH my neck from left to right and back again, stretching the tight muscles. It's been a long few days. Between the job, Vegas, meeting with O'Boyle, and helping Rosie settle in, I feel like I could sleep for a week.

Not to mention the delightful little ache between my legs. And the fingerprint-shaped bruises along my hips.

I've had a busy week.

And if my sister wasn't so excitedly preoccupied with moving into her dorm room, I'm sure I would've faced her special brand of inquisition. For someone who spends most of her time behind computer screens, she's ridiculously adept at reading people. Especially me.

The radio plays softly in the background, some melancholy song I haven't heard before. I don't hate it, and if I already didn't have a belly full of dread, I might appreciate it more.

The flight home was long, but not long enough to prepare me for the conversation with Da. At least I got to sleep a little.

Between the power nap on the plane and the double espresso

I grabbed for the drive home, I should have some of my wits about me.

I exhale and toss my shoulders back. Time to do this. I throw my purse over my head and let it settle against my waist, but I don't bring anything else inside. I'm not sure how the conversation is going to go, and I'd rather have a quick getaway.

The sky is still dark, with the first rays of the sun just barely skimming the horizon. It's so quiet here compared to Chicago. The sharp contrast raises the hair on the back of my neck. I give the length of the driveway and the yard I can see a cursory glance, but everything looks as it should be.

I carefully twist the doorknob, silently pushing the mudroom door open enough to slip inside. I lean on my skills to slink into the house, damn near holding my breath as I do. It's nearly six o'clock here, and I don't want to wake Da if he's still asleep. That man is a bear when he's woken up suddenly.

I toe off my boots in the mudroom and tuck them underneath the coat rack. I pad into the kitchen on socked feet, clutching the strap of my purse across my chest.

My steps falter for just a moment when I see him. I guess I didn't need to worry about waking him up.

Da sits at the dining room table, hands steepled in front of his mouth. A bottle of whiskey casts a golden-hued ring on the table, an old fashioned glass next to it. Breakfast of champions.

"Cutting it close, yeah?"

"I had plenty of time." I didn't. I had ninety minutes to spare.

It takes effort, but I don't quicken my pace. I keep a steady gait as I cross the kitchen and stop in front of him.

"Sit down, Maeve." His tone is just shy of barking at me like I'm one of the grunts that work under him, cleaning up his messes.

I take my time pulling out the chair across from him and

settling into it. A reminder of who I am—who we are to each other. Or who we should be: equals.

The cushions are normally soft, but I've been traveling too long. I need the comfort of my bed to soothe the stress lining my body.

I sweep my hands out on either side, palms up. "Not a family chat?"

He shakes his head and pours himself a drink with a heavy hand. "Today it's between us."

I swallow past the boulder in my throat. An irrational fear skitters across my brain then. I know it's ridiculous and physically impossible, but I'm suddenly terrified that he'll know what I did. How I slept with Santorini *and* a random guy at a pub.

That he'll know and he'll condemn me for it.

I'd like to think my father is a progressive man. Not a feminist, but cares for his five daughters enough that he could see past his own Syndicate programming about women.

But his marriage contract has proven that I don't really know my father at all. It pains me to think that, but I console myself with the fact that means he doesn't know me either.

And that's the thing about always being underestimated: no one ever sees you coming. I used to loathe it, fight against it for years. But I've learned to embrace it. Mostly.

"Here I am, Da. What do you want to talk about?"

He leans back in his chair, bringing his glass with him. "Where are your bags?"

It wasn't what I was expecting, and his question throws me off. "I'm headed out as soon as we're done chatting."

He clucks his tongue. "Ah, see, that's where you're wrong."

My muscles tense as I brace. "How so?"

With measured movements, he takes a sip of his drink and sets the glass on the table. "Your contract has been revised."

My shoulders hitch, and my eyebrows crash over my eyes. "I don't understand."

Da flashes a sad sort of half smile at me. "I don't know what you did, but I know you had a hand in the termination of your contract with Las Vegas."

He talks so casually of the rest of my life like we're discussing nothing more pressing than if Mrs. Schroeder from down the road dropped off extra tomatoes today. And he reduced the man he wanted to irrevocably tie my life to nothing more than a city name.

"I don't know what you're talking about—"

He holds out his hand, palm toward me, and looks to the side for a moment. "Save it." He looks at me and drops his hand. "I don't really care how you did it or which one of your sisters helped you. It doesn't matter. Vegas agreed to keep their mouths shut for a small price, and I've already secured you another one."

My jaw drops as I stare at the man in front of me. I don't recognize him. It takes me several long moments to find my voice, and when I do, pure venom slithers out. "Are you kidding me?"

"I told you this was your future. You should've believed me the first time. Maybe then I wouldn't have had to take such drastic measures."

The hair on the back of my neck stands up, but I force down the uneasiness. It takes effort but I relax my tense muscles and lift a shoulder in a careless shrug. "Don't be surprised when this contract ends. And the next one and the one after that and so on."

He's shaking his head before I even finish talking. "See, I knew you'd say something like that, and I just can't risk it."

My blood starts to boil, this warming, churning feeling in my gut. It spreads outward, toward my fingers and my toes, heating up with each inch it claims. My gaze ping-pongs between his eyes, looking for a shred of the man I used to idolize when I was younger.

A stranger stares back at me.

The thought is so crushing, I have to stifle the pain in my chest.

I push my chair back abruptly and stand up. "What did you do?"

He tips his head back and holds my gaze. "What I had to."

"Tell me." I keep my voice low, but I add every ounce of authority that *he* taught me.

The side of his mouth hooks up. "I've made arrangements with Camarillo."

My mind races as I struggle to pinpoint who he's talking about. My thoughts come to a screeching halt. He never mentioned a city the last time. We found that information out ourselves. So what's changed now?

I narrow my eyes at him. "Why are you telling me this?"

The pad of his index finger taps an even beat on the rim of his glass and he continues like I never asked him a question. "You will become a Milano in six weeks."

My anger short-circuits my common sense. I slap my palm against the table and lean forward. "I will always be a King."

"Not in the eyes of the United States government you won't."

I straighten up and press my other palm flat against the table, using the hard oak to ground me. "I don't give a fuck about the government and neither do you. I will always be a King. And no one, not even *you*, can take that away from me."

He stills. The mask of The Hammer descends over his face, obscuring any sort of warmth I associated with the man I called my da.

"The Milanos are old school. They make their fortune in their California vineyards . . . among other things. Taking your new husband's last name is non-negotiable. And if, for any reason, you don't fulfill the contract, Ava will go in your place."

White-hot rage flashes before my eyes. I step toward him on instinct, the edge of the table digging into my hip bones. Adrenaline floods my veins as I stare him down. "Are you really going to sit at my mum's table and blackmail me? With my sister—your own daughter?"

He doesn't respond, just calmly holds my gaze. And I might've been able to forgive him had he offered a single morsel of regret or apology or fucking explanation. But his silence, it's unforgivable.

"I will *never* forgive you for this."

A muscle in his jaw twitches and he offers me a sharp nod. Like my wrath and punishment are acceptable to him. It only infuriates me further.

"But you'll be alive."

I throw my arms out on either side of me. "I'm already alive!"

He exhales through his nose, his face holding its unnatural stillness.

I drop my arms, letting my palms hit my bare thighs with a slap. My brows furrow as I stare at him. At this point, there are so many tumultuous emotions churning around in my gut, I can't distinguish one from another.

A bone-deep exhaustion rolls over me in a soft wave. I sigh and sink into the chair behind me. "Tell me the truth. You owe me that much."

He swallows the rest of his cocktail in one gulp and gently places it next to the whiskey bottle. "War."

My lips part, and I reel back. "That's it? I've been hearing those three letters for as long as I can remember, and never—not once—did anything ever come from it. How is this any different?"

"War *is* coming, Maeve."

"With who? When? What happened?" My questions are rapid-fire, louder with each word.

He folds his arms across his chest and arches a brow. "You know I can't tell you that."

I scoff. "Of course. How silly of me to think that I'd be privy to Syndicate information when I don't have a dick."

"You test my patience, Maeve. All you need to know is that people are missing. From factions in several different cities across the world."

"And so what? You think shipping me off to some fucking winemakers is the way to—do, what, exactly? Protect me? Stop lying. To yourself and to me."

"They're winemakers *and* gun experts, imported straight from Italy."

He offers the information so freely like I haven't been starving for Syndicate information and begging him for ten years to include me. The fact that he does it right now only adds salt to the gaping wound.

Realization dawns on me with a special sort of horror. My lips part, and my eyes widen as I stare at my da. "You sold me for a piece of their gun business, then?"

He doesn't answer me, which is all the confirmation I needed.

"How much was I worth to you? To the Syndicate? Hm? A million? Two?"

"Ten million euros in cash and guns and a piece of their business." His voice is so quiet, so matter of fact, it breaks my goddamn heart.

I suck the inside of my cheek between my molars and look away. My sinuses sting but I would rather eat glass than let him see me cry.

I give him my profile, staring off into the backyard patio to my left. "And my sisters? Will you sell them for your war?"

"If you hold up your end of this contract, marry the Milano kid, then I won't need to arrange contracts for your sisters."

The threat hangs heavy between us. I turn my head toward him once more, wiping my face clean of emotion.

"Your word isn't good enough. I want a binding contract from a lawyer of my choosing. My sisters are off-limits. Forever."

His gaze roams my face, his expression drawn, his mouth turned down in the corners. After a moment, he nods. "Alright."

I nod a few times, an unconscious movement, and push to stand once more. "I'll have it drawn up today. And I want to see the Milano contract first."

"It's on your nightstand upstairs."

I nod again, feeling like a bobblehead as I scramble to lay preliminary terms. "I'll meet them in six weeks. My time between now and then is mine."

"Aye, I'll make sure it's understood." His voice is softer now, and I hate him all the more for it.

I step around the chair and push it in, my fingers curling over the top of the back. "I'll be back for my things later."

Da reaches across the table, palm down. "Thank you, Maeve—"

"Don't," I snap. "I'm not doing this for you. I'm doing this for them."

"I know," he murmurs. "But I'm thankful all the same."

I look at him then, memorize the way the overhead light shadows his face. His proud nose and the laugh lines around his eyes. The dark hair covering his jaw, always kept short and tidy.

I allow myself one single minute of nostalgia.

Because when I leave this kitchen, I will never look at him the same way again.

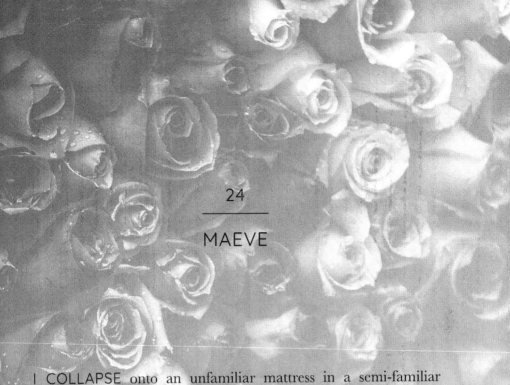

24

MAEVE

I COLLAPSE onto an unfamiliar mattress in a semi-familiar apartment three hours away from home. It's an open floor plan with two bedrooms, a decently-sized kitchen, and wraparound windows taking up two walls.

It's a place my sisters and I own, somewhere to crash when we can't make it home.

Or in my case, when we don't want to.

I haven't spent a ton of time here, preferring to unwind in our penthouse in New York City, but there are touches of my sisters everywhere.

The mattress is softer than I like, but the blankets are that cozy sherpa material Ava loves. A vanilla pumpkin cupcake oil diffuser in the corner makes the whole room smell like a bakery.

It reminds me of the times Fiona and I would spend in the kitchen together, whipping up cinnamon bread and pumpkin muffins.

I close my eyes and let the memories wash over me.

My mum used to say that a woman had to be well-rounded in

her skills. If we were going to be independent women who could sneak around undetected and handle weapons with respect, then we should know how to feed ourselves.

It's odd how the brain works. I can vividly remember things she taught us, but in my memories, her face is fuzzy. Time has chipped away at my recollection of her, blurring her edges.

But the feelings are still there. The way my heart felt two sizes two big when Mum dragged chairs over to the island for me and Fi to stand on. She stood behind us and guided our movements as we whisked and stirred in the big metal mixing bowls she loved to use.

And then after she was gone, it was me standing behind my younger sisters, passing her knowledge on.

A tear slides down my cheek, disappearing into my hair.

I'll never bake in Mum's kitchen with my sisters again.

I open my eyes, and tears slip free. I look at the crisp white ceiling above me, so pristine and perfect, not a watermark or brushstroke in sight.

One more minute. One more minute of dipping my toes into my grief.

I'm trying to figure out when the switch happened. When my da turned into this cold, harsh version of himself. Or maybe he was always this way but I didn't realize it.

Or I didn't *want to* realize it.

Was this always my path? What would my life look like had Mum not died?

Exhausted and despondent, I'm feeling low. Too low to ponder such things that could send me into an existential crisis spiral.

I can't allow myself to wallow any further, or I fear I won't be able to pull myself out in time.

I swipe my fingers underneath my eyes, wiping away the moisture and mascara smudges.

I need a long, hot shower, food, and sleep. In that order.

And when I wake up, everything will look better.

I've showered—even used Fi's fancy shampoo and conditioner for icy blonde hair—changed into something clean and over-sized, and eaten one of Ava's fresh-frozen breakfast burritos.

And I still can't sleep.

Every fiber in my body begs for sleep, but I can't shut my brain off. I tap the back of my phone against my bottom lip, debating on what to do.

I don't think I can stomach another read-through of the contract right now. I've already read it three times on the plane, another might push me too far. And I know I need to start planning. Six weeks is going to go fast.

But I'm just not ready to tell my sisters yet. I can't temper their anger and betrayal when I'm still working through my own.

I've never been resentful for being the oldest, for bearing the burden so my sisters don't have to.

But sometimes it's fucking hard. And this is one of those times.

I know I have to tell them soon, I need their help. But I need a day or two to process first.

Fi and Rosie are busy with school and Ava's already traveling. Their plates are full enough that they won't be hounding me for answers for a couple days.

Keira's the only one I'm worried about. She's around some-where, and if she comes looking for me here, she's going to know something's wrong right away. Her intuition is annoyingly good. So I'll have to avoid her.

It's fine. Totally fine. I'll just avoid my one sister who can sniff out a lie even by omission like a hound with a scent. She's determined on her worst days and obstinate on her best.

I guess if I'm not going to sleep, then I can get some work done. I've been avoiding my phone since I left Da's house, knowing one of my sisters would've texted me.

Sure enough, I have seven messages from Rosie. Anxiety churns in my gut, my finger hovering over our message thread. I blow out a breath, toss the blanket over my bare legs, and open the message.

> Roisin: I know you're on a flight right now, but I wanted to show you what I found before I went to bed. I have class at 8AM! Why the hell did you let me pick a class for 8AM?! Never again, Maeve, never again! LY!

> Roisin: I amped up our security measures, rerouted some funds, and shut down one of the Fairy Godmothers forums the conspiracy theorists loved. That should stop them for a little while until I can figure out who's texting you. I'll know more next week.

The next five texts are screenshots of Rosie's computer screens. They're actually several screenshots made into a collage. I pinch my index and thumb together and then flick it outward to zoom in.

Holy shit.

Martin Bendtsten Jr., embezzled from a children's charity his parents started.

Hal Kristofferson, all three wives disappeared.

Steven Woodridge, suspected health care fraud and his victims are all patients with terminal illnesses.

Brock Lampshire, suspected serial killer and his victims are sex workers.

Devon Carlton, his daddy's a judge and wiped the last four cases of domestic violence clean.

She made dossiers for all five of the names I sent her. The ones from him—*Romeo*. Rosie only makes dossiers this extensive for those who qualify for our justice. Which means . . . he was telling me the truth.

But why? Why would some stranger take the time to find me —which is another problem we need to figure out—and then hand-deliver me people to mete out justice? Why didn't he do something himself if he knew what kind of people they are?

I spend a few minutes zooming in as far as possible and trying to read the pixelated screenshots. From her preliminary research, it seems like these guys fit the criteria of our usual marks. I close out of our text thread and toss my phone next to me. There's always an inherent urgency to what we do. The sooner we take these guys off the board, the safer everyone is.

But that doesn't mean we rush it. Whether it's a solo vacation or not, we always bring a candidate to the table for a vote. Only if they pass do we move forward.

Considering we're all scattered around the globe, we'll have to bring these guys to a virtual vote. But not today. Or tomorrow. Next week, maybe.

I want Rosie to be able to enjoy her first week of school. Fi too. She acts like it's just a job, but I saw the way she looked at the course schedule when she didn't think anyone was watching. She's excited.

College never appealed to me the way it does to Fi and Rosie. It seemed too far-fetched of an idea for me to do something so normal as go to college. Not when I knew my da was known around the world as The Hammer. And not for his sunny disposition.

Just the thought of Da sends a sharp pain behind my ribs.

Time for another distraction. I lean over the side of the bed and rummage around in my carry-on bag for my favorite back-pack. Inside the back pocket is the phone Romeo texted me on earlier. I know I should've destroyed the sim card. It's the smart thing to do.

But I didn't.

Call it curiosity or self-preservation or some other attribute I'm too tired to overthink right now.

I find the right phone and swipe it on, flicking to our previous text thread. I don't hesitate, tapping out three words and hitting send before I second-guess myself.

> Me: Tell me why.

His reply is instant. I must've caught him on the phone unless he was already awake. I wonder where he lives, if he's getting ready for work or if it's the middle of the night. If I had to guess, I'd bet he's the kind of person who stays up all night, trolling the message boards. It's probably how he found me.

> Romeo: So you did get my messages.

> Me: Aye, I got them.

> Romeo: And? Did you like them?

> Me: I have questions.

> Romeo: They're a gift, Juliet.

> Me: My name's not Juliet you know.

> Romeo: I know, but isn't this more fun than me calling you the Wren?

> Me: Tell me why you sent the list of names.

> Romeo: I told you. It was a gift. I'm a generous man.

I scoff, my fingers flying across the screen.

> Me: People who are sincerely generous never have to tell someone they are.

> Romeo: I'll prove it.

> Romeo: Gregor Markham, Alanzo Caruso, Chet Beaufort.

> Me: More gifts?

> Romeo: Until next time, Juliet.

I read his text three times before I can accurately describe what the feeling underneath my breastbone is. Disappointment.

That doesn't make sense though. I shouldn't be disappointed by someone I've literally never met. We owe each other nothing.

It must be a leftover emotion from everything with Da.

Still, I tap out another text before I can think better of it.

> Me: Wait. I want to know who you are.

> Romeo: You will. Soon.

I stare at my phone for a moment, waiting to see if he'll say anything else. When three minutes pass, I turn it off and toss it next to my other phone on the other side of the bed.

Three more names to our never-ending list. If they check out. But maybe the most important name that should be on the list is his—Romeo's.

I need to figure out who he is and what he really wants. In my experience, most people don't give without expectation. And he's going to be in for a rude awakening when he realizes that I don't bend for anyone. Not anymore.

25

MAEVE

I WAKE up to my phone buzzing next to my head, this persistent vibration over and over again. I crack one eye open and blindly flop my hand around until it hits the hard plastic case. It's tucked underneath the pillow next to me.

I have to blink a few times to get my vision to clear. I roll over onto my back and bring my phone up above my face. I have to squint to see the little bar under the image of Keira's smiling face. It takes a few times, but I finally manage to answer it with a muffled noise.

"Oh good, you finally decided to answer." Keira shouts.

I pull the phone away from my ear and look at the screen for a moment before bringing it back. "What's going on?"

"Where have you been?"

"Jesus, Keira. You don't have to yell," I grumble.

"Aye, I fucking do have to yell. I've been calling you for hours."

I put her on speakerphone and push to sit up. "What? Really? I must've slept through it."

"Where are you, Maeve?"

The tone of her voice wipes the fuzzy tendrils of sleep from my brain. "What's wrong? Is it Fiona?"

I wasn't sure about her going to that school alone. It's a huge risk—too big, if you ask me.

She sighs, a car horn blaring wherever she is. "No, it's not Fiona or any of our sisters. It's you."

Some of the panic dissipates at her assurances our sisters are okay. I scrape my fingers through my hair, lightly combing through the tousled waves. "What? I'm fine."

"Oh, you're *fine*?"

"It's too early for sarcasm," I say, a yawn stealing my last word.

"It's five o'clock in the evening."

I check the time on my phone. "Huh. I guess so. I'm a little jet-lagged, and I fell asleep watching old Vampire Diaries episodes a few hours ago."

"Great. I haven't seen it in a couple years, so I'm overdue for a binge-watch."

"Oh, well, I'm not at—"

The lock on the apartment door turns and the door creaks open, interrupting me.

"I know where you are, sister." Keira's voice echoes from inside my phone and the front of our apartment.

A moment later, she appears in the bedroom doorway, a duffel bag thrown over her shoulder. Her hair is thrown up in a messy bun on the top of her head, smaller pieces that have fallen curling around her face and neck. Dressed in all black, she looks like she's just come from the gym: tight black bike shorts, a black cropped workout shirt, and black sneakers.

But I know my sister better than that. The only thing she hates more than being ignored is cardio. She wants people to glance at her and think she's coming from the gym, when I know she's really just come from The Cavern.

The Cavern is a weapons specialty gym in a way. It's a safe space to practice with things that might otherwise be illegal or frowned upon. Keira lives for learning and honing her skills with weapons.

I end our call and lay back on the bed, my energy dwindling now that I know there's not an emergency. "What are you doing here?"

She stares at me, her mouth tipped down in the corners. "I was home. Earlier." Her voice is soft, low. It's not pity in her gaze, but something worse—sadness. A deep, profound sadness.

My brows lift toward my hairline. I hadn't realized she was there. I didn't exactly search the house though. "Oh."

I clear my throat and look away for a moment. My skin gets that prickly hot feeling of embarrassment. Which is completely ridiculous.

I look back at her. "Why didn't you say anything?"

She shrugs a shoulder. "I thought it might be better if I didn't make myself known. See what happened after you left."

I settle back into bed, pulling the comforter up to my chest. "And? What happened after?"

She pulls both lips inward for a moment before releasing them. "Nothing. Da left ten minutes after you did."

I nod a few times and shift my gaze toward the TV across from the bed, staring at nothing. "How did you find me?"

She dumps her duffel bag just inside the room with a thump and beelines toward me. "Please. Like it was hard. I knew you weren't going to turn around and hop back on another plane. This was the next logical place."

She toes off her sneakers. "Scoot over."

I oblige and shuffle over a little to make room for her. "I thought about leaving."

She grabs the top corner of blankets and peels them back

enough for her to climb in. She lays on her side, facing me with her hands tucked underneath her cheek.

I turn toward her, mimicking her pose. It reminds me of the days we would have sister sleepovers and two—or sometimes three—of us would fall asleep in my California king-sized bed.

"You're a better woman than me. I would've left," she murmurs.

I smile and shake my head a little. "No, you wouldn't have. Not if you know one of us was close by."

"So you knew I'd find you, is that what you're saying?" Her sass doesn't pack quite the same punch when she's quietly talking.

I chuckle under my breath. "No, but I knew I was going to tell you guys soon. I just need some time to process."

A glassy sheen covers her eyes. "What are we going to do?"

I exhale a big breath and let the edge of my mouth turn up into a smile. "I'm going to marry what's-his-name."

"What *is* his name?"

"Milano."

"Maeve Milano," she draws the name out, her nose wrinkling up like she smelled something bad. "Sounds terrible together."

I chuckle and nod. "A terrible name. But I'll always be a King."

"We'll find a way out of the contract," she vows, her voice hushed.

My stomach swoops at the mention of the contract—of the terms. "If we do, he'll send Ava. They already agreed to it."

"This is bullshit, Maeve. We can't let him do this. We're not fucking sheep. We're fucking Kings, you said so yourself."

My throat gets tight, but I force the words out anyway. "Aye, we are. But I won't risk you guys. If I don't do this, every single one of you will be in the same position within six months. And I'd never be able to live with myself."

Her chin trembles as she rolls her lips into her mouth for a second. "How are you so calm?"

"I'm terrified," I admit. "But I know it's the right choice—it's the *only choice*. For now."

Her eyes brighten. "I knew it. You have a plan."

"Not yet, but I will."

"Tell me what to do to help," she says, her jaw set.

"I will. I'm just glad you're here."

The side of her face lifts into a smirk. "As if I'd miss a chance to mother you like you've been doing for us for years."

My stomach rumbles, breaking the tension. We both huff out a giggle.

"Alright, time for food. I'll run out and grab those gourmet grilled cheese sandwiches you love from the place around the corner," she says, but she doesn't move yet.

"You're the best, sister."

She smiles, her grin infectious, as she rolls over and off the bed. She shakes her finger at me before slipping her sneakers back on. "I'm totally going to quote you on that, and as soon as Rosie's out of class, I'm sending it to her. *Maeve said I'm the best sister.*"

I roll off the bed, straightening my oversized band tee. We went to see one of our favorites a few years ago, and I loved this shirt's design. They didn't have my normal size, but I like the comfy, oversized look too, so it works.

I laugh, my chest feeling light at our familiar banter. "There was a comma in there! You're the best—comma—sister."

"That's not how I heard it." She gives me her best innocent face, but I'm not fooled. She's the most conniving out of all of us. She'll be out for blood on my behalf soon enough.

"You're all the best," I tell her.

"Yeah, yeah. You said *I* was the best first though, and I'm totally going to rub it in their faces." She grabs a crossbody belt bag from her duffel in the corner and slips it over her head. "Okay, I'll be back in thirty minutes."

I nod. "I'll be here."

"Love you, bye," she says in a sing-song voice.

My other phone buzzes a few minutes after she leaves, and like Pavlov's dogs, my heart skips a beat. There's only one person who uses this number right now.

I round the bed to the other night stand and unplug my other from the charger. The home screen lights up with a new text notification. From him.

> Romeo: Did you like my presents yesterday then? Would they make good additions to your menagerie?

> Me: Some girls might think chocolates and roses make good gifts and you send me names of despicable men.

> Romeo: Is that what you want? You want me to send you flowers and chocolates and edible fruit arrangements?

> Me: What? No. I was pointing out the differences.

> Romeo: Roses are too generic for someone with your exquisite talents. And the best chocolate comes from Belgium.

> Me: Is that where you live? Belgium?

The three little dots bounce up and down in a little wave for a minute before they stop altogether. Almost like he's typing and deleting. I wait for another two minutes, but he doesn't reply.

I tilt my chin down and frown, disappointment sitting on my shoulders. It's quickly followed by swift annoyance with myself.

I'm not usually one to attach so many feelings to anyone or thing, and here I am, placing expectations on an actual stranger who somehow found me.

It must be some sort of break in my normal emotional wall. Another thing to blame Da for.

26

TOMMY

I WHISTLE the last song from a show I watched a couple days ago. It's a tragic story but the music is excellent.

I discovered a long time ago that my whistling and general enjoyment of life has the added bonus of freaking the fuck out of the people I have to chat with. Like the two little fuckwits in front of me.

Two of our grunts sit on hard metal chairs in front of me. They haven't put in enough time to be soldiers yet, and considering the reason I pulled them in here today, they'll probably never make it.

They're known associates of Marco Colombo, and since I can't seem to locate that motherfucker today, these two will have to do.

Their wrists are zip tied behind them, but if they really wanted to, they could stand up and walk out of here. My reputation alone holds them here. Well, that and the fact that I brought them to The Side Winder.

The Side Winder Motel takes up one small block of our territory. It's an L-shaped building with sixteen single rooms renovated into eight deluxe rooms, spread out over two floors. We upgraded each room to include a little living space, so it's more like a suite. Plus, they're all soundproofed.

We never advertise any vacancy, and on the rare occasion someone walks in off the street looking for lodging, the girl at the front desk directs them to our other motel, The Maple Inn.

We keep The Side Winder open for any of our guys who need a place to crash for a few days or if we need to conduct certain types of business.

One of the dipshit friends grunts, the noise muffled behind his gag. I stop whistling in the middle of the chorus and glare at the one who just won't shut up.

The urge to finish the song is strong, but time waits for no man. And I'm already running late.

I've lost too many hours to a certain dark-haired beauty lately. I've played out too many variations in my head. I let myself get tangled up in the idea of her. I don't even fucking know her, but in the moment, it felt like I did. Like it was destiny or some other fairytale bullshit.

Not that I said a word of it to my brothers. If Rome caught me waxing poetic about a random woman, he'd start digging. And we can't have that.

I thought about finding her, but if merely thinking about her distracts me this much, searching for her will take me out.

It's too dangerous when my brothers and I are taking out our father in just a couple days. Not to mention we still have to keep our hold on the city.

I sigh and refocus on the task at hand.

"Do you have any idea how hard it is to simply stop singing a song that's been playing on repeat in your head? It's nearly painful."

He mumbles something unintelligible behind his gag, and I

sigh. I unbutton the bottom of my black sleeve and begin methodically cuffing my shirt halfway up my forearms.

"Do either of you know who I am?"

They both jerk their heads forward in a swift nod. Good, that definitely makes things easier.

"I'm disappointed in you boys. I thought you understood your place here. Understood my brother when he gave you a final warning last week." I glance from the guy on his right to one on the left. "Was a bullet hole in Marco's shoulder not enough to make you understand?"

The kid on the left's dark eyes flare with fire, but he doesn't try to speak like his friend. More than likely, he already knows he's fucked.

Nic gave him a final warning, and if you ask me, he should've just put him down. It's not that I don't believe in second chances, because I do. But it's a sliding scale.

I turn around and grab my steel-tipped darts. I've grown quite the reputation with darts over the last few months. I don't know if I would say that I'm good, but I think what I lack in skill I make up for in presentation.

At least that's what the judging panel said at our last tournament.

"You know, I'm actually surprised. Not that you're trying to peddle your shitty laced drugs in my city and in my fucking club. That I believe. You're young and greedy and you think it's the fastest way to make a quick buck. The hustle, I can respect."

I run the edge of my finger over the tip of the dart, enjoying the way it stings a little. They're not sharp, not compared to a blade. But with enough force, they make quite an impact.

"It's the self-preservation I don't understand. Or the lack thereof. What kind of fucking moron ignores his bosses orders? Especially the ones that explicitly say if you keep selling your fentanyl-laced shit in our town, we're going to kill you."

The one kid pretending to be tough glares at me, his shoulders thrown back and his chin tipped up. I let the maniacal grin spread across my face at his feeble attempt at intimidation.

I grew up with Vito for a father and Alfred as a grandfather. No one intimidates me, certainly not some snot-nosed kid.

"Alright, which one of you is going to tell me where Marco Colombo is?"

The kid on the left cuts a sharp look to the other one, but his buddy doesn't even see it. He's too busy staring at me, all wide-eyed and slack-jawed. It could be because I'm rolling a dart around my fingers like a magic trick with a coin.

But I'm betting it's because they heard all about that one time I used a man as my own personal dart board.

I jerk my head to the kid on the right but look at the one with the paltry glare. "I see your friend appreciates a man who can play darts. Here, let me show you how good I've gotten over the last few months."

Without another warning, I squint and bring my arm back and snap my wrist forward, curving the angle a little at the last second. The dart sails through the air like a rocket, landing perfectly in the guy's thigh.

He cries out in pain, his eyes screwing up tight. I spare him a brief look, my gaze turning back to the glaring kid. He doesn't look rattled yet.

I sigh, like the whole thing is a chore and fire three more darts in rapid succession. I hold the stubborn one's gaze as they land in his friend's leg, letting him see the deadened darkness in my eyes.

His buddy starts talking then, mumbling something between cries of pain.

I stretch my neck from side to side, mentally gearing myself up for what has to happen next. I think they're ready to talk.

Hopefully, they don't need too much more convincing because I have a meeting to get to today.

I place the last three darts on the table behind me and cross the room to stand in front of the crier. I assess him with the sort of cold detachment my father would be proud of. After all, I am his greatest creation.

I often think of my father as Frankenstein and me, his monster. True, he didn't create me in a lab but rather the streets. He taught me how to interrogate someone, which bones to break for the maximum amount of pain and which places to slice to inflict the most torment.

But just like Frankenstein's monster, I've surpassed him. Outgrew him and his archaic ways. I've found more beneficial ways to get the information I need.

I don't need to pull fingernails and slice off ears to get the answers I need. I can simply sing show tunes, pick up my favorite burgers from the place down the road, and practice darts. Admittedly, using someone as a dart board would be considered maiming.

But it's all relative.

And if Nic tells me someone has to go, then they have to go. But I take no pleasure in ending a life. Unless they're a threat to my brothers, then I take quite a bit of enjoyment in extinguishing their light.

But these two in front of me? They're just kids. Dumbass kids with misplaced loyalty to another dumbass kid. They all got caught up in a game they didn't even realize they were playing. And I intend to find out who's pulling their strings.

I stare at the crying guy again. Dark hair slicked back with too much gel, a thick gold chain-link necklace around his neck, wearing too much cologne.

I take the gag out of his mouth, pulling it over his chin and letting it fall to his neck. Crouching down with my hands on my thighs, I ask him, "What's your name, kid?"

I tune out the yelling from next to me and give him my full attention. But he's not as practiced as I am, so he keeps turning his fearful gaze to the side.

"Hey," I say with a snap of my fingers. "Ignore him. Look at me."

He faces me once more, his lower lashes wet with pain. "Rosco."

"Rosco what?"

"Martinez, sir," he says with a sniff.

"Alright, Rosco Martinez, what's your buddy's name?"

"Ralph Madden, sir."

"And how long have you and your buddy been running with Marco Colombo?"

He swallows audibly. "Six months, sir."

"And where is your boy Marco?"

"I-I don't know, sir, I swear. I haven't seen him in two days. He told us to lie low for a few weeks."

I nod a few times, trying my best to contort my face into the semblance of understanding and compassion. "And why would you need to lie low?"

He licks his lips and side-eyes Ralph. "He didn't say."

I clap his shoulder twice. I didn't think he would know too much, and I was right. But Ralph might. "Alright, Rosco."

Standing up from my crouching position, I turn to face the broody one. "I'll give you a choice. You can answer my questions or I can turn you into my personal dart board with knives instead of darts."

It's not exactly a bluff. I will get the information out of him by any means necessary, but I don't want to have to resort to straight-up torture. That shit gives me insomnia for days.

Ralph clenches his jaw before nodding twice, two sharp jerks of his head. I lean forward and slip the gag out of his mouth, but before I let go, I tighten my fingers around the cloth and jerk him forward. He squeaks in surprise, his eyes widening.

"Don't lie to me, Ralph. I'll know, and then I'll take your choice off of the table, yeah?"

He jerks his head forward several times. Sweat beads at his temple, darkening his brown hair.

I slap his cheek in a gesture more playful than painful and stand up. I take a few steps backward until my legs hit the end of the bed behind me. I fold my arms across my chest and widen my legs a little.

"Now, you boys ever been in love?"

Almost as one, they exchange a look and shake their heads.

I scoff. "Of course not. How old are you, anyway?"

"Eighteen, sir," Rosco says.

"Nineteen," Ralph says.

"You're young," I concede, tilting my head to the side and lifting my brows. "Plus, you act like a bunch of wannabe Sopranos after watching your mama's HBO subscription. You play dress-up. Wear your cheap suits and hand out drugs that kill people in our clubs and casinos."

"We didn't know about that," Ralph interjects.

"See, that I have a hard time believing. I thought you two were Marco's boys?"

Ralph clenches his jaw, his gaze narrowing.

I tsk, pivoting to snatch the darts from the table. In rapid fire succession, I launch them at Ralph, nailing him in the thigh just like his buddy.

He yelps in surprise and grimaces. From underneath low-lidded eyes, he glares at me. I keep my expression neutral, taking care not to let him see a glimpse of the monster that lives inside me. He's not the one I'm really after. If he were, then we'd be having a different conversation at a different location.

I slip my hands into my pockets. "Now, Ralph. I thought we came to an understanding. I ask you a question, and you answer. If you don't, I have to get creative."

Ralph's gaze slides away from me and fixates on the partially-opened blinds. "Marco started hanging around with a new crew."

I lean toward him. The prospect of new information is alluring. There's nothing I love more than sniffing out traitors. "Tell me about Marco's new friends."

"Italian."

I narrow my eyes and take a step to the side, blocking his view of the blinds he can't stop staring at. "We're all Italian here, Ralph. That doesn't help me at all."

He flicks his stare from my chest to my eyes. His gaze flattens and his shoulders slump. "He's going to kill us for snitching."

"Maybe," I say with a slow nod. "But think of it this way: if you don't start talking, I definitely will."

"West Coast Italians. Marco said they're older than us."

I rock back on my heels and glance between the two of them. "Where'd you get the coke from?"

Ralph's eyebrows crash together over his eyes. I see the lie on his tongue before it leaves his lips.

I slash my hand through the air, my patience drying up. "Don't feed me that bullshit about it being ours either. I'm not a fucking idiot. Don't forget that you work for me, your allegiance is to the Santorinis. Not Marco fucking Colombo or any of his motherfucking friends."

Ralph's eyes widen almost comically big, his head bobbing quickly in a nod.

"You've had your chance, now it's Rosco's turn." I pivot on my heels to face him. "Tell me where you got the laced coke."

Rosco looks at Ralph out of the corner of his eye, then

quickly shifts his gaze back to me. The tendons in his neck stick out, his pulse beating frantically on his skin.

"Ralph gave you the laced coke?" I ask, scanning him for any signs of lying.

He shakes his head. "No, sir. Marco did. He told us it was new product."

I walk over to him and pat him on the shoulder. "Two more questions, then we can be done, okay?"

He frantically nods.

I lean down so I can look him in the eye. "If you answer this correctly, you just might save yourself, so think carefully."

"I will, sir. I promise," Rosco says.

"I know you will, Rosco. Now, does pineapple belong on pizza?"

"Uh, I—I don't understand."

"It's an easy but important question. So answer truthfully. Pineapple on pizza—yes or no?"

His gaze flies between my eyes, his brows disappearing into his hairline. "Uh, I mean, yes?"

I don't react, just pivot my attention to Ralph. "And you? Same question."

He doesn't hesitate with his answer. "Yes but only on pies with olive oil based sauce."

God damnit, now I'm gonna owe Nic twenty bucks. I sigh and straighten, exhaling through my nose and rubbing my chin. When will people learn that tropical fruit belongs in smoothies and not on savory pizzas?

"You're both wrong, but I don't have the time to educate you right now. So if Marco was lying low, where would he go? He have a girlfriend? A mama he goes home to for Sunday dinner?"

Rosco licks his lips, his hair damp with sweat and cheeks flushed with fear. Or pain. Probably both, honestly. "Uh, I think he has a couple girls he's seeing. I'm not sure."

"Names, addresses, phone numbers. I need more information than that."

"I don't know the address, but I can take you there," Ralph says.

I check my watch. I have three hours until I have to meet my brothers at Violet Oak. Plenty of time to track down a defector and extract a little information.

27

MAEVE

I DRUM my fingers against my thigh, going over all the reasons I shouldn't text him again.

It's been two days. He didn't answer me last time. He'll know I'm trying to dig for information.

All valid reasonings, but not the most alarming. It's the startling realization that I want to talk to him. I'm oddly intrigued by our exchanges—by him. What kind of person follows our work long enough, possesses enough skills to actually track my phone number down, and offers more men to feed the fire? Blackmail, I expected. Maybe even revenge for one of the men we've taken down. But this is all just so . . . unexpected.

And surprisingly, I don't hate it.

I flop back on my bed, bringing my phone up in front of my face. Without thinking too hard about it, I open up our text exchange.

> Me: I've been thinking.

> Romeo: About me? I'm flattered.

Me: Not exactly. I've been trying to figure out why you didn't turn those men over to the authorities?

Romeo: C'mon, Juliet. We both know the cops don't have the real power.

Me: And who does? Not you, obviously.

Romeo: You wound me, mon chéri.

Me: I don't know you.

Romeo: You will.

I bristle. There's no context in texts. Is he . . . flirting with me or threatening me?

Me: That's the second time you've said that. And yet, I don't know anything about you.

Romeo: What do you want to know?

I tug the corner of my lip between my teeth and stare at the screen. I suppose I should try to get some more information out of him. Rosie said any information is helpful.

Me: Tell me something real about you.

Romeo: I'm good with computers.

Me: I could've guessed that already. How did you find me?

Romeo: A magician never reveals his secrets.

> Me: What kind of magician are you? The one who books children's parties or the one who practices with his friends in his parents' basement?

> Romeo: Shakespeare wrote "If there's magic, let it be art." I'm paraphrasing but the message is the same.

A chuckle floats past my lips, lighting the air around me. The laugh dies instantly, brows drawn in confusion.

> Me: What's with the Shakespeare quotes.

> Romeo: Shakespeare is one of the most influential people in our history. I like to do my part in keeping him alive.

> Me: And how's that? Texting strangers paraphrased Shakespeare?

> Romeo: Exactly.

> Me: And what made you find me?

> Romeo: I've been waiting my entire life for you, Juliet.

My brows knit together. That's more than just flirty, that's bordering on obsessive. For all I know, I'm being catfished by some lonely person with too much time on their hands.

> Romeo: Was that too much?

> Me: Yes.

Romeo: Okay how about this. I've been following your work for some time, and I think you're fascinating.

Me: So you're a web detective then.

Romeo: I'm not an amateur.

Me: What is it you do exactly?

Romeo: I work in the family business.

Me: Like me?

Romeo: Something like that. Are you a night owl?

Me: Aye, but it's more out of necessity. I travel a lot for work, so I work all hours. You know that already though.

Romeo: I work all hours too. Another thing we have in common.

I shake my head a few times, the smile never leaving my lips.

Me: I didn't think we had anything else in common.

Romeo: We share a hatred for evil men who do evil things.

Something in my belly stirs to life, a small little caterpillar of warmth. I smother the smile on my face by leaning my face half onto the pillow. Keira's going to be back any minute with our late-night snack: fish tacos. The last thing I need is for her to come in and see me all moon-eyed over a text.

TOMMY

I saunter into the second-floor office of Violet Oak with a scowl and a bottle of bourbon.

"You're late," Nic snaps. He's not even looking at me, instead watching the empty first floor of the club.

"No, I'm not. I'm five minutes early, and I've had a fucking day, so don't start in on me, man," I grumble.

Nic spins around and stalks toward the chair behind the desk. I slump into my preferred seat across from him and unscrew the top of the bottle. He pushes the old fashioned glass with his index finger, sliding it across the desk and stopping in front of me.

I ignore it and take a pull from the bottle itself. My tongue smacks the roof of my mouth and my face pinches in a little. It's a harsh burn that somehow feels good too.

I sigh and set the bottle on my thigh and reach into my pocket with my free hand. Slipping some cash free, I thumb out two tens and toss them on the desk between us.

Nic arches a brow and glances at the bills. "What's this?"

"Toss it in the pineapple jar," I grumble.

A laugh splits his face into a grin before he swipes the money from the desk. He spins his chair around and stuffs the bills into the opening of the bronzed pineapple bank on the shelf behind him. He had it custom-made when we started this stupid bet five years ago. At the end of every year, he takes the money and buys as much pineapple pizza as possible and treats the staff at our various businesses.

It's all tongue in cheek, and normally I take the L on the chin. But I'm having a fucking day today, and I'm in no mood for his ribbing.

"Ah," he says, his laugh petering out. "So that's why you're in a shitty mood then?"

I lean back in my chair and widen my legs. "You know that kid you put one in the shoulder last week?"

Nic grips his old fashioned glass with the tips of his index finger and thumb and swirls around the whiskey. He gives me a long look as if to ask if I'm serious.

I've been on the receiving end of this look more times than I can remember. It stopped phasing me years ago.

"Of course I remember. Do you think I shoot so many people that I lose track of them?"

I lift a shoulder. "How should I know what the boss does?"

He sets his glass on the desk, his palm resting on the top. "Is there something you want to say, brother?"

I scrub my free hand down my face. "Nah, man. I'm just frustrated. I spent three hours scouring the city for Colombo."

"No shit? Where do you think he is?"

The door behind me squeaks as it opens and then closes, and I crane my neck over my shoulder to see Rome stroll in, his smile a mile long and an extra swagger in his step. His head is bent over his phone, his thumbs flying across the screen.

"Oh, good, so you didn't lose your phone," Nic drawls.

Rome smirks at his phone with a low laugh. He weaves around the low-profile coffee table in front of the couch and around his normal chair, sinking into it without a word to either of us.

I side-eye my baby brother, my scowl deepening the longer he doesn't acknowledge us. I glance at Nic. "The fuck?"

Nic swirls his whiskey before bringing his glass to his mouth and swallowing the rest down in one sip. "Don't ask me. I haven't seen him in days."

I take another pull from my bottle, letting the burn coat my throat all the way down. "What do you think he's doing on there that he can't tear himself away?"

"Probably watching porn," Nic says.

"Nah, I bet he's sexting with his catfish," I say with a smirk.

"I can hear you both you know," Rome says, taking his time looking up at us. He presses the button on the side of his phone and places it face-down on his thigh. "Sorry I'm late. What did I miss?"

I blink at him a few times. "What's wrong with you?"

"What's wrong with you?" he parrots. He scans my face with a clinical sort of look. "Usually, you're much happier when you have someone in your sights. Honestly, I don't understand how the fuck you can go from extracting information from people in the after-noon to watching fucking Broadway shows at night with such ease."

I bristle at the casual judgment in his voice. He doesn't mean it maliciously, but my nerves are too frayed today.

"First of all, those shows are works of art, and you would understand that if you ever bothered to peel yourself away from a fucking computer screen once in a while." He opens his mouth to reply, but I slash my hand in the air between us. "And secondly, I didn't actually find that slippery fuck Colombo today."

Rome lifts his shoulders and lets them drop in a dramatic shrug, never losing that smile. "I'm away from my computer screen now, aren't I?"

I glare at his phone resting on his thigh. "Hardly."

"Alright. That's enough posturing bullshit for right now," Nic interjects. "Tommy, tell me more about Colombo."

I stretch my neck from side to side and take another pull from the bottle resting on my leg. "He's in the fucking wind."

"Are you sure?" Rome asks.

I pin him with a harsh look over my shoulder and he has the decency to lose some of the defiance in his gaze.

"I snagged two of the guys he runs with and brought them back to the Side Winder. We had a nice little chat and they gave him up pretty quickly. He's the one who's been supplying our guys the laced coke."

"Motherfucker," Nic grits out between clenched teeth.

I nod a few times. "Exactly. I spent my afternoon running around town to all his usual spots. No one has seen him in at least two days, maybe longer."

"I can set up a profile for him using my facial recognition software. I'll find him," Rome says.

Nic taps his index finger on the rim of his glass, his gaze unfocused.

"What are you thinking?" I ask.

His gaze sharpens on me. "I'm not sure. Could he be a plant from Vito?"

Rome drags his fingers over his jaw. "That doesn't make sense though. People dying in the casinos and clubs is bad for business. If anything, he wants to increase the drugs in the city, not bring more heat."

"So someone else then," Nic muses.

"Someone who's trying to weasel their way in and take our territory?" Rome asks.

"Or someone who's trying to overthrow us?" I muse.

The three of us sit for a moment, nothing but the loud thoughts turning over themselves in my head. I don't have the head for games like Nic or puzzles like Rome. Mostly, I'm just the fucking muscle. Occasionally, I've been known to have a good idea or two. But today is not that day.

After another minute of silence, I slap my hand on the edge of the desk. "Alright, let's move on. I'll find Colombo soon enough. Until then, let's talk about our pal Vito."

Nic sits back in his seat, resting his elbows on the arms of his chair and steepling his fingers by his mouth. "Tommy's right.

We'll ice this until we have Vito sorted. Let's go through the plan again."

My blood quickens in my veins, a strange mix of urgency and dread. They both think I have this mounting bloodlust for our father, like I'm some kind of crazed vampire. Personally, I think it's the perfect amount of contempt.

I don't hate him for the fact that he failed me as a child, that he ripped away every scrap of normalcy when I was still in elementary school.

No, I loathe Vito Santorini for what he turned me into. The monster who lives and breathes inside of my chest, snarling and snapping at anyone who gets too close to us. He honed me into a blade that he wielded for far too long.

And that—that's on me.

It took me years to realize his affection was expertly disguised manipulation. Vito Santorini is many things, a master manipulator among them. I've learned a lifetime's worth of control in the last fifteen years.

So what if I'm delighted to finally rip him from his cushy little life and live the rest of mine free of him? I've fucking earned it.

28

MAEVE

"HELLO, EARTH TO MAEVE," Keira says, waving her hand in front of my face.

I blink, her gorgeous big brown eyes coming into focus. "What? Sorry. I'm tired, I guess."

She raises her brow and glances at my lap. "Is that why you've been clutching your phone all day?"

I blink a few times, flashing her a tight-lipped smile. "It's nothing. I just thought I'd hear from someone."

It's been twenty-four hours since Romeo and I were texting. One minute, I was making a great case for why The Smiths are superior to The Cure, and then next minute, he goes radio silent. Again.

I've learned some important things about myself in the last month. My hard limits, what I would do for my sisters, that I am decidedly not a clam chowder person. But the most interesting thing I've learned about myself is my intense dislike of feeling ignored.

It's stupid really. I'm the oldest of five girls, who has lived half of her life with a dead mother and a mob boss father who was gone more than he wasn't. I'm used to being overlooked.

I turned my insecurity and sharpened it into a successful career path.

And yet, after a day of silence from a stranger I've only known for a week, I'm feeling unraveled.

And I don't fucking like it.

Keira's mouth parts before it curls into a slow grin. "I knew it! You totally have a man on the side. No wonder you were all-in on ending the marriage contract." She pauses, her mouth flattening. "Well, the original one, at least."

I'm shaking my head before she even finishes speaking. "No, I ended the original contract because it's archaic and demeaning to a woman with my kind of experience in this life." I flutter my fingers in front of her face. "I see it written all over your face, and that's not true either."

She sits taller in the seat across from me. "Hey! You don't even know what I was thinking," she protests.

"You mean you weren't thinking about something romantic involving me and my nonexistent boyfriend?"

She covers a smile behind her hand, her elbow on the table between us. She picked up food from one of our favorite local restaurants. They make the best poke bowls I've ever had. I got salmon with mango, rice, and greens, and Keira opted for the ahi tuna with pineapple and greens.

It's our last night together before she heads to the countryside for some weapons exhibition. I have to head back to the house—to my old house, I guess, and pack my things up. I have five weeks of freedom left before I'm irrevocably tied to a stranger.

She sets her fork down next to her bowl with a sigh and pins me with her big brown eyes. It's earnest and pleading, and I already know I need to doubly fortify my mental barriers. When Keira drops her tough-as-nails exterior and allows herself to be vulnerable, I know it's going to get my emotions going.

My sister isn't the one you call when you need someone to talk you down from a rash decision. She's the one you call when you need a lighter to torch the building you already soaked in gasoline.

I exhale softly and mirror her pose, setting my fork down next to my bowl.

She scrapes her bottom teeth along her top lip before releasing it. "If I can't change your mind—"

"You can't," I interrupt with a shake of my head.

She nods a few times, these absentminded small movements. "I know. Then I want you to do something for you. And don't try to tell me you are because we don't lie to each other, yeah?"

I reach across the table and clasp my hand over hers. "I'm going to New York, remember?"

She places her free hand over mine. "Aye, I remember. But I want you to do more than that. If it were up to you, you'd hole up in our apartment, only emerging to get coffee from your favorite place a few blocks down."

I swallow past the tickle in the back of my throat. "What's wrong with getting coffee? You know I love their seasonal lattes."

"I know, and there's nothing wrong with that. But I want you to do more than that. I want you to explore the city and meet new people and dance in Central Park to one of those acoustic shows they have in Strawberry Fields and to close a karaoke bar and to sleep with someone—sleep with several someones —and—"

"Okay, okay," I say around a laugh. "I get it. You want me to live it up while I'm in New York City. But I've done all those things before, so if I stay inside—"

"No," she interrupts me, flipping her hands around to grip mine. "Promise me you'll do all your favorite things and be adventurous and do everything you always wanted to do. Or I'll call Da right now and swap places with you."

I lean forward and increase my grip. We're holding on to one another like our strength alone can hold me here with her.

Her eyes are glassy and the tip of her nose turns pink. "I mean it, Maeve. You promise me you'll do these things, if not for yourself, then do it for us."

My sinuses tingle and my eyes prickle with tears. "I thought we were just going to have a nice dinner together. I wasn't expecting this."

Keira sniffs. "I know, but I had to try. I love you, and it's not fair that your freedom is the cost of ours."

"It's worth it," I whisper, a tear breaking free from my lashes and rolling down my cheek.

"No," she says with a shake of her head, freeing two tears from the sides of her eyes. "It's not."

Not for the first time, my chest aches at the whole situation. I lean forward even further, the edge of the table digging into my ribs. "I have a plan. It'll all be okay."

"Even the best laid plans fail. You can't account for every-thing, Maeve."

"I know, but I have something far more powerful than control: hope."

She blinks a few times, sending another wave of tears down her cheeks. "Tell me the plan then."

I roll my lips inward, stuffing the words in my mouth. "I bet my husband-to-be has very high blood pressure. It's a common ailment for men involved in the mafia. It's the kind of silent killer that steals men in the middle of the night without a trace."

She sniffs again and pulls a hand free of mine. She slides the side of her index finger underneath her eyes, clearing any smudged mascara away. "Good. That's good. Tell me what to do to help."

I give her hand another squeeze and settle back into my chair. "I will. When the time's right."

I know I never will though. There's nothing her or any of my other sisters can do. And I would never risk their lives for something so selfish. I have to do this on my own.

The words resonate deeply with me in more ways than one.

My phone rings, breaking the tension. Both of us laugh, this watery sort of sound that has our grins growing wider. I reach over and grab my phone, flipping it around to see a photo of Rosie's smiling face.

I glance at Keira, my chest tightening at the prospect of telling her the new terms of my arrangement. "Don't tell her. Not yet, okay?"

Keira's smile falls, her lips pursing into a frown.

"Please, Keira. I'll tell her eventually, but I don't want her to worry. I want her to enjoy school," I plead with her.

Her scowl melts, her shoulders drooping. "Of course."

I look upward and blink a few times to clear any glassiness from my eyes before swiping to answer. An up-close view of half of Rosie's face is the first thing I see.

"Uh, hello?" I say around a laugh. "Is this an accidental call?"

"What? No," she says, pulling the phone further away so I can see more of her. "Sorry, I forgot I called you."

"What?" I sputter out with a laugh. "I answered after like five seconds."

She glances at the screen before looking at something to the right. "It took you eleven seconds, actually. I almost hung up."

"Okay," I stretch the word out. "What's going on? Are you okay?"

"I'm great. Classes are great. Found a little coffee shop on campus that makes a proper cup of espresso. Met some hot guy in my Intro to Coding class—which is shit I learned in fifth grade, by the way. But that's not why I'm calling." She speeds through her sentences, like she's rattling off an intricate coffee order at a chain restaurant.

"Hi, Rosie," Keira sings her voice.

Rosie jerks her head to the side. "Where are you?"

"I'm in our little apartment a few hours from home. Keira showed up a few days ago, and we've been spending time together before I leave for New York."

"I'm only a little jealous. I love sister sleepovers," Rosie says with a grin.

"I'll come visit you in a few weeks, okay?" I promise her.

"I'll hold you to it. But first, check this out. Your mystery texter is a total ghost."

"What do you mean?" I ask.

"Mystery texter?" Keira asks at the same time, brows raised.

I feel Keira's gaze on my face, and my cheeks heat, but I keep my focus on my phone. "You couldn't trace him?"

"Him?" Keira asks, her voice a little higher in pitch.

I clear my throat. "It. You couldn't trace the phone number?"

Rosie shakes her head. "No. My best guess is he's using a burner that consistently recycles the phone numbers on the backend while still maintaining the same phone number for outward calls and texts. Plus, he probably has a scrubber installed. I mean, it's what I do for all of us. Which is why it's a little alarming to me that this guy found us."

I lift a shoulder. "He said he's been following the Fairy Godmothers for some time. And he said he's good with computers."

Rosie's eyes widen. "What else did he say? Anything we can use?"

I bite the inside of my cheek and think over our text messages. "He said his name is Romeo but he called me Juliet, so I kind of think that's bullshit."

"That sounds like a terrible pick-up line. I'm shocked you fell for it," Keira mumbles.

I cut her a look, my shoulders bristling. "I didn't fall for anything."

Keira gives me a deadpan look, her perfectly manicured brow arching over her left eye. "You've been texting with some random person for days, Maeve."

My mouth opens but before I can try to think of something witty to come back with, Rosie jumps in.

"That's because I told her to get information from him. Anyway, keep talking to him, Maeve. Until we can figure out who he is and what he wants, you're the best source for information from him. Rush Fitzgerald is digging through it right now, so I'll let you know in a few days. It's the only time I'll happily admit defeat if he cracks it before I do," Rosie says.

A beeping noise in the background pierces the air.

"What is that?" Keira asks.

Rosie's face brightens and a wide smile spreads across her face. "Oh nothing. Just an alert I set up to let me know when this douchey amateur hacker begins my obstacle course."

"Obstacle course?" Keira asks.

She lifts a shoulder, eyebrows raised to show nonchalance. But it's all a ruse. She's practically vibrating with glee. "He's been talking shit up and down the Forum for weeks. So I decided to have a little fun."

I purse my lips to the side, letting a small smile play over my face. "I know you're dying to tell us, so get on with it."

She leans in close and faux whispers, "I created a set of obstacles, a web, really. He has to complete each one before he can move onto the next one."

Keira comes around the table to stand behind my shoulder. "I don't know what that even means, but if you're excited, then I'm excited."

Rosie laughs. "It'll be great. I can't wait to watch him eat his words. But I have to go, okay? Love you, bye." She sings the last three words, barely waiting for Keira and I to respond with "love you" before she disconnects.

The knot inside my chest eases a little, reassurance that I'm doing the right thing by accepting the contract and letting my sisters live their lives. That knowledge makes it all so much more bearable.

I guess the only thing left to do is pack up my room at home.

29

MAEVE

THE CREAKING floorboards precede his presence. If he came for my forgiveness, he's going to leave disappointed. I don't have anything else to offer him, so I keep my mouth shut and continue packing.

My bedroom is almost completely boxed up, only my bookshelf and the things I'm taking with me right away are left. Keira arranged for all my things to be shipped to our New York City apartment for now. Including Mum's favorite wine glasses, a few framed family portraits from years ago, when Mum was still here, and a few keepsake boxes from when we were little. She's going to put my bedroom furniture in storage for now. We'll get it the next time we need to furnish a safe space somewhere.

I have a few vacations I'm going to take care of before I head to the west coast. But even then, I'm not bringing everything with me to California. It'll only weigh me down when I leave.

And one way or another, I'll be leaving. I'll be there long enough for the ink to dry on the marriage certificate. A few weeks —six tops, and then I'm gone.

I'll head back to New York City and lie low for a while, make sure no one suspects anything or follows me. And from there . . . well, I haven't figured that out yet.

I place the last stack of books in the cardboard box and use the tape gun to seal it closed. I scrawl books across the top flap and push to my feet. Dusting my hands off on my black leggings, I cross the room to my bed. The bedding has been stripped off, washed, and packed in a box.

Two rose-gold suitcases sit open, both of them almost empty. Everything I need to pack and take with me sits in neat little piles on my bed. I start with the stack of laundry, unfolding my clothes and rolling them into small little pinwheels and tucking them on one side of the suitcase nearest to me.

I feel Da's gaze like an uncomfortable itch just out of reach between my shoulder blades.

"Roisin won't return my calls."

I don't know if I was expecting him to say something specifically, but I wasn't expecting this. I'm a little surprised he said anything at all.

"I guess you'll have to figure out how to handle them without me now."

It's snarky and bitter, but I'd be lying if I said it didn't ease the sharp sting of betrayal a little bit. Not by anything measurable, but enough to get me through.

"Aye, I guess I will." He clears his throat. "They know then?"

I stretch across the suitcase to grab the next pile of things. This group of things needs to go in my carry-on bag—a couple paperbacks, my laptop, all my chargers, and my black backpack with rose gold stitching.

"Are you asking me if they know that our father sold his oldest daughter to a bunch of strangers in California to fund some war—fictional or otherwise? Then yes." I keep my tone even, matter of fact, but I hope he realizes just how fucking crazy it sounds when it's reduced to a single sentence.

"You told them then."

"Not that it matters, but I didn't," I say with a huff. "Keira was home last week. Heard the whole thing straight from the source."

If I had to guess, Keira told Ava so I wouldn't have to, and Ava told Fi and Rosie. I was planning on telling them all myself, but I'd be lying if I said I wasn't a little relieved that I don't have to now.

"I'll deal with it."

I snort. "Good luck."

He's going to need it. The only thing more dangerous than a King is one with a thirst for vengeance. And my sisters are nothing if not loyal.

To me.

Our loyalty shifted over the years, each time edging our father out further and further. He might as well be on another continent now.

He doesn't say anything for a few minutes, and I continue to pack in silence. The quicker I get this done, the quicker I can leave. I won't stay here a moment longer than necessary.

I tug the zipper closed on my oversized tote carry-on bag with an exhale.

I'm done.

This was my room for almost my entire childhood.

Countless nights of sister sleepovers, as we called them, where all five of us slept in the same room.

There were a few years where Ava and Rosie were afraid of thunderstorms, so they'd poke my arms until I'd wake up and let them bunk in my room.

Afternoons spent listening to music and creating silly dances.

All of us pooling our money to buy a big TV so we could binge-watch shows in my room without any interruptions.

School mornings spent in a mad dash to get ready, and Fi helping herself to my closet.

That one time Keira wanted red hair like Fi and Rosie, so she bought shitty box dye and burst into my room one night, crying because it turned her hair neon orange. If you look closely, there's still traces of neon orange dye on the carpet by the closet.

I swallow and look around my room again.

When my mum was alive, she would tuck us in every night, no matter what. She always saved me for last, said I was the oldest, so I could stay up a little longer than my sisters. She'd lay next to me, playing with my hair until I fell asleep. Sometimes we would talk, but most of the time, we didn't need to.

It's a lifetime of happiness in two hundred square feet.

But without my things, without my mum or sisters, without me—it's just four walls.

It's reduced to nothing but the echoes of laughter and love.

My sisters and I will continue to make memories for many, many years to come. I'm sure of it.

So why does my chest ache like it's being cleaved in two?

"You didn't have to pack everything."

His voice startles me, not because it's loud or aggressive. Quite the opposite. It's soft, almost melancholy.

"I'm getting married, remember?" I work hard to keep the contempt out of my tone.

"Aye, I remember. But that's not for another five weeks."

I scoff, this derisive noise that belies the sadness sinking deep into my skin. "Don't be ridiculous. I'm not staying here, watching the clock on my freedom run out."

"Where will you go?"

I look over my shoulder at him. He's standing in the hallway, not a hair over the threshold into my room.

His dark brown hair is messy, the gray at his temples more prominent than six months ago. His expression solemn and hands tucked into the pockets of his well-loved jeans. Dark green flannel thrown over a gray Henley—his staple outfit.

I used to find comfort in the soft material of his many flannel shirts, burying my face in his shoulder when he would wrap me up in his arms.

Hate and grief make strange bedfellows. They're entangled so deeply inside of me that I can't experience one without the other. I'm afraid that I'll never be able to think of my da again without experiencing this tidal wave of emotion. My memories from childhood will forever be knotted with the cloying tar of grief and profound sadness.

"Not here."

It's the only answer he's going to get, and it's honestly more than he deserves.

He nods, his brow wrinkled low over his eyes.

"Don't worry. I'll be stateside in five weeks."

"I wasn't worried. I know you'll keep your word."

O'Boyle's words come to mind. A King always keeps his word. It's a well-known detail about our family. That conversation in Chicago feels like a year ago, not a couple weeks.

He smooths his hand down the front of his flannel shirt and clears his throat again. "I should be there. To give you away."

"It's not a real wedding."

"The state of California would disagree with you," he counters.

I lift my gaze to his, letting the mask I've glued to my face slough off like mud.

The lines around his eyes deepen and his shoulders hitch when he sees my expression. Good. I want him to know.

"I'll never know the joy of walking down the aisle with my heart so full of love it's ready to burst. To look up and see the man I'm hopelessly in love with waiting for me. To spend hours with my sisters trying on too many dresses and drinking too much champagne and giggling until our sides hurt. To say I do and mean it." My breath catches and my eyes fill with tears, blurring my view of him.

I don't wipe my tears away. He should bear witness to my anguish.

"Instead, I will have the impersonal touch of a stranger sliding a wedding band I didn't pick out onto my finger. I will recite vows I don't mean wearing a wedding dress my sisters have never seen. And I will drink champagne to forget it all the moment it's done."

His gaze scans my face for a moment, tracking the tear slipping down my cheek. "I'm sorry, Maeve."

"Your apology means nothing to me."

He flinches, this small jerking of his shoulders and nods. "Still, I am sorry. If there were another way—"

"Stop. Just—just stop. You've made your choice. Now you have to live with it."

I refuse to take on his guilt, to assure him that I'm fine. I've been the fixer in our family for so long, it feels physically uncomfortable not to step in and smooth it over. Like a wool sweater that went through the dryer—itchy and too tight on my skin.

I toss my carry-on over my shoulder and grab the handles of my suitcases, crossing my room to stop in front of him.

"Keira's arranged for my things to be shipped to me."

"She told me."

"Good." The urge to fall into his chest, to feel the comfort of his arms wrapped around me sucker-punches me in the gut and steals my breath. It's the wish of a child though. Da hasn't comforted me like that in more years than I can count. "I have to go."

He takes a slow step backward, shuffling to the side so I can leave. "Here, let me help you."

"I don't want your help," I snap.

His face falls, like those five words are the ones that pushed him over the edge. "Maeve, I—" He cuts himself off and shoves his hands into his pockets. His eyes look a little misty and blood-shot, but it's probably a trick of the old overhead lighting in the hallway.

I wait, my stupid bleeding heart aching to hear words of regret and vows to make amends.

They don't come.

I nod a few times, sniff and straighten my shoulders. "Right," I mumble under my breath.

I adjust my grip on the handles and maneuver the suitcases down the hall and down the stairs carefully.

When I hit the first floor landing I hear him. It's not words of comfort or love or regret. They're worse. Meaningless and empty.

"I'm sorry, Maeve," he whispers.

I wheel my suitcases out of the front door without looking back.

30

NICO

I STOP in front of the mirror in our hallway, adjusting my shirtsleeves so you can see a quarter of an inch of my midnight black button-down. I like my jacket sleeves tailored a hair shorter than others, so you can see the shirt underneath. The European style of mens suits is my personal favorite, that crisp, fitted look. It's nearly impossible to find a reputable tailor within a thousand miles who understands the look I'm going for, so I've resorted to flying one in from Italy every few months. He's an older gentleman who helps me brush up on my Italian while he works.

"Stop obsessing over your suit. It looks fine," Tommy calls from the living room.

My shoulders stiffen. "I'm not obsessing. I'm making sure I look presentable."

"Listen to yourself, bro. Presentable? You're going to a meeting with Dad at Bistro 908 not the fucking prom."

"Like you would know anything about the prom." I regret the scorn as soon as it leaves my lips.

For an entire year, Tommy got it in his head that he wanted to go to the prom. It didn't matter that we barely went to school, and when we did, the girls whispered behind their hands. Sure, they all wanted to walk on the wild side with the town bad boys, but underneath all that posturing and hairspray was a mountain of ridicule and shame.

And Tommy, well, he took that shit to heart.

I let my head fall backward and look at the ceiling for a moment. I blow out a breath. "Fuck, I'm sorry——"

"It's fine," he says. It's a brush-off, a kindness that I don't deserve.

"I didn't mean it. I'm just on edge today."

"No shit. You reorganized the flatware drawer at six o'clock in the morning," Tommy deadpans.

I fiddle with my tie, adjusting it again. "I never liked the small spoons on that side, and you know that."

I grit my teeth at the uncomfortable churning of my stomach. Anxiety claws at my skin like ants foraging for a new home.

I feel like I'm one misstep away from losing control and that makes me want to rage to regain it. It's a fucking vicious cycle, a Santorini special.

"Where's Rome?" I frown at my watch. We have to leave in thirty minutes if we want to arrive on time.

"I'm right here," Rome says from behind me. "But Tommy's wrong. It's not your appearance that will tip Dad off. It's the stick in your ass. Chill out a little, brother."

I stop messing with my shirtsleeves and drop my hands, clenching them into fists. I'm not sure how, but I can almost feel the vein in my forehead throbbing in annoyance. I turn around with narrowed eyes. "I do not have a stick up my ass."

"Alright," Tommy says, lifting his shoulders up a little.

He's sitting on one end of our overstuffed couch, his ankle crossed over his opposite knee and his arms extended wide along the back of the couch. Dressed in black athletic pants and a black hoodie, he looks like he's going to relax on the couch for the rest of the night, not commit armed carjacking.

Rome sits on the other side, dressed similarly and looking at something on his phone.

I cross the room to stand in front of them, on the other side of the coffee table. "Ready?"

Rome pockets his phone, leaning back into the couch. "We're ready."

I exhale a breath, trapping what little air I have left in my lungs for a moment. "Let's go through the plan again."

Tommy and Rome groan in unison.

"We've been through this a dozen times already," Rome says.

"At least," Tommy adds.

I slip my hands in my pockets and force my shoulders to relax. "Then it'll be easy to go through it again."

"Fine," Rome says on a sigh.

"Dad thinks I'm in the Midwest, meeting some prospects to expand our reach east," Tommy says.

"You're meeting Dad at Bistro 908 for drinks like you always do to debrief or whatever the fuck you talk about at these biweekly things. I'll already be there, in the office in the back, watching the cameras. Specifically, looking for any moves Dad would make against us," Rome says.

Tommy picks up where Rome ends, "Which is unlikely, by the way. When you're done, you're going to tell Dad you're going to Violet Oak to oversee tryouts for new dancers, which we corroborated with actual tryouts happening tonight."

"But we won't be there, because Jenny is already handling it like she's done for the last three years," Rome says.

I nod, running my index finger along my bottom lip. Thankfully, our plans for our father perfectly timed up with Jenny's tryout schedule for new dancers.

"Naturally, Dad will want to join you, the disgusting fuck, so he'll call his driver, Ric, and that is where you'll have to sell it, brother," Tommy says.

"I've got it all figured out. I'll tell him about my new car during drinks, and I'll offer to let him drive it to Violet Oak," I muse.

"And his ego won't let him refuse such an offer, so he'll call Ric off, and hop in your car," Rome says.

Tommy nods, his face falling into a neutral expression. "Then Rome and I will cut you off on the side street by the old Reed Motel, ski masks and all."

The Reed Motel is in a vacant lot, half torn down. The new owners lost their loan at the beginning of their project, and it's been abandoned ever since. It's a breeding ground for violence and drugs, which is perfect for our needs.

My mind spins with the possibilities of how this plan can unravel. "I'll put two in Dad, and one of you has to clip me too. We have to make sure it looks like an armed carjacking."

Tommy drums a beat on the back of the couch with his fingers. "I already told you I'll take Dad out."

I sigh through my nose, frustration crawling up my throat. We don't have time to deviate from this plan again. "I'm not having this conversation again. It's my responsibility, Tommy."

Tommy sits forward, dropping his feet to the floor and hands to his knees. "It's not though, so just know the offer stands."

"I appreciate it, but I'll handle it." I smooth down my jacket lapel and check my watch reflexively. "We better go now if we want Rome to have enough time to get into position."

The three of us leave our shared penthouse apartment, each taking a different car, all of them with illegally dark tint. The last thing we need is an overzealous cop tying us to the scene of the crime by traffic cameras before Rome can scrub them.

If I don't develop an ulcer by the end of this day, it'll be a fucking miracle. Dad is on his fourth gin and tonic, and it's only been an hour. The conversation is unbearably mundane or maybe it only feels that way because I know it's pointless. By the time the sun rises again, my father will cease to exist.

So what the fuck do I care about his complaints of the waitresses at our casino, The Meridian, pouring with a heavy hand? The Meridian is one of our bread and butter businesses. It earns legitimately while washing our illegitimate cash.

And he wants to slow it down because he doesn't want to eat the cost of the booze? It's barely a dent in our profits.

Just another reason why he's unfit to lead us any longer. He's been content to sit on his throne of money, amassing more and more off the labors of our loyal soldiers.

He's the cliché type of boss who would cut off his nose just to spite his face. And then go on a killing spree to exercise his rage.

My father swirls the last dredges of his drink around his glass before swallowing it down. "And the situation with our streets? Did you handle whoever is flooding our town with bad narcotics?"

I widen my legs and adjust myself in the seat. My ass started falling asleep ten minutes ago, and it's distracting me. "We're working on it. Tommy's following a few leads."

"Tommaso is good at that, isn't he?" He flashes a shark like smile before raising two fingers in the air to signal our waitress tonight, Charlene.

She's already ahead of him though, weaving her way through the empty tables of our VIP section with a fresh drink for both of us. We're seated in the middle of the private section, each of us facing the opposite direction. It's the best way to ensure we won't be snuck up on by curious eyes and ears, but it requires a level of trust that I've never been comfortable with.

It would be all too easy for my father to simply not alert me to someone approaching me from behind. It would be a stupid move considering I've been handling over half of our operations for years.

Bistro 908 is a modern gastropub. Serving elevated comfort food for lunch and dinner and drinks at night, we do great with the tourists.

Rich mahogany floors with darker cherry tables and chairs, a custom-made bar top. Modern yellow light fixtures hang from the ceiling, warming the entire restaurant. Accents of dark bronze and metal, Bistro 908 is one of our most unique businesses.

"Here you go, Mr. Santorini," she murmurs, placing a fresh gin and tonic in front of Dad.

"Thank you, sweetheart." He grabs the drink with one hand and taps her on the ass with the other. It's gone in a blink, but even if I missed it, there's no mistaking the way she stiffens.

"That's enough, Dad." My voice cracks through the air like a whip.

Charlene flinches but it's Dad's reaction that I'm watching closely. He raises his brows, letting his smile widen into something far more sinister. "Excuse me, son?"

I tip my chin up and let a sliver of the beast inside of my chest poke through. I take a measured sip of my drink and stare at my father. I can't fuck this all up now, so I need to play this carefully. "This is my restaurant, and she's my employee, so hands off."

Dad's face flushes, a red sea that starts at his neck and rises all the way to his hairline. "Are you sure you want to do this right now, son?"

"That'll be all for tonight, Charlene. Take tomorrow off," I say instead of answering him.

Charlene turns and practically dashes through the section, disappearing down the stairs to the main floor of the restaurant. I put a cork in my rapidly rising rage, vowing to let it out another way. Soon.

"I'm heading to Violet Oak after this. Why don't you join me in overseeing the new dancer tryouts?"

Predictably, his face smooths out into something more jovial. I do the best I can to tamper down the disgust that threatens to bubble up.

Dad rubs his hands together, the rings on his pinkies clinking. "Now you're talking, son. Let's head over there now. It's been too long since I visited your private rooms."

I toss my drink in one gulp and push my chair back, swallowing my revulsion. If there's one thing I'm thankful for tonight, it's the fact that he'll never make it to those rooms. Not tonight. Not ever.

31

NICO

DAD PUSHES to stand and buttons his coat. He opens his arms wide, a large smile spreading across his face. A light sheen coats his forehead. "Sweetheart, you made it."

My mother steps into his arms, embracing him with genuine affection. I watch their interaction, a silent observer to the spectacle that is my parents marriage. I'll never understand their relationship. Or how she could so easily abandon half of her children.

But I don't have time to ponder one of my life's greatest mysteries. Her showing up here throws a wrench in my plans.

I check my watch and purposely stay seated.

"Nico, aren't you happy to see your mother?" He narrows his eyes at me as he takes his seat.

"Sloane." I greet my mother with the same amount of affection I reserve for strangers I bump into on the street.

Dad reaches over and claps me on the back, his meaty hand clamping on my shoulder and his thumb digging into the sensitive spot beneath my collar bone. "Now, is that any way to greet your mother, son?"

I don't temper my disdain, giving my father an exaggerated glare between his hand and his face.

"Oh, sorry, son. I forget my own strength sometimes," he says with fake sincerity, removing his hand. His lips purse in some sort of apologetic grimace that only provides further proof that he needs to see a better technician.

Vito Santorini is a powerful man with far too much vanity for someone in his position. The average person gets fine lines and wrinkles by their thirties, but if you account for the fact that you're the boss of a west coast outfit? You're looking to bump that age down by ten years, at least.

But not our father. Things like fine lines, wrinkles, and sun spots are unacceptable for him. Like he's better than time itself.

And that might be the root of his problems: my father thinks everyone is beneath him. His sons, his wife, his estranged daughters. No one is safe from his prideful wrath.

He's a category five tornado, picking and choosing who to destroy on a whim. His power goes continuously unchecked, and I know it in my bones that if he merges our family with another one, he'll grow too big to contain.

It's why we have to strike now before we lose our chance. Every day that passes with my father still breathing is a twenty-four-hour opportunity for him to fuck up my life further.

"Nico?" My mom's voice is soft, hesitant even. She hovers at the end of the table, wringing her fingers together in front of her.

I dip my chin in greeting. It's the best I can offer under the circumstances. I'm thirty minutes away from facilitating my father's murder, and I don't have it within me to offer her empty pleasantries.

And I still haven't forgiven her for keeping my sisters from me for years.

Sloane tucks her chin toward her dress for a moment, her fingernails tapping on the edge of the table. She's dressed for a night out on the town, which isn't unusual for her. Every weekend she's back home, she seems to spend most of it out doing stuff, never staying too long at the house she shares with Dad. Not that I blame her. I got my brothers and I out years ago for the very same reason.

"Sit with us, Sloane. Nico and I were just discussing the prospect of marriage," Dad says.

I stifle my surprise behind my hand, running it across my jaw. Marriage was never brought up tonight, at least not that I can recall. Maybe it was when I tuned him out.

Or maybe he's full of shit.

"Oh, I don't want to intrude," she says. She's so fucking demure in front of him, it's a stark difference to how my sister had described her to Rome.

"Nonsense, my dear. Scoot over, Nico, give your mother some room."

I grit my teeth and slide my chair over, giving her plenty of room to pull out her own chair and sit down.

She's wearing a short icy-cream-colored sleeveless dress with textured fabric and jewels sewn-in. Jewels on her ears, wrists, and fingers and big bouncy curls. She's certainly dressed the part to spend more of Dad's money in his clubs and casinos tonight.

"Oh, no, really. I'm just passing through. I heard two of my favorite boys were here tonight, and I couldn't pass up an opportunity to say hello," she says with a smile worthy of a pageant.

"I'm on my way to one of our clubs now, anyway." I stand up and rebutton my jacket, smoothing my lapels down with one hand. "It was nice to see you, Sloane."

I have to choke the words out, but I deliver a performance I'm sure Tommy would be proud of. If I can get out of here before I get trapped in another meaningless conversation, the night is still salvageable. I'm putting a lot of trust in my father's inability to say no to see tits.

263

"That's right. Don't wait up, sweetheart," Dad says as he stands. He leans over and kisses her cheek.

"Don't work too hard tonight, boys," she says.

"Anything for you, dear." Dad lets his mouth linger against her cheek until she turns her head and gives him her mouth.

I clear my throat and turn away, winding my way through the tables toward the staircase behind me. Dad joins me a moment later, clapping his hand on my shoulder again, this time without the added pressure. We take the stairs down to the main floor and follow the hallway to the employee parking in the back.

"Let me call Ric to pull the car around. We can ride together to Violet Oak," Dad says.

"Actually," I say, slipping my keyring from my pocket. I flip the keys around, the keyring balancing on my index finger. "I thought we could take mine."

Dad's eyes light up, honing in on the Aston Martin logo on the key fob. "You've been holding out on me, Nico?"

I jerk my head to the side and head toward one of the six reserved parking spots for my family. I pause next to my brick red Aston Martin Vantage.

Dad whistles under his breath. "How'd you get the new model?"

I lift a shoulder and hold up the keys. "I have a connection. I'll reach out if you're interested."

He snatches them with lightning speed. "I don't buy anything without a test drive. You'd do well to remember that, son."

My lips pinch together like they do when lemonade is too sour, but he's too busy drooling over my car to notice my glare. I turn away from him and round the car, slipping into the passenger seat. Dad settles in behind the steering wheel, muttering something too low for me to hear.

He grips the steering wheel and stomps on the gas pedal. The tires screech as we rocket out of the parking lot. If this were one of those cartoons Rome used to watch when he was younger, there'd be a trail of burnt rubber and fire behind us.

The tires squeal as Dad whips us around the corner and we fly down the busy roads. Even this late at night, there are hundreds of people crowding the sidewalks.

Las Vegas truly is the city that never sleeps.

I grit my teeth every time he shifts too hard, jerking the transitions roughly. I glance out of the window, watching the city flash by as Dad hurdles us toward Violet Oak. He takes a hard right on Charm Boulevard, and my heart beats hard inside my chest. We're close now.

No sooner than the thought flits by, a dark SUV comes out of nowhere and parks horizontally on the narrow street. Dad slams on the brakes, and I have to brace myself with a hand on the dash. It feels like my brain slams against the front of my skull, and I rub it with my free hand.

"What the fuck, Dad?" I snap, lifting my head in time to see two figures emerge from the dark SUV six inches in front of my bumper.

"Why don't you tell me, *son*?" He says *son* like it tastes rancid on his tongue, and the tone is so unexpected, I jerk to face him.

Three inches in front of my face is the barrel of his favorite gun.

"What the fuck, *Vito*?" I grit through clenched teeth, dropping the familial pretense.

"Get the fuck out," he says, using the same calm tone he reserves for ordering drinks.

"What the fuck are you talking about—get out?" I snap, my muscles coiled tight.

"I said get the fuck out before I decide I don't care about detailing and paint the seats red."

"Are you kidding me? This is my fucking car," I yell, my

blood whooshing in my ears. I don't know what happened or where we went wrong, but I'm desperately clinging to the plan.

"Consider it a down payment on your debt." He says it all so casually like we're back in Bistro 908 talking about bullshit.

The two figures advance closer, only five feet away now. I notice the familiar gait of my brothers, but I can't relax. Not when my fucking father has a gun to my face and a twitchy trigger finger. He makes *unhinged* look like a fucking walk in the park and he's currently got a gun in my face. Even the worst shot would do serious damage this close.

"If I were you, I'd get out of my car and tell your brothers to back the fuck off before they start to resemble Swiss cheese."

I stare at him for a moment, the streetlight shining at the perfect angle to highlight a rectangle of his face. His eyes are bottomless pits of black, swirling with a detached sort of mania I've only ever seen in him.

"Now, son."

I unbuckle my seatbelt and open the door with one hand, keeping my eyes trained on him. I take a giant step backward out of the car.

"Good. Close the door and get in the fucking SUV and get the fuck out of my sight before I decide to change my mind."

I flatten my palm on the door of my new car, lingering for a moment. I've only had her for a few weeks, and even though I don't want to just give her over to my dad, walking away like this feels . . . wrong.

I need to know how the fuck he figured it out. Neither of my brothers would turn, so it has to be something else. Could we have been overheard? Did Vito bug my office at Violet Oak? My thoughts rapid-fire, flitting across my consciousness faster than I have time to process.

"I expect all three of my treacherous sons at the house at ten o'clock in the morning tomorrow. If you're not there, I'll consider you a traitor not only to the family but to the outfit. You'll be hunted down like dogs and hung like yesterday's laundry as a warning for those who wish to betray me."

My molars grind together as I push the door closed without a word. The loud slam does nothing to ease my frustration though.

Dad reverses in hyperspeed, squeals the tires again as he rights the car, and zooms away. The darkened sky and city lights swallow him in four seconds flat.

"What the fuck just happened?" Tommy asks, pulling off his ski mask.

"He knew," I answer.

"How?" Rome asks.

"Fuck if I know. He took my car as a *down payment* on our debt." My gaze narrows as if the answers will suddenly appear in the bright lights of the casinos in the distance. "But he summoned us to the house tomorrow. So expect our punishment to be brutal."

32

TOMMY

THE THREE OF us sit around the ostentatious twenty-person dining room table, sipping on expensive coffee in fancy mugs as we wait for Vito to show up.

The earthy tones of brown and cream in their Renaissance style wallpaper make the room feel small despite its mammoth size. Crown molding that leans more cream than white and a recessed ceiling. An elaborate bronze chandelier hangs over the middle of the table with actual candles in the holders.

They're rarely used if the thick layer of dust is any indication. Instead, the room is brightened by the matching bronze metal sconces every few feet around the room. A large bay window takes up most of one wall, parallel to the wall with the six foot sideboard buffet.

I have no idea how often they still entertain guests, but they used to host people often. All the ass-kissers and people in positions of power who want to make a deal. They wine and dine them in this room. The kitchen, breakfast nook, and smaller dining room are where we ate together when we still lived here.

The ever-present classical music plays through the dining room's built-in speaker system. Vito had almost the entire house outfitted with an intercom and speaker system when we were kids. He used to press the call button to find us in the house instead of actually walking to the second floor.

Now it's mostly used to play Beethoven.

The air between us is thick, not with animosity but tension. Anxiety and unease.

Whatever Vito's demands are, they'll be harsh. There's only one thing he loves more than money: violence.

Nic and I are well-acquainted with his preferences, and we've tried our best to shield Rome as much as possible growing up. But some things are unavoidable, out of our control.

This will be no different.

Nic twists his wrist to look at his watch. It's one of his only tells, and it's hardly even one at that. But I know my brother well enough to know he's crawling out of his skin right now. This situation is the definition of chaos, spiraled so far out of our touch that we can't even grasp the strings any longer.

Rome sits unmoving on the other side of me, his fingers still where they're normally flying across a phone or a keyboard.

None of us got any sleep last night, not that we did much talking either. When we got back to our apartment, we went our separate ways without a word. What is there really to say?

We tried to kill our father.

And we failed.

Now we have to pay the price.

I heard Nic in the kitchen three hours ago, starting up his elaborate espresso machine. So I'm sure he'll be jittery before the day's end. Actually, I should probably make him stop for something greasy on the way home.

And I don't think Rome left his workspace all night, because I heard the clacking of his keyboard throughout the night. I'm actually surprised how composed he looks, but I guess I shouldn't be. He pulls all-nighters for fun.

All three of us have been combing through every small detail since last night, trying to find out where we went wrong.

I've temporarily suspended my quest through Vito's possible motivations. It doesn't matter right now anyway, so I'll enjoy the music and the coffee and the freshly baked blueberry scones.

Ten minutes later, Vito walks in. He's dressed sharply in a true blue suit, crisp white button-down, and a pale pink pocket square.

I arch a brow and resist the urge to roll my eyes. Another intimidation tactic like making us wait? It's fucking child's play. I mentally urge him to get on with it, and by some divine intervention, he does.

He goes to the sideboard buffet and pours himself a cup of coffee from the metal carafe. He takes his time stirring it, like we don't know he takes his coffee black.

After exactly seven swirls around the cup, he removes the spoon and leaves it on the buffet. He takes his seat at the opposite end of the table, directly across from Nic.

Loathing starts gurgling in my gut. It's not a new feeling, but sometimes it takes me by surprise. The ferocity in which I'm capable of hating one singular person should be alarming.

But I think the most concerning part is how calm I am.

"Boys." He takes a measured sip, smacking his lips together. "Ah, that's good stuff."

"Why are we here?" Nic asks. His voice is gruff from disuse.

Vito glances down the expanse of the table at us from underneath his brow. "Oh, I think you know exactly why you're here."

Nic slides his hands from the table to rest them presumably on his lap, out of sight. "And my car?"

Vito chuckles, this delirious snort that makes the whites of his eyes look exceptionally big. "I think you're mistaken. The Vantage is mine. Call it." He pauses, waving his hand in the air. "An act of good faith."

I settle my weight against the back of the chair and eye the two exits in this room. The doorway that leads to the kitchen and the entire open wall that leads to the front of the house.

"See, I've failed you. All of you," Vito says, looking at each of us. "I thought I taught you better than that."

He pauses and takes another sip. His lip twitches, his amusement evident. None of us give him the satisfaction of asking what the fuck he's talking about, so he sighs.

"Surely I taught Tommaso that if you want to kill someone, you don't pussyfoot around it. You pull the fucking trigger."

Quicker than a snake, Vito whips out his favorite handgun and fires a shot at Nic. I'm out of my seat in an instant, my gun already in my hand.

"Like that." Vito beams.

"What the fuck," Rome yells.

I whip my head from Vito to Nic, my hand steady as I hold the gun aimed at our father. I scan my brother from head to toe, searching for a wound but there is none. He's whole. For now.

Nic is as still as I've ever seen him, every emotion locked down tight, his muscles coiled and ready to spring.

"Nico, tell your brother to sit down before I give him a real reason to pull a gun on me," Vito says.

"It's fine, Tommy. He didn't even graze me," Nic says, glancing from me to Rome and back to me again.

"You always were a lousy shot, Vito," I snarl, slamming myself into my seat. All pretense of civility has been wiped clean from this meeting.

Vito sets his gun on the table, the sight of it next to the delicate coffee cup paints a ridiculous image.

It's the fucking story of my life.

"Now that I've got your attention. Here are my terms: you tried to kill me last night. I don't care what your reasoning was or what excuses you have. You failed regardless of your motivations. I'm in a particularly forgiving mood, all things considered, so I'll give you boys a critique, free of charge." He pauses, but no one takes his bait.

"See, son, when you're trying to kill someone close to you, you don't do things out of character," Vito says, staring intently at Nic.

Nic's jaw tics, but still, he says nothing.

What did Nic do at the meeting that was out of character?

Oh fuck. *Oh fuck.*

I battle against the urge to slam my fist against the table as realization slams into me with the weight of a truck.

We're fucking idiots for not realizing the fatal flaw in our plan.

Nic has never offered to drive Vito anywhere, let alone hand over his keys.

Vito lifts a hand in the air. "But since I'm a kind father, I'll give you a choice. It's not something I'd offer to anyone else, and trust me when I tell you it's a one-time offer."

"We're listening," Nic says. Though his jaw is clenched so tight, it's a wonder he can even speak at all.

"You have two choices to earn my trust back: take out every single member of the west coast family encroaching on our territory." He pauses, stretching one second into ten. I hate him a little more for the way my heart kicks up a notch. "Or one of you die. I don't have a preference either way."

He sits back in his chair, leaving his gun on the table untouched and sipping his coffee like he's some fucking regular joe starting his workday.

The urge to double-tap Vito rides me hard, and it takes

everything I have inside of me not to comply. The only reason I'm not already staring at his lifeless eyes is because he's a sneaky motherfucker. I wouldn't put it past him to have some sort of contingency plan in place. And I'll be fucking damned if I'm going to pull the trigger that takes him *and* all of us down.

All of us don't need to go down with his ship. Vito's sins have bled all over this town, staining the streets with his vendettas and plans for domination. And there's only one man in this room who can change the tide, who can right some of Vito's many, many wrongs.

My brother.

I look between my brothers for a moment, knowing before Nic opens his mouth what he's going to say. But I can't let him do that.

I won't let him wipe an entire family from the map just to save me. What Vito didn't spell out is he means women, children, elderly—*everyone*. If he wants a family gone, he expects us to exterminate them like fucking mosquitos in the summertime.

That's the sort of stain that never leaves you, no matter how hard you scrub it clean. No amount of good deeds will ever erase the blot on your soul.

But me? I'm already too far gone.

"Fine," Nic says, pushing his chair back and standing up. His gun is clutched in his right hand, so I know he's rattled.

But he doesn't need to worry. I'm going to make this easy for him—for both of them.

"I'll send you the information on the family later today," Vito says, a Cheshire smile on his smarmy face. "Lovely catching up with you boys today."

Nic jerks his head to the side and Rome and I push back from the table as one and follow him out of the room. Vito's humorous laughter chases us out as we stalk out of our childhood home.

I slide into the passenger seat as Nic gets behind the wheel.

Normally, I like to drive but I know he needs the control right now.

He peels away with an angry screech of tires. The engine purrs, a humming balm to my racing thoughts. I clasp my hands together loosely, letting my elbows hang off my knees as I wait.

We're flying through the streets, and after another minute of silence, I open my mouth to tell them the solution.

"Shut your fucking mouth, Tommy," Nic snaps.

His ire isn't unexpected, but I am surprised it's aimed at me. "You don't even know what I was going to say."

Nic takes a hard right. "The fuck I don't. Tell me you aren't trying to sacrifice yourself."

I snap my mouth closed and lean my head back against the headrest, rolling it from side to side. "It makes sense, Nic. You won't survive the kind of toll it will take to wipe out a family like that."

"Fuck you, brother. Fuck you for thinking that you're expendable and fuck you for thinking I can't handle it. That I haven't handled much worse," Nic snarls.

"Damn, man. I didn't say you couldn't handle it. I just don't think you should *have to*. That's all I'm saying." I lift my hands up, palms in the air with a small shrug.

"Whatever stupid fucking plan you're thinking of, shut it down. You're not dying today, asshole," Rome says from the backseat. The heat in his words matches Nic's.

"I thought it was a good plan," I grumble.

"In what fucking universe do you think it's a *good plan* to sacrifice yourself to the whims of our fucking psychopath of a father?" Nic shakes his head, speeding down the open road.

"We'll figure something else out, Tommy. But you're not checking out yet, so knock that shit off." Rome reaches forward and shoves my shoulder.

"Whatever, man," I huff out.

It's a front to cover the sapling of warmth that grows inside my barren wasteland of a heart. The one that gets watered and fed by my brothers and their unending loyalty.

Planning has never been my strong suit anyway.

33

MAEVE

I'VE BEEN in New York City for four weeks. And true to my word to Keira, I've been taking each day as an adventure. In between daily calls from my sisters—on a rotating schedule, no less—I've been exploring one of my favorite cities.

I've done all the touristy things like visiting the eighty-eighth floor of the Empire State Building, where I discovered I'm not a huge fan of heights. I traipsed up and down Fifth Avenue, indulging myself with three new dresses, a gorgeous pair of red-soled shoes, and the most perfect black quilted, buttery-soft leather crossbody purse.

I spent some time in St. Patrick's Cathedral and imagined myself standing in the middle of a packed Catholic church with a long veil and a heavy heart.

I lost almost an entire day to the Museum of Modern Art, offering my undivided attention to every exhibit. Something I've never done before. New York City has been a haven to me for many years, but I never had enough time to explore it properly.

I spent time in Greenwich Village perusing vintage clothing

stores. A vintage Dior dress from the 1950s spring collection now hangs in my closet.

I've been one in eight million for weeks, my sisters halfway around the world from me. But I've never really felt alone. My phone vibrates in my pocket, and I slip it out, expecting it to be a text from the reason I haven't felt lonely.

Somewhere in the midst of our countless text exchanges, I lost my way. I stopped looking at our conversations as ways to gather information and started seeing them as something more. I recognize the absurdity of it all, and the irony isn't lost on me. But I can't make myself feel guilty for it.

And I can't make myself stop.

But it doesn't matter because it's not him. He hasn't texted me since late two nights ago, and I need to stop checking my phone every five seconds for a new text. I don't love the way it makes *me* feel obsessive, like I crave it.

I answer the call and bring my phone to my ear. "Fitzgerald, to what do I owe the pleasure? Need another favor, perhaps?" I tease, strolling down Central Park.

It wasn't too long ago that I helped the Fitzgeralds out of a few binds. For a few favors, of course. We're friends who often do business.

I stop at a bench to the right and sit down, holding my double-decker chocolate lava cake ice cream cone to the side so it doesn't drip down my leg. It's unseasonably warm for September here, and the humidity makes it feel like I'm wading through jello when I'm outside.

But it makes me feel alive, so I'm going with it.

"Yes, actually. We're having a little event tonight, and you're invited. I know you're in the city, so don't bother using that excuse," Rush says.

"How do you know th—Roisin." I answer my question before he can, realization dawning on me. "That sneaky little sister."

"About that. I wasn't able to crack your little stalker problem Roisin sent me."

"I bet she loved that," I say around a smile.

"Aye, she fucking did. She sent me coursework for some beginner computer science class, said maybe I should *brush up*."

It's all posturing, and he's not even doing a halfway decent job of his faux annoyance today. There's too much mirth in his voice.

He's always had a soft spot for Rosie, said she was like the little sister he never wanted. She always responds with some dig about his age or his computer skills. It's all very entertaining when our families get together.

I twist my lips to the side to stifle some of the laughter. "I can imagine how well that went over. And don't worry about tracking him. It's fine for now," I say, waving the ice cream cone in the air like I'm dismissing the whole thing. Truthfully, I stopped thinking of him as a stalker-type.

"Are you close to O'Malley's? Stop by for a drink."

The trees above me rustle with the soft breeze. It's oddly warmer with the breeze, but I appreciate the wind stirring the sweaty strands of hair stuck on the back of my neck. "I'm in Central Park."

"By yourself?" Skepticism is thick in his voice.

I roll my eyes. "You do remember who you're talking to, right?"

He clucks his tongue softly. "Ah, of course. How could I forget that the almighty Maeve King herself has deigned me worthy of a phone call."

"You're an asshole, you know that?" I say around a laugh. "And you've been spending too much time with your brother."

"When you share your girlfriend with your brothers, it comes with the territory," he deadpans.

"Aye, I bet. Things are good then?"

Rush and his brothers went through the fucking wringer in the last year with their girl. They have a unique relationship, as in the three of them date one woman and she only dates the three of them. It's unconventional, but I applaud them all for living their lives unapologetically.

It doesn't hurt that all three Fitzgerald brothers have been known to shoot first, ask questions *never* on more than one occasion. And when it comes to the love of their life? Well, let's just say the gloves really come off.

The thing is, I really like Alaina. My sisters and I got to know her last year when we spent time at the Fitzgerald house. In fact, the five of us had Alaina on a rotating schedule while we were there, we each taught her different things from our skill sets.

"Alaina's still adjusting now that everything has settled. But you know how it goes, Maeve, as soon as you get used to the quiet, shit blows up again."

I can't help but think of my predicament. "Aye, I know." I lean over and take a bite of my ice cream. It's getting dangerously close to dripping down my hand, and considering it's the time of year for those aggressive dumpster bees, I'd rather not advertise myself as a sugar source.

"Five o'clock at The Fjord. And bring a present." He sounds distracted with murmuring in the background.

My mind jumps to the date, quickly trying to remember when their birthdays are. "Wait. Your birthdays aren't any time soon. Did I miss an engagement announcement?"

Rush scoffs. "As if I would announce it to the world and make her an even larger target."

Rush is the president of the junior Brotherhood council. When his da's council steps down, Rush and his brothers will ascend. They all have more than enough experience with enemies, but I get it. You don't want to make it easier for your enemies or ladder-climbers to pull one over on you.

"No, it's a party for Alaina's birthday."

"But her birthday isn't for months," I protest, my face scrunching up in confusion.

"It's Wolf's grand plan for a surprise party. Ever since he found out she's never had one before when they were watching some movie, he's been obsessed with it."

"I heard that," Wolf yells from the background of Rush's line.

Their banter always makes me laugh and today is no exception.

"Good, you were meant to," Rush snaps.

"Don't listen to him, Maeve. It's a fucking brilliant plan, and my girl's gonna be so surprised. Don't be late, yeah?" Wolf yells.

"See you boys tonight at The Fjord." I nod a few times, even knowing they can't see me.

They say their goodbyes, and we disconnect the call. I finish my melting ice cream cone and make my way back to our apartment. I need to shower this sticky treat off of me and freshen up before I get ready for tonight.

I remember seeing a vintage vinyl record store the other day, so I'll have to make a detour to snag a few I think Alaina will like. She's got an impressive vinyl collection from her da, so I know she'll enjoy adding to it.

I PULL open the door to The Fjord, pausing in the threshold to let my eyes adjust to the dim interior. Soft yellow fairy lights illuminate the short hallway to the black pedestal hostess stand.

"Good evening, we're closed to the public tonight for a private event," the hostess greets me.

I offer her a smile. "I'm a guest of the Fitzgeralds."

"Oh, of course. Right this way." She comes around the corner and tilts her head toward the dining room.

I adjust my new crossbody purse across my chest and follow behind her. The heathered gray floors do nothing to absorb the sound of my heels, and we announce my presence long before anyone sees us.

"Mr. Fitzgerald has reserved the entire venue for the evening, so feel free to utilize any of our rooms. Here's the main dining room and our largest bar," she says, fanning her arm out wide, palm up, to encompass the room.

The dining room of The Fjord looks nothing like I expected it. Where I anticipated crisp whites and modern lines, there's soft oranges and minty greens. Giant potted blue ferns make up a gorgeous focal point in the middle of the room, their large creamy beige pots clustered together on a small riser.

The four and eight top tables are evenly spaced in two-thirds of the space, the bar taking up the last third of the room. The bar top is a modern industrial style with dark wood, matching the tables and chairs.

Champagne-colored fabric art pieces hang from the interior wall and the outer wall is floor-to-ceiling windows. The kind of garage door windows that slide open horizontally, sort of like an accordion.

"To the right are our private banquet rooms for more intimate gatherings," the hostess says as we pass a smaller display of plants in muted cream pots at the other end of the dining room. "And to our left is our rooftop lounge. This is where Mr. Fitzgerald directed all the guests be escorted too."

I follow the hostess as she leads me outside to their wraparound patio enclosed in a glass half-wall. Strings of Edison bulbs and fairy lights give the space a more intimate vibe. A long bar in the same design sits against the shared wall to our right.

Two and four top bar tables and stools dot the space closest to the bar, but the rest of the patio has low profile patio furniture. Overstuffed pale orange cushions on loveseats, sectionals, and couches. Champagne-colored coffee tables and side tables. Five foot arborvitaes in soft minty-green planters between lounge spaces give the impression of privacy. Not that it matters if you rent the entire restaurant out for an evening.

"Please let one of the staff know if you need anything," the hostess says just as I spot Rush by the end of the bar. He's dressed in a dark charcoal suit with a black button-down shirt. His tattoos peek through the opened collar of his suit, and if I didn't view him as a brother *and* adore his girl, I'd be tempted to hit on him.

But as it stands, he's more familial than fuckable.

"I will, thank you." I flash her a warm smile before I stroll toward my friend.

"You made it," he greets me with a drink in a martini glass in his outstretched hand.

I accept it with an arched brow. "What's this?"

"Ah, another one of Wolf's ideas: espresso martinis."

My brows raise in interest. "Yum. But first, take this." I hold up the gold gift bag by the string with one finger.

He grabs it from me. "You didn't really have to do that."

"Please," I say, rolling my eyes. "Like I would show up to a birthday party without a present. My mum raised me better than that."

"Aye, she did. She taught all her girls to raise hell." He places my gift bag on the bar behind him.

I slip my trusted vial out of my purse and squeeze a drop inside the martini. I wait thirty seconds to make sure it's safe before I take my first sip.

Rush scoffs, this deep noise from the back of his throat. "I'm offended, Maeve."

I lift a shoulder as I bring the glass to my lips. "Don't be. It's not personal."

"What's going on over here, brother? Ah, Maeve, you made it," Wolf says, coming up behind Rush. He leans over and snatches a full martini glass off the counter behind the bar.

"Maeve here thinks to check her drink for foul play," Rush says, folding his arms across his chest and glaring at me.

"What?" I look at them both from underneath my lashes and I let the smooth, rich taste of espresso mellow on my tongue. "It's not like I thought you would personally, but I don't know these bartenders. And to be honest, you have a lot of enemies. So I thought it might be aimed at you, and I'm not looking to be anyone's collateral damage."

"Damn, Maeve, it's good to see you," Wolf says, letting a wide smile spread across his face. He's dressed similarly to his brother. A tailored black suit, the jacket ditched already, his matte black button-down rolled halfway up his forearms showing his tattoos.

"I know you haven't missed me, not with Alaina keeping you boys busy." I look to the side to disguise my amusement. There was a point in their relationship where the three of them struggled to get along and share her together. And from an outside perspective, I enjoyed watching her put all three of them on their asses more than once.

Wolf takes a drink of his own martini and rocks back on his heels. "Yeah, I've been meaning to call Keira and tell her to stop sending Red so many fucking weapons. Our front hall closet looks more like an armory than a place to store coats."

I laugh at the mental image. I'm not even a little surprised. Keira's probably been sending Alaina new toys every month to try out since we first started training her. "If I know my sister, I'm betting her collection is quite impressive by now."

"Aye, it is. But she nearly took out Sully's head when she tossed her throwing stars at him last month," Rush says.

I lift a shoulder and turn to look at the view of the city. "Then he probably deserved it."

"How did I know you would take her side without even hearing the specifics?" Wolf muses.

"Girl power and all that."

The hostess ushers a group of people in, a few familiar faces, but mostly not. Wolf swallows the rest of his drink in one sip. "Time to get ready. They'll be here any minute."

"Thanks for coming, Maeve. Enjoy yourself, yeah?" Rush says, pausing to glance at me and waiting for my nod before he heads toward the door as well.

34

MAEVE

I TAKE another sip of my martini, enjoying the way the espresso smooths out the vodka. I tip my head back on the soft orange cushion behind me, letting the Edison bulb lights create a bright border of my view of the night sky.

It's too bright in the city to really see the stars, not the way you can see them back home. But even without the view, I still love this city.

The surprise went off without a hitch, and Alaina was suitably shocked. I guess that happens when your boyfriends throw you a surprise birthday party four months in advance.

I've never had a surprise party, and I'm not sure I would even enjoy it. But Alaina was clearly having the time of her life. She's currently standing on top of the bar at the end of the balcony, singing her karaoke-loving heart out. Wolf stands behind the bar, playing his acoustic guitar and singing along with her. Sully's been rooted to her side the entire night. He's playing sentinel, planted in front of her, head brushing against her shins.

I've been nursing my drink for a while now, trying to make it last a little longer. I don't want to wade through the small crowd of people to get another drink. I suppose I could always go to one of the bars inside.

These drinks go down a little too easily, and considering the last time I let myself get wrapped up in the warmth of alcohol and the loving embrace of freedom, I fucked a stranger in the bathroom of The Red Lion Pub. I better slow down.

Thoughts of that night flash before me without warning. The way his cock felt stretching me wide, the way he tongue-fucked my pussy and then spread my ass cheeks apart.

Warmth rolls over my body, a slow cascade from my cheeks to my toes. My fingers curl around the slender stem of the martini glass, and my thighs clench automatically.

I blow out a breath and physically force myself to think about something else—anything else.

The cushion next to me depresses, and I roll my head along the backrest. I expected Rush, maybe one of our acquaintances, but I wasn't expecting a stranger.

He glances at me as he settles against the seat, smoothing down his tie with one hand and clutching an espresso martini in the other. "Is anyone sitting here?"

I let my gaze roll over him, the finer details becoming clearer as my eyes adjust to the different lighting. The curve of his lips tilt upward slightly, like my slow perusal is amusing to him. Long dark lashes frame deep blue eyes the color of the depths of the ocean. Dark scruff covers his jaw, the kind of beard that's not quite a beard but more than a five o'clock shadow. I idly wonder how it would feel between my thighs.

Dark hair, blue eyes, dresses well—I'm sure he's used to being perused.

"Sure," I murmur, taking in the way his black button-down shirt stretches around his biceps. I follow the line of his arm, my gaze snagging on the sleeves rolled-up to his elbows and the whorls and lines of black tattoos. There's just enough light to see a shape but too many shadows to make it out clearly.

"Sure, someone's sitting here, or sure, it's available?" His voice is like honeyed bourbon. Deep and smooth with a little rasp.

My gaze flashes from his forearm to his eyes. He cocks his head to the side and scans my face, like he's trying to place familiar features.

"No one's sitting there," I murmur.

The fairy lights above us twinkle, highlighting the deep brown strands of his hair. It's one of those colors that looks nearly black unless it's in the right light.

"How do you know the birthday girl?"

Disappointment pierces my buzz. Small talk is arguably one of the worst forms of communication. I'd rather get on that bar with Alaina, belting pop songs, than make small talk with someone I'll never see again.

I tilt my head, the ends of my hair tickling my shoulder and take him in again. He sure is pretty though.

Maybe I could make an exception for my aversion to small talk tonight. After all, I only have another weekend here before I sign my life away.

I exhale and mentally roll my eyes at myself. I sound like Rosie—she's always the most dramatic in the family.

I angle my body toward him a fraction and toss my hair over my shoulder. My beachy waves have fallen considerably since I left the house hours ago. The humidity should be going down soon, leaving the city for a crisp fall season. Unfortunately, I won't be here to witness it this time.

"How do *you* know the birthday girl?" I counter.

He chuckles. "I should've expected the paranoia with this crowd."

I arch a brow. "This crowd?"

His grin grows wider, a faint dimple flashing in his left cheek. My stupid, traitorous knees go a little weak at the sight. He has to do a lot more than flash a nice smile with a dimple to win me over.

Right?

He drags his hand along his jaw, trying to wipe the smile from his face. He doesn't succeed, but I don't think he was trying all that hard. His gaze tracks my own, watching me watch him like we're in a locked game of cat and mouse.

Only he mistook me for the mouse, when I am very much the predator here.

"I'm sort of a friend of the family," he says, angling his knees toward me and sinking into the corner of the lounger.

"What family?"

"The Rossis. And now the Fitzgeralds, by extension."

"Hm." It's a noncommittal noise, but really, his presence here tells me all I really need to know about his allegiance. Rush would never invite anyone here who poses a threat to his girl.

I don't offer him my connection to Rush or Alaina. If he's here, then he's clever enough to deduce that I'm an ally already. And I'm not in the habit of broadcasting my relationship to either of them, for all of our sakes.

I think between the Syndicate, the Brotherhood, and our vigilante justice system, we have enough enemies to last a lifetime. No need to make unnecessary connections. They only cause problems in the end.

Not that I wouldn't take tall, dark, and dangerous home tonight, because I'm increasingly open to that idea. But I won't exchange information.

I finish the last sip of my drink and balance the empty glass on my knee, the stem between my index and middle fingers.

"Ready for another?" He gestures to my glass with his nearly empty one.

I look over his shoulder and see more people on the bar top singing into the microphone. "I'll wait."

He glances over his shoulder and chuckles. "How about I take one for the team and get us fresh drinks?"

I tug the inside of my bottom lip with my teeth. "Sure."

He gets to his feet, snagging my empty glass from my knee. "Save my seat?"

I dip my chin in a nod. "Sure."

I watch him head toward the bar, appreciating the unobstructed view of his ass. Damn, he does look good in a suit. It seems I have a habit of finding dark-haired, dangerous men lately. I run the edge of my thumbnail across my bottom lip, contemplating the logistics of hooking up with him.

Two different women stop to talk to him, but he doesn't linger. More points in his favor. He steps in front of someone, and I lose sight of him.

My purse vibrates against my lap, and I reach for it without thinking. I've already talked to Ava today, so I know it's not my sisterly daily check-in.

I glance at my phone, seeing the notification from *him*. I haven't heard from him in days, and I sort of hate the way my heart skips a beat at just seeing his name flash across the screen.

> Romeo: Did anyone ever tell you that red is your color?

I glance down at the dress I picked on fifth avenue last week. Deep brick-red satin with a finely detailed lace overlay. It's stunning, and more importantly, it makes me *feel* stunning. Like I could slay dragons and conquer worlds in this dress.

It's sleeveless with an A-line waist and flared skirt that hits mid-thigh. A double soft and steep V-neck on the front and back, plunging nearly to my navel. But that's not my favorite part. My very favorite thing about this dress is the staggering

293

sides. Where a normal dress's armscyes—armholes—lay right above your typical bra line, these plunge to an inch above the A-line seam.

It gives the entire dress a fitted, dramatic look, and the flared skirt gives me a little more height.

> Me: What are you up to, Romeo?

> Romeo: I've missed you.

I roll my eyes, my heart thumping hard against my ribs.

> Me: You don't know me well enough to miss me.

> Romeo: And yet, I still do.

I glance up, checking to see if my handsome stranger is on his way back from the bar. I crane my head to the side and see his dark hair bent toward the bartender still.

> Me: I'm surprised you texted today. I thought you lost my number.

"Fuck," I chastise myself as soon as my thumb hits send. I don't even know why I sent him that. It's forward and snippy and gives away too much.

But I was annoyed that he suddenly went radio silent on me for two days after five weeks of daily communication.

My phone vibrates in my hand, startling me. I jump a little in my seat, my eyebrows crashing low over my narrowed eyes. Why is Romeo calling me?

I push to my feet and let the call ring out. I'm not going to answer it in the middle of a party with Alaina singing Britney Spears in the background.

I weave around a few tables with people, my gaze locked on

the door to the inside of the restaurant. My fingers curl around the handle when someone yells my name.

I look over my shoulder and see Rush five feet behind me, worry etched all over his face.

I wave him off with my hand clutching my phone and a smirk. He tips his chin in my direction and I take it as my cue.

I slink by the waitstaff, squeezing my phone in my hand hard enough to sting. I walk down the hallway, dipping into one of the private rooms to the right.

It's a slightly different theme in here from the main space. Eight light wood circular tables and matching chairs, a much smaller bar against the entire back wall, two low-profile loungers in the same soft orange as the cushions outside, and an entire wall of windows overlooking the city.

Blackout blinds are partially closed, casting only the center strip of the room in city lights. It's a wild contrast to the other-wise dimly lit room.

I close the door behind me, twisting the knob slowly so it clicks quietly. I know the hostess said it was available to any of the night's guests, but it still feels like I *shouldn't* be in here.

And the last thing I need is Rush sneaking up on me and overhearing something he shouldn't. If my sisters find out I've been talking to Romeo like this whole time, they might actually kill me.

Spinning around in a circle, I confirm that I'm alone. My thumb hovers over his name for a moment. I exhale and press his name before bringing the phone to my ear.

"Ah, *mon chéri*. Did you miss me?"

My lower belly clenches at the smooth tenor of his voice. It sounds different than I imagined over the last month, and yet, it's not unfamiliar. "Are you watching me?"

He chuckles, this quiet exhale of breath. "Ah, I'm always watching."

I stalk toward the side of the window and push the drape to the side with my index finger. We're too high up to see anything, at least not without proper equipment. But that doesn't mean he isn't in one of those luxury apartments across the street with a fancy telephoto lens.

"Where are you, Romeo? No more riddles."

"I thought you liked our games, *mon chéri*."

I scan the rooftops across the street. "I do. Are you in New York City?"

He tsks. "Would you like me to be?"

I hesitate, letting the drape fall back in place. Our texting sparring matches have been the highlight of my days. The last few times, the flirting devolved into more explicit conversation. Which I definitely cannot do right now.

"I can't talk right now."

"Are you ashamed of me, Juliet?"

My lips curl up into a smirk. "Are you going to serenade me with more Shakespeare?"

"Did my heart love till now? Forswear it, sight, for I ne'er saw true beauty till this night."

My hair whips around my shoulders as I spin on the ball of my foot. My lips part on a gasp as I hear the voice from the doorway *and* my phone. I take a step back, my ass skimming the wall.

Dark hair, piercing blue eyes, dressed to impress with his sleeves rolled up to showcase his ink.

"It's you."

35

ROMEO

I SHOVE my hands in the pockets of my pants and nudge the door closed with the heel of my boot. I've waited a long time to see her in person. The pixels on my computer screens didn't do her justice.

My fingers ache to touch her. It was the most divine torture being so close to her without being able to touch her.

To tuck the strand of hair behind her ear, to lace my fingers with hers and tug her onto my lap, to feel her lips against mine, taste her exhale on my tongue.

I've thought about this moment too many times to count, and now that it's here, I'm plagued with a moment of indecision. The air in my lungs crystalizes, making it hard to breathe.

She's so fucking exquisite it hurts.

"Romeo?" She tilts her head to the side, but she doesn't step away from the wall, telling me exactly how to play this.

It doesn't matter. I'm a patient man.

"*Mon chéri*. Juliet. Wren. Maeve King." I take a step toward her with each name. "So many names for one woman."

"A rose by any other name would smell as sweet."

My grin is quick. "Ah, so you do like Shakespeare."

Her hair slides over her shoulder when she tilts her head to the side. "How do you know them?"

I keep my leisurely pace, prowling toward her. "They're family. Sort of."

"I meant my names."

"Remember when I told you I was a magician?"

"Aye, I remember," she breathes, her chest rising faster the closer I get.

"Then you should know I never reveal my secrets, *mon chéri.*"

Her fingertips press into the wall behind her. "How are you here? Do you really know the Rossis or was that a lie too?"

I arch a brow. "I'm many things, Juliet, but a liar is not one of them."

She pushes off the wall, her eyes narrowing on me. "I've known the Fitzgerald boys for most of our lives. I would've remembered you."

I press my palm flat against my chest, my fingers splayed wide. "I'm touched."

She rolls her eyes, her face relaxing marginally, but her shoulders remain tense. "Why are you here?"

I take another step forward, eliminating the space between us to a meager two feet. "Because you are," I breathe out.

Her breath hitches and her lips part. "Another game then?"

It takes a Herculean amount of effort to not reach out and touch her, but somehow I manage to keep my hands in my pocket. "No, Maeve. It's not a game."

"How long have you known where I was? Who I was?"

"Not long," I murmur.

"How long, Romeo—if that's even your real name," she snaps.

There's more heat in her voice now. And fuck me because it's only turning me on more. Dominance hasn't ever been my thing, but I have a feeling that *anything* Maeve King does will suddenly be my thing.

I lick my lips and proverbially cross my fingers that this all works out the way I've been envisioning it. "My real name is Romeo. And I've known you were in New York City for a few days."

"Is that why you went dark for the last few days?" she challenges, her hands balling into fists at her sides.

I lift my shoulder. "Not really. I was caught up in some work things."

"And what do you do for *work* things if you're at a Fitzgerald birthday party and friends with the Rossis? Steal candy from children? Make cement boots at the docks? Graffiti the railroad tracks?"

My brows hit my hairline as I roll my lips inward to stop the cackle of laughter at her little meltdown.

She relaxes her fists and tosses her hand in the air, letting it hit her side with a thwack. "Shut up. I don't know, okay?"

"So you default to a very random list of what you think I really do?" I smirk.

She bristles. "I'm caught off-guard and I don't fucking like surprises."

"Don't throw Juliet a surprise party, got it," I say softly.

She cuts me a look, glaring at me. "Stop flirting with me."

I shrug my shoulders and press a hand to my chest. "Who's flirting? I'm just taking notes."

She narrows her gaze, but the corner of her mouth ticks up on the side. She's fighting a smile.

I shuffle forward a half step, the tips of my favorite boots a half-centimeter away from the points of her heels. "Now that we got that out of the way, there's been something I've been dreaming of doing for weeks, months, even."

"Months?"

I bridge the gap between us before the word even leaves her lips and claim her mouth. I deny myself the pounding savagery demanding I ravage her mouth and fucking claim her as mine once and for all.

Instead, I go slow. Savoring the way her lips feel against mine, relishing the way she parts her lips on a sigh, memorizing the way her body arches into mine.

She pulls back, her lashes slow to open, her pupils wide with lust. She reaches out slowly, her palm flattening against my chest. She pauses over my heart, and I swear it beats a rhythm only for her. She smooths her palm across my chest, taking her time to feel the results of my time spent in the gym in our home.

I force myself to remain still, to let her explore without rushing her. Even if waiting feels like my veins are parched and my skin too tight.

She curls her fingers around my tie, winding her fist around and around until it's a taut line between us. "If this is an elaborate game, my sisters and I will take turns cutting you into tiny pieces and scattering you across the Atlantic."

She murmurs her threat so softly, almost lovingly that my wires get crossed in my brain, and my cock swells in my pants. I groan, nearly panting with desire. "It's not a game. I swear it."

She licks her lips and holds my gaze. "Then take me home, Romeo."

MAEVE

My mind is on overdrive as I follow Romeo down the hallway of the Prism Hotel to his suite. He tightens his hold on my hand and looks over his shoulder again, like he's double-checking I'm still walking a half step behind him.

I'm no amateur when it comes to heels, but I can't quite keep up with his long strides. Even with the added inches, he's nearly seven inches taller than me.

"We're almost there," he says, almost distractedly.

Ever since I told him to take me home, he was a man on a mission. The playful, flirty banter was replaced with a steely determination that I suspect is a temporary leash on his lust.

I've been thinking about this man every single day for over a month, sharing parts of my life and meaningless thoughts. And the truth is, I have precious time left before the clock strikes midnight and I get turned into a metaphorical pumpkin.

At least until I can get out.

If I can get out.

And as strange as it happened, this is a gift. Maybe the fates felt bad for the cards I've been dealt and gave me a boon.

A six-foot-two, dark-haired boon who smells like sandalwood and sandy beaches.

Romeo stops next to room twenty-three and holds his phone to the black pad next to the door handle. It beeps and flashes green a moment later. He opens the door and tugs me in behind him.

The lights are off, but the blackout blinds on the opposite wall are open, casting the room in muted yellows and whites.

A ten-by-twelve beige-and-navy patterned rug takes up most of the main space, from underneath the platform King-sized bed to the small lounge area in front of the window.

A slim light-beige couch is centered in front of the window, overlooking the city. Two arm chairs on either side and a small dark mahogany wood coffee table in the center.

White walls with grey artwork expertly framed and hung around the room. An oatmeal-colored tufted low-profile headboard, eight pillows in two neat rows, a light gray plush comforter. Small cream-colored nightstands on either side of the bed with modern-style lamps.

A wide doorway leading into the bathroom is just beyond the nightstand closest to the window. I let our fingers drift apart as I stop a few paces in front of him.

"Does it meet your standards?" His breath rustles the hair behind my ear, tickling that sensitive spot on my neck.

I step toward the bed, out of his reach, and trail my finger along the edge of the comforter. The stitching from the embroidered design pricks against my skin, giving me something tangible to focus on. Something to ground me against the rising tide of need swelling inside of me.

Romeo and I have been verbally dancing around each other for weeks. The tension between us sizzles hotter and hotter.

I don't know what it is about him. But I can't stop the insatiable longing that burns inside my chest. It's a heady feeling, especially when it tangles with lust.

I've created this idea of him inside my head, placed him in an unattainable position. The realist part of me understands what I've done and accepts that I need to curb my expectations.

But the tiny romantic butterflies quivering inside my chest urge me to let him try. They're convinced he'll not only meet my expectations, but he'll *exceed* them.

"How did you find me?" It's a question that's plagued me since I realized who he was.

I saunter toward the bathroom and peek inside. It's spacious with a double vanity sink with cream and gray marble countertops and a half wall mirror. Square, heated tiles on the floor, three different lighting settings.

But the showstopper is the shower.

In the middle of the back wall, three tall panes of glass frame a huge rectangular rainforest showerhead. There's a built-in bench on one side closest to the window, next to a towel warming rack.

It's the kind of shower that you could spend some serious time in.

I cock my head to the side and imagine myself in the shower . . . with him. I've never fucked anyone in a shower before. It didn't seem like the payoff would be worth the effort.

But with a shower like that and a man like this?

I'm willing to give it a try.

I'm so lost in my fantasy about Romeo bending me over the shower bench that it takes me a moment to realize he never answered my question.

I toss my hair over my shoulder and look at him. He's exactly where I left him. Standing in the middle of the room, hands shoved into the pockets of his trousers.

The look on his face seizes my breath. It reminds me of this tiger I saw at the zoo once.

Rosie had begged me to take her and Ava years ago. But I couldn't stop staring at this beast of an animal. He prowled the enclosure, back and forth and back again. All day, that's all he did. Prowl and stare at anyone bold enough to get close enough.

I wasn't convinced that piece of glass would protect us, not from power so explosive. The ferocity in the tiger's gaze assured he was going to make a meal out of us, even if it was the last thing he did. And still, I couldn't stop watching him.

Romeo reminds me of that tiger, a caged beast just patiently waiting until the right moment to strike. I already know I'm going to let him consume me whole. It's just a matter of how much I'm going to make him work for it.

36

MAEVE

AWARENESS ROLLS OVER ME, prickling the roots of my hair at my scalp, cascading down my neck and over my shoulders, free-falling to my lower stomach, where it settles into something warm.

My chest rises and falls quicker the longer he stares at me with that expression. Lips wet like he just ran his tongue across them, eyes a shade darker than they were under the fairy lights, muscles coiled like he's preparing to pounce.

He watches me like he's deciding how he's going to devour me. And just like the tiger, he's unapologetic about his hunger.

I turn and face him, my spin so exaggerated and slow. It feels like a lifetime before I face him fully.

I feel my lids lowering as I take him in, my chest rising and falling faster in a rhythm that matches his.

My nipples pebble from the heat in our exchange, pressing against the lace cups of my bra, and my lower belly clenches with desire.

Perhaps I have it all wrong. Perhaps *I* am the beast, finally set free from my own prison, even if only momentarily. Maybe it's *me* who's going to devour *him*.

My muscles coil, and I shift on the balls of my feet, fingertips tingling in anticipation.

Romeo tracks my movement and clocks the shift in the air immediately. His head drops a little, so he's looking at me from underneath his dark lashes. His tongue peeks out to swipe across his lower lip. I don't know if it's an unconscious move or a deliberate one, but my reaction is the same.

Desire wraps around my legs like vines, spreading until my whole body feels heavy with it. I desperately want to erase the space between us. To claim his mouth as my own. To push him on to the bed and explore the body that I've been fantasizing about for weeks.

"I've thought of you often, you know." My voice is a smooth, almost conspiratorial.

He arches a brow but doesn't reply, seemingly content to hear where I'm going with this.

"For weeks I've wondered what your arms would feel like wrapped around me." I take a step toward him. "What your lips would taste like against my own." I take another step. "I'd fantasize about how you would feel inside me." Another step. "Your fingers." Step. "Your tongue." Step. "Your cock," I whisper, stopping right in front of him.

A vein in his jaw tics as he stares down at me with a smirk. "You want to play, *mon chéri?*"

I push onto my toes and whisper against his lips, "Aye, I want to play."

He slides a hand on either side of my head, sinking his fingers into my hair. He tilts my face toward his, and murmurs, "'Thou art more lovely and more temperate.'"

The hushed words of Shakespeare snap the tenuous hold on my lust, and I find I no longer want to play. If you would've asked me six months ago if whispered literature quotes would turn me on, I would've buried my blade in your thigh for the insult.

And then I would've eaten my words. Because the way Romeo's tongue curls around the consonants of his whispered sonnet sends a flare of arousal straight to my clit.

I imagine how it would feel to have his mouth recite lines against my clit, and I feel almost feverish.

I can't wait a moment longer.

So I claim his mouth this time. Sighs fall from parted lips, his or mine, I can no longer tell. Our kiss deepens, pulling a groan from him. With eager hands, I start unbuttoning his shirt and untucking it from his trousers.

"Eager little thing, aren't you," he says with a chuckle, dragging his lips down my neck.

I tilt my head to the side to give him better access and peel his shirt over his shoulders and down his sculpted arms. I don't have time to properly appreciate his warm skin or how he's used it as a canvas for art. It's too dark, and I'm too impatient. "Tell me how you found me."

He pauses with his mouth on my pulse point. "I thought you knew a magician never—"

"Reveals his secrets," I finish for him. "I remember what you said. But I need to know how worried I should be. Will I wake up tomorrow with you inside my apartment?"

He nips my neck. "Of course not. You'll still be in my bed."

"How presumptuous of you." I trail my hands over him, marveling at the dips and grooves of his chest and abs. And oh my god, is that . . . an eight-pack? I slide the strap of his belt through the buckle and unzip his pants.

"Hopeful, maybe. Determined, even. But definitely—"

Impatience burns the back of my throat. "Kiss me, Romeo, or lose me forever."

It's not Shakespeare but one of those recognizable movie quotes, even if I adjusted it slightly. He drops his hands from my head and palms the back of my thighs. He picks me up with ease and walks us toward the bed. I wrap myself around him, keeping him pressed tightly against me.

The heat of his bare chest against my inner thighs makes my pussy clench. I sink my hands into his hair, tugging on the strands enough to elicit a groan. But he still doesn't kiss me.

Frustration wars with lust, fighting a battle inside my chest. How long will I let him hold out before I take charge?

He places me on top of the comforter, and I reluctantly let my legs fall open. I take my time sliding my hands from around his neck, marveling at the way he looks up close.

Keira would call him a *pretty boy*—the kind of man who's almost too good-looking. Classically handsome by today's modern standards.

Thin coils of wonder weave their way around my ribcage.

In a sea of eight million, he is the one who kept me from feeling lonely. And like I dreamt him to life, suddenly, he's here.

But fate demands balance. For every gift she gives, she takes something in return.

She gave me Romeo—but only for the weekend.

What if I found him four weeks ago instead of tonight?

I don't allow myself to wander down the *what if* path. It's dangerous and fruitless.

I arch my back, softly grinding against his cock. The pressure feels amazing, but it does nothing to quench the growing need inside of me. He makes this low sound from the back of his throat, and I reach for him. He dodges my hands, sliding down my body and falling to his knees.

My heart slams against my ribs, and I push to my elbows to watch him. "What are you doing?" My voice is breathy and hushed, an unrecognizable tone.

His hands land on my thighs, his thumbs wrapping around my calves. I jump at the contact, and he smiles at me. He holds my gaze as he smooths his hands upward, over my knees and thighs. He pauses an inch away from that sensitive area between my thighs and my pussy.

Lips parted, eyes wide, I stare at Romeo like I've never properly seen him until now. He holds my gaze with a mischievous glint in his eyes.

"I'm going to kiss you now, *mon chéri*." The heat of his whispered words warms the thin lace barrier between his mouth and my clit.

I dip my head in acknowledgment. His answering smile is pure sin, somehow both smooth and sharp. The sight of it sends my heart slamming against my ribs even harder.

He yanks my underwear off my body in one hard pull, and before I have time to appreciate the dominant move or the bite of the fabric on my skin, his mouth is on me. He licks me from my ass all the way to my clit, pausing to swirl around once before starting the journey over again.

"I will live in thy heart, die in thy lap, and be buried in thy eyes," he moans against my pussy, fucking devouring my cunt like it's his last meal.

I can't focus on his words when he pins my right knee to the bed with one hand, his fingertips digging into my thigh. His other hand spreads me open so he can better tease me. Tight, high-pitched noises fly from the back of my throat, and my hips start rocking at the same tempo.

I sink my hands into his hair, tugging on the strands hard enough to hurt. He grunts at the contact, but doesn't apply any more pressure.

"Please, Romeo," I beg.

I'm climbing that peak too early. I scrunch up my eyes, my toes curling into the comforter, and I try to slow my progression. I want it to last longer, to always feel the way he worships me with his tongue.

"What is it, *mon chéri?*"

"Don't stop." I roll my hips against his face, searching for more.

"I would never," he breathes against my clit.

I'm hurtling toward the edge of the cliff, and before I even jump, he slides two fingers inside my pussy and sucks in my clit. And I'm fucking gone. He shoves me off the cliff and I dissolve into a swirling, needy mass of nerve endings

I astral project, flying high as he tongue-fucks me through my orgasm. When I finally make it back to this plane, I open my eyes in time to catch him licking his fingers clean.

But it's not enough. I won't be satisfied until he fulfills every one of my fantasies that have been on repeat for weeks.

37

MAEVE

I WAKE up to midmorning sun streaming through gauzy curtains. A muscular, tattooed arm pins me to an unbelievably comfortable bed. Soft cream-colored sheets pool around my waist, and a gentle breeze from the ceiling fan rolls over my bare skin.

I squint open an eye and look around. I'm still in Romeo's hotel room somewhere in New York City.

We haven't come up for air except to eat our weight in room service and occasionally shower. Which always led to things that got us both sufficiently dirty.

That man's tongue is a gift from the universe itself.

And if I were any other girl in any other situation, I would close my eyes and roll over. Maybe even initiate another round.

But I'm not.

And I'm out of time.

I need to be in Camarillo tomorrow to start the wedding *festivities*, as ordered of me. Dress fitting, signing documents, and, you know, meeting my fucking betrothed.

I've put it off as long as I could, lived these last five weeks like

I promised Keira I would. I can't wait for her to hear about my weekend with my mysterious stalker turned lover?

Ugh, no. That makes me sound like some divorcee who seduces the young pool boy next door or something.

Acquaintance? No, that doesn't feel right either. We're a category of our own, one yet to be labeled.

Not that it matters, because as soon as I leave this hotel room, I'll never see or talk to Romeo again.

I listen to the steady cadence of his breathing for another minute, assured that he's still asleep. I don't want to have to lie to him, make up an excuse to slip out of the room for a coffee run or something. But I will.

He mumbles something in his sleep and rolls over, taking his arm off of me. I exhale and count to thirty before I slip out of bed. I grab the clothes closest to me which happen to be a pair of Romeo's black athletic shorts and his white tee.

I vaguely remember him rummaging around in his suitcase and throwing on the first clothes he could find to answer the door. He'd ordered us stuffed French toast and strips of bacon with freshly squeezed juice and lavender lattes.

My stomach rumbles at the thought of food, and I quicken my pace. I step into his shorts, roll down the waist a few times and tug the string taut to make them stay on my hips. His shirt hits me almost mid-thigh, but it's the least of my worries right now. I can't find my dress.

I spin around on the ball of my foot, looking for the swath of red fabric, and I can't see it anywhere. Shit. I don't want to leave it behind. It's too pretty to never wear again.

My internal clock is ticking, winding down in more ways than one, so I don't have the luxury of taking my time to search through the room to find it.

I release a frustrated breath and slip my purse over my head to rest across my chest and gather my shoes. There's no way I'm leaving these red-soled beauties behind.

I tiptoe to the door, pausing at the small table with two chairs. Romeo's phone and laptop sit in the center of the table, untouched for the entire weekend. I hesitate, two warring emotions swirling around inside my chest.

I should take his phone, smash it and scatter the broken pieces in the river along with mine on my way out of town. A clean, swift break.

If he found me once, he might be able to find me again, a nagging voice whispers in the back of my mind. It sounds an awful lot like my youngest sister.

I can't live my life on maybes though. I can only control what I do in the now. And right now, cutting ties with Romeo is the best decision for the both of us.

In a week, I'll be someone else's *wife*.

So whatever this is—whatever it could've been—doesn't matter. Not anymore.

After I walk out of this door, Romeo will be firmly slotted into the folder that I'll only reopen on those especially lonely nights. He'll sit pretty next to the two other reckless decisions I've made in the last couple of months.

I can't bring myself to regret any of it. Not Las Vegas or Chicago or anything I've done in my month in New York City.

But the time for living freely is over now. I have a role to play, and it's one of a lifetime.

No man, no matter how well he uses his dick *and* tongue, is worth jeopardizing my sisters' lives.

With the consequences of my father's agreement in the forefront of my mind, I swipe Romeo's phone, keys, and laptop off the table. There, bundled up on the seat of the chair, is my dress. I exhale a sigh and grab it by the fistful and tuck it under my arm.

I quietly hustle to the door, taking care to juggle everything in one arm while I open the door with the other. Slipping into the hallway, I allow myself one final look.

My heart clenches at the sight of him. Hair tousled from my fingers running through it all night, sculpted muscles decorated with swirls and fine lined artwork, and a fucking eight-pack. I ran my tongue through those grooves last night.

He's a total fucking catch, and I have to throw him back to sea like he's not worth keeping.

I ease the door shut, cutting off my view of him and stoking the embers of rage to life. They've cooled a bit since I've been here, more so in the last forty-eight hours.

Yet another item to add to Da's growing list of offenses.

ROMEO

I stretch my arms out to the side, fingers searching for the warmth of my Juliet. All I find are cool sheets. Half of my face is smushed into the pillow, so I crack one eye open.

Bright light sears my vision, and I slam my eye shut. Damn, I forgot to close the blackout blinds after I took her against the windows last night. Her naked silhouette against the backdrop of twinkling lights will go down as one of the most beautiful things I've ever seen.

Speaking of my gorgeous girl, I crawl my fingers over the sheets again, extending my arm as far as possible. I expect to find her soft skin, but I come up empty again.

I roll to my back with a groan, throwing my arm over my eyes to block out some of the light. Fuck it's bright early on the east coast.

There's a stillness in the room, a tangible absence. I already know she's gone before I look around. Still, I can't help but call out to her.

"Juliet?"

The low hum of the air conditioner is the only thing to greet me. I blow out a heavy breath and sit up, looking around the room.

Just as I assumed: no sign of my midnight-haired temptress.

A low laugh rumbles through my chest, and I drag my hand down my face. My girl is feeling playful, and lucky for her, I love a good puzzle.

The only question is how much of a head start should I give her?

Coffee and a quick breakfast. That's all I'll give her, then I'm dragging her ass back here. I've got nearly a week before I have to be back in Las Vegas. I plan to spend it between her thighs.

Fuck it. I'm too eager for her.

I need to find my phone. I remember checking it yesterday after we had dinner, but I don't remember where I left it. see it anywhere. I toss the comforter off of my lap and step over my discarded shoes toward the table. I lift up the trays and toss the napkins on the seat of the chair. Nothing.

Startling realization dawns slowly and then all at once. It washes over me in a cool wave, and on the heels is the kind of stunned disbelief.

"That tricky vixen," I murmur on a laugh.

She took my phone, my car keys, *and* my fucking laptop. I'm not worried about her accessing anything she shouldn't. Everything of mine is password protected within an inch of its life.

But it does throw a kink in my grand plans of a reunion today. Now I don't have the necessary equipment to find her. Which means I have to go home earlier than planned.

I shake my head, scratching at my scruff absentmindedly. I

was planning to find her regardless, but now? Now I'm on a fucking mission.

She should really know better than to wave a red flag in my face. I spent months looking for her, before I even knew the taste of her and noises she makes when she comes.

But now that I've had her, I'll never fucking let her go. Never.

I could have a lifetime with her and it would never be enough.

She can run to the ends of the earth, and I'll track that sweet ass down and give her another reminder of who she belongs to. She just doesn't realize it yet, but she will.

Next time I see her, I'm going to make damn sure she understands that I always play to win.

38

MAEVE

I'VE BEEN in Camarillo for three days, and I couldn't tell you a single thing I've done. It's been a blur of dress fittings with strangers poking and prodding me, unfamiliar faces of the women in the family hemming and hawing over my appearance, a sea of people claiming me as family and loudly discussing my ability to bear them sons for whatever fucked-up business their family is in.

I think Da mentioned they're into wine and guns. An interesting combination, if you ask me. Which no one has.

For three days, I've been surrounded by a swarm of my betrothed's family, chattering nonstop and refusing to let me get a word in. Not that I've tried that much.

It was all too easy to let them talk over and around me, to sink further into the swirling pit of anxiety that grows with each passing second.

And now it's time.

I slip out of the hotel room I've been in since I got here and take the back stairs to the parking garage. It's a nice enough hotel, but I can't help but compare it to the last one I stayed in.

With *him*.

This boutique hotel in Southern California is cozy chic with only fifty rooms on four floors. The décor is bright blues and greens with soft grays and rustic woods. The hallways are painted light gray with dark gray and navy patterned carpet.

It's not the décor that attracted the family to this hotel, it's the proximity to the church down the block. I overheard one of the great aunts talking about how all four hotels within a three block radius are sold out for the wedding, so I imagine it's going to be a full house.

It makes my plan so much more difficult but not impossible.

I walk halfway through the bottom level of the parking garage before I jump over the concrete half wall that runs along the first level. I quicken my pace four blocks to the south and one block east. I parked a conveniently borrowed SUV Ava arranged there on my way into town. It's my ticket for an easy getaway, if I need it.

And I have a sneaking suspicion I'll need it.

I double-check that my backup wallet, alternate ID, and fake passport are in the front pocket of my favorite bag. It's a slimline black backpack with rose gold stitching and flair. It's been with me almost as long as we started going on *family vacations*.

All of my sisters have one: a go bag. One easy-to-carry bag that you can grab quickly and get the hell out of dodge if you're pressed for time. To anyone else, it looks like a normal bag with the usual contents: wallet, hair ties, chapstick and lip gloss, a couple of those nearly-never-expiring energy bars, a change of clothes.

But that's hardly what makes it important, though all of those things have become essential a time or two.

No, what separates my bag from anyone else's bag is the false back sewn in.

Most backpacks have a cushioned back panel for comfort and

mine is no exception. But mine also has an entire secret compartment fitted in between the layers of padding. Passports with different names and countries of birth, money in a few different currencies, a couple slim profile burner flip phones, and a tiny black tracking device that only Rosie knows how to access.

I drop my backpack in the faux bottom of the drivers' seat, concealing it from any prying eyes. I make quick work of locking it up and getting back to my hotel room. I need to start getting ready if I'm going to be to the church on time. I just need to stop at the store around the corner on the way back, grab a few things to make my sudden errand believable.

While I have no intentions of actually starting a life with the slimy fuck—whatever his name is—I have to play the part. Am I being petty by refusing to acknowledge Milano's name? Probably. But I just don't fucking care right now.

A reluctant Irish mafia princess in an arranged marriage for the Syndicate.

It's easy enough to fake. They won't realize their mistake until the damage is done.

———————

THE WEDDING DRESS is heavier than I thought it would be. Layers of satin and tulle form a wide ballroom skirt. The chapel train sweeps eighteen inches behind me. A stunning look from behind, I'm told.

One of my two appointed attendants is in charge of bustling it up at the reception. I met them less than twenty-four hours ago, and I'm supposed to let them get underneath my dress without a blink.

The bodice is ivory satin, the neckline skimming my collarbone. It extends all the way to my wrists, but thankfully the fabric isn't overly tight along my arms. I already feel claustrophobic enough wearing it, if it were any tighter, I might cut them off before I walk down the aisle.

The material feels expensive with elaborate stitching, but the design is rather plain. The best feature is probably the back, where it dips into a low vee to my lower back.

But the best thing about this dress is the many, many layers in my skirt provide the perfect cover to hide things.

Sewing isn't my best skill, but I manage well enough. I tore off some satin from one of the layers closest to my legs and made them into two pockets. Then I sewed the pockets into the lining of my skirt.

I won't be able to easily access anything in them, but that's fine. Anything I need will be in my pre-approved wedding clutch. So I stuffed it full of everything I could. My wallet, a phone, a wedding emergency kit which is really just a bunch of things I can use to get myself out of a sticky situation. Plus my favorite lip gloss, cash, and the key to a car parked a few blocks away in a parking structure.

My passport and burner phone are in the interior pockets sewn in.

My phone buzzes on the vanity next to me. It's a new phone that I had Rosie overnight to me while I was traveling from New York. I had her scrub my other phone and send me all new replacements.

I glance down and see an incoming video call from Rosie. I take a deep breath and practice my best smile before swiping to answer.

All of my sisters' smiling faces stare at me from my phone screen.

"You look gorgeous," Rosie blurts.

I roll my eyes and lift a shoulder. "Don't act so shocked, Rosie."

"Puh-lease. I know you're a total smokeshow, sis, but like,

damn." Rosie drags out the last word and gives it a different inflection.

It works as she intended to, I'm sure, and a wide smile spreads across my face. "I mean, I guess I look pretty good for a girl who's getting fake married today."

I meant it as a joke, but none of my sisters are laughing. In fact, the smiles they were sporting earlier slip from their faces, dropping low into frowns.

Heat prickles along the back of my neck. "C'mon, it was just a joke."

"Yeah, but was it? I mean, you really are marrying him, Maeve," Fiona says.

I stare at my blue-eyed sister and try to figure out where she is. The background is dark behind her—behind all of them, really. It's just as well. I'm sure they wouldn't be casually chatting with me if they were in trouble.

"In name only, Fi."

My assurance doesn't help and Fiona shakes her head a little.

"And if he wants to consummate?" Rosie asks.

Ava leans to the left and raises her brows with a low whistle. "Damn, in college for a week and already using ten-cent words."

"Whatever. It's a valid question." Rosie rolls her eyes.

I shake my head. "I'm not going to let it get that far."

"Say the word, Maeve, and we're there," Ava says.

"Yeah, we're right here, Maeve," Keira says. Her voice sounds weird, almost like it's in surround sound. "Like right here."

I whirl around at the distinct sound of my sister's voice behind me.

Blonde hair piled high on top of her head and dressed in head-to-toe black, my younger sister stands in front of me, waggling her phone with our video chat.

"Keira!" I push to my feet and launch myself the three steps to reach her, throwing my arms around her neck.

"Surprise!" She rocks back on her heels, wrapping her arms around me.

We stand like that for a few quiet moments, the two of us squeezing each other tight. To my absolute horror, my sinuses start to tingle and my eyes fill with tears.

I didn't realize how much I needed someone here. No not someone—one of my sisters.

"Uhm, hello? Did you forget about us?"

I pull back with a watery laugh, resting my hands on her shoulders. I scan her face for anything out of place, but all I find is her whiskey-colored eyes darkening by the second.

"Why are you crying? I know you said you didn't want us here because it's not a real wedding, but we all agreed that was total bullshit. So we pulled the sister card," Keira says.

Another soft laugh bubbles up and I squeeze her shoulders. "Of course you did."

The sister card was something we made up when we were younger when someone was being stubborn and petulant. Mum used to tell us when the times we refused a hug from her were the times we needed it most.

"Now tell me what's wrong," she demands.

"Yeah, but come back over here when you do because it's hard to hear you two," Rosie says from my phone behind us.

I turn around and swipe my middle fingers underneath my eyes, catching any smudged makeup. I plaster a smile on my face and face three of my sisters on the small screen. "Nothing's wrong."

I settle back into the cherry-wood-colored wicker chair and look at Keira. "I thought you were back home with Ava?"

"I'm in Monaco with some friends, remember?" Ava says.

"That's right. I forgot."

Keira drags the other over and places it next to mine. She sinks into it with a soft thud and pockets her phone. "You've been understandably busy, but after this, I'm taking you with me. We'll meet up with Ava for a bit. Sister trip."

"Hey, what about me?" Fiona's voice pitches higher than normal.

"Not cool, Keira," Rosie says at the same time.

I can't help the smile that tips up the corners of my mouth. In an ironic twist, hearing their good-natured bickering settles my nerves more than anything could.

The conversation devolves from there, laughter between half-hearted teasing and well-wishes for me. Anyone overhearing might believe they're intended for my wedding. But we all know what they're really for, and that's enough for now.

"Okay. I'm walking down the aisle soon, and I need to get to the bridal suite at least twenty minutes beforehand. I need to finish getting ready." Regret thickens my tongue.

"We love you, Maeve. Call me the moment you can," Ava says.

"It better be a video call because I will be tracking your phone to make sure you're okay," Rosie says.

"Love you, Maeve. I'll see you soon, okay?" Fiona worries her bottom lip as she stares at me.

"I love you all. So, so much." I kiss my fingers, lean forward, and press them to the screen.

All three of them mimic the movement at the same time Keira leans her head on my bare shoulder.

"Love you, bye," they all say in unison.

The call disconnects, and I stare at the home screen of my phone. The background is a Polaroid of the five of us at a carnival from a few years ago.

"I love you for coming, but you have to leave."

Keira lifts her head from my shoulder, and I look over at her.

I make sure to keep my expression soft, locking up my panic somewhere under my ribs.

"Maeve, I'm not leaving. The whole point of being here is to *be here*."

I clasp her hands in mine. "I know. But when I take the elevator downstairs toward the small skywalk to the church, you need to take the one at the opposite end of the hall to the lobby and walk out of here. I mean it. I already told them that all my sisters couldn't leave the country—our country—so if any one of the family sees you here, they'll know I was lying. And the goal is to have the least amount of suspicion as possible."

Her gaze ping-pongs between mine before she dips her chin once. "Alright. But I'm staying until you get in that elevator."

"Thank you." I release her hands and pull her in for a hug. "Who else is going to help me touch up my makeup?"

Her laughter tickles the loose hair around my neck, and I give her an extra squeeze.

"You laugh but I wasn't kidding. C'mon." I pull back and stand up, holding out my hand to her. She places her hand in mine and follows me across the room to the bathroom.

39

MAEVE

I TUCK my small stick of perfume on the top of my makeup bag. I zip it closed and toss it next to my peach-and-pink quilted toiletries bag. It's this loud print that screams my youngest sister, which is fitting since she gifted it to me last Christmas.

"It's not too late, you know. We can come up with a different plan." Keira's voice is low, just above a whisper.

Her determination brings a rueful smile to my face. It was exactly the thing I didn't know I needed to hear.

"There's no other plan but this one. It'll be fine. It'll all be fine." The last few words are quieter, and I'm not sure if they're more for her or me.

"Okay, I'm going to use the restroom before I take off then. Since you insist on me missing your nuptials."

"You know how I feel."

"I know, I know, but I had to try again," she says, disappearing into the bathroom.

I press my palms flat against the cool countertop and lift my head to stare at my reflection in the large vanity mirror.

Keira's the kind of naturally beautiful that doesn't require any makeup—all my sisters are really, but she has that effortlessly gorgeous look. Of course, she's amazing at makeup too.

Stress has left its mark on me physically. Darkened half-moons have claimed permanent residence underneath my eyes. I feel like I haven't slept in weeks even though I got a solid five hours last night.

I've never been the kind of person who needs nine hours of sleep, but seven is my sweet spot. And I can't remember the last time I got seven hours of sleep.

Without preamble, my mind conjures up images of the last good night's sleep I've had in years.

Romeo curled around me after he fucked me into a sleepy haze. The post-orgasmic bliss faded quicker than I'd hoped it would.

A knock on the bathroom door shatters the memories playing like a highlight reel behind my eyelids. I blink my lashes open, the warm, fuzzy memories scattering away like dandelion fuzz on the breeze. I don't even remember closing my eyes.

"Maeve?" she calls from inside the bathroom

I have to clear my throat before I can answer. "Yeah?"

"I got my period early, so I need to borrow a tampon."

I nod even though she can't see me. My fingers splay wide on the countertop, the pad of each finger digging into the hard surface. "Got it. Let me grab you one."

I push off the counter and go to my open suitcase on my bed. I rummage around through the toiletries side of my bag. I remember packing a whole box of tampons because I was expecting my period that second week in New York.

Did I forget them at our apartment?

My fingers brush over the cardboard box underneath a beach waver curling wand. Ah, here they are. I snag the box, untangling the cord as I go and yell, "Got them. Hang on a second."

I pick up my skirts and hustle the box to the bathroom. The

sooner she leaves, the better. I don't want her getting caught up in this.

I knock on the bathroom door and stick the box in. "Here you go."

She grabs the box from me with a murmur, "Ooh a fresh box?"

I adjust my skirts and fluff my hair for the tenth time. Keira comes out a moment later.

"Uh, Maeve?"

"Hm?" I ask distractedly.

"These are from back home. I recognize the brand from the corner store we go to. How long have you had these?"

"They're not that old. I just got them a few months ago," I say, trailing off. A swell of pure ice washes over me, and my head spins.

"Oh my god, are you okay? You just got really pale. Have you eaten anything today?"

Her questions are rapid-fire, but they bounce right off of me. I'm stuck on one alarming fact, blaring in my brain like a megaphone.

"Maeve? Talk to me. Want me to go grab you some juice or a muffin?"

I look from the floor to my sister's face. Concern etches in the lines around her beautiful eyes. I reach out and grab her forearm. "I need you to run to the pharmacy. There's one around the corner."

She's nodding before I even finish my request. "Of course, tell me what you need. Allergy medicine? Aspirin? Antacid—"

"A pregnancy test."

40

ROMEO

WIND SWEEPS in through Tommy's open window, a witness to us *before*. It dances between the three of us, lifting my hair and sending a chill down my back. Our hands are far from clean, but they've never been quite so bloody as they will be this afternoon.

I can't shake the idea that we're on a precipice here, straddling the line. But it's not as easy as good and evil, it's murkier and muddled with moral dilemmas.

The silence weighs heavy between us, expanding to take up every inch of available space. I run the pad of my index finger along my bottom lip, a tic that I can't seem to shake ever since her lips touched mine.

Thoughts of her are my escape, distracting me. If I were a better man, I might be inclined to think of her as my salvation. But I'm not that naïve. And nothing in this world can save me. I've accepted my fate.

I wonder what she's doing right now. If she's thinking of me. If she recalls our time together as often as I do. It's been only days since I've tasted her, and I already miss it. I thought I'd be able to find her before we had to complete Father's task, but she's living up to her potential and making me work for it.

My lips twist to the side with a perverse sort of realization: even on the way to execute a horrendous order from our father, she still invades my thoughts.

She's a Valkyrie, a harbinger of justice.

I slide my phone out of my pocket. It's one of my secondary ones, a burner phone that I only use to contact one person.

Hitting the button on the side to light up the home screen, I will myself not to let the pang of disappointment pierce my chest.

It's been days since she left me in New York City.

Days since we last spoke or texted.

When I got home, I tracked her sim card down and mine, but they both shorted out somewhere in the middle of the river. I knew she would dump them—it's what I would do.

And the first thing I'm going to do when we get back home is catch a flight back to New York City and go find my girl. If I know my girl, and I like to think I do, I'm betting she's still there, hiding in plain sight, probably waiting for me to find her.

And if she's not, I don't mind. I'm excellent at hunting.

It's been a while since I faced a challenge as complex as her. It'll make our reunion all that more rewarding.

The four-hour car ride through the desert has been quiet, and not that comfortable kind either. It's the kind full of expectations and dreaded anticipation. What's more curious is that neither of my brothers felt inclined to fill it either.

Nic pulls into a narrow driveway, the blacktop cracked wide enough for weeds to spring up. He shifts it into park and turns off the car.

No one moves to get out yet.

I look between the two of them. "Are we sure this is the only way?"

Nic swallows, the action audible in the quiet of the car. "It's the only way to win his trust, to play his game."

"We should've just fucking killed him when we had the chance," Tommy murmurs. There's no heat in his words. He's not hurling accusations or blame, just working through this shitty situation the best he can.

I glance at my brothers, my gut churning with worry. I can't really see them from back here, only the back of Tommy's head and Nic's profile, but I don't need to see their faces to know they're both seeped in guilt and shame.

Our bond was forged through more than just siblinghood. Being Vito Santorini's sons gave us all front row seats to horrors no one should ever have to witness, let alone participate in.

Because we had each other, we not only survived, we shattered the glass ceiling of the gilded cage Dad kept us in.

At least, I thought we did. It wasn't until last night that I realized how wrong I was.

We didn't break out of our cage—he just built us a bigger one without us realizing it.

And here we are, flying in circles again, puppets on his string.

"He knew we were trying to kill him, Tommy. Somehow," Nic reminds him.

"Then we should've taken him out at the house then. Something—anything would be better than this," Tommy grumbles.

I shake my head. "It's not that simple. What about Mom? She's innocent in all of Dad's dealings, and she would've gotten swept up in it," I remind him.

Tommy lifts a shoulder and looks out the window. "She's made her choice many times over the years."

"Maybe, but between the security and staff at the house, it was too many eyes and ears to manage. You know his death had to appear random, something we can easily explain to the Outfit as a random act of violence. We don't have their favor, not yet," Nic says.

I nod a few times, reluctantly impressed with Dad's manipulation tactics. "Which is probably another one of Dad's brilliant plans: keep you away from the big Outfit dealings, keep you hidden. Keep you *small.*"

"Well it doesn't fucking matter now because this is where we are. Sending dozens, maybe hundreds, of innocents to early graves."

Thick, oppressive shame wraps around my shoulders like one of those gaudy fur shawls women love to wear at the high-roller's tables.

Frustration looks different on everyone, and my brothers wear theirs disguised as rage, tied tightly around their necks.

"What makes our lives better than any of theirs?" Nic mutters.

I stare out my window, my gaze unfocused. A dark thought slithers through my consciousness, the kind that might make my brothers look at me differently if I voice.

Fuck it.

"And if what Dad says is true? If those assholes are running narcotics and women from Mexico to Canada and trying to use Las Vegas as a shortcut and to wash cash? This could be a good thing."

"Don't be so naïve, Rome," Nic snaps at me.

I rake my fingers through my hair, pushing it off my forehead. "I'm not. I'm being as impartial as I can. But what's the alternative?" I pause, waiting for an answer that we haven't found yet. "We say no to his demands, and then he kills one of us. It sets a precedent, and before long, he'll take all of us out. And then there's nothing between him and our sisters. Who will protect them if we're gone? Not our mother."

I lean into my bitterness and let it fuel my ire and hatred for not only our father but the position he put us in. His loyal *soldiers*.

"We've been reduced to doing his bidding like fucking lapdogs," Tommy grits through clenched jaw.

"So our sisters are better than these innocent people?" Nic counters.

"Are they innocent though? If they're running guns and skin from one end of the continent to the other, they have more blood on their hands than Dad does," I say.

Nic's gaze clashes with mine in the rearview mirror. "Are you *actually* trying to talk us into killing a roomful of people? Who the fuck *are you* right now?"

I scoff. "Of course I'm not. I'm saying we make some adjustments to Dad's grand plan while still delivering results. Buy us some fucking time so we don't have to worry about Tommy sacrificing himself again." I glare at the back of his head, but all he does is lift his shoulders high before dropping them again.

"I stand by my choice, but that was yesterday, little brother. Today is a new day, so *c'est la vie*," Tommy says.

Nic drums his fingers on the steering wheel, a fast-paced pattern. "I'm listening."

I lean forward between the two seats and look out the front windshield. "We'll need to make a few stops to get everything we need."

41

MAEVE

I'VE NEVER BEEN MORE thankful to have my sisters surprise me in my entire life. I don't know what I would do if Keira wasn't here—wasn't able to run around the corner to the pharmacy.

I haul my eighteen layers of tulle and satin in my right arm and pace the length of the hotel room. Twenty-two steps from the doorway to the window and back again. I kick off the ridiculously high satin white vintage style heels, flipping them toward the dresser along one wall.

A tidal wave of warmth rolls over my head, spilling down my chest and arms and sinking all the way to my toes. I dig them into the plush carpet as sweat breaks out along the back of my neck.

"Fuck, it's hot in here. Did the heat kick on?" I swipe my hair over my shoulder and divert from my path to the thermostat on the wall. I bump the air conditioning down, and almost immediately, the fan kicks on and pours cool air in the room.

And then I continue pacing. Back and forth, over and over again as my mind fractures.

I've had unpredictable periods my entire life, so this—this is no different. Just my hormones playing Connect Four inside my body, making me panic for nothing.

Have I had sex recently? Yes, I have. But I used protection each time.

Didn't I?

My inner monologue of thoughts sounds shaky—fearful. A sharp pain lances across my temple. Fuck, I can't remember. I was caught up, angry at Da and cursing the world, and things got out of hand.

I press my fingertips to my temple, easing some of the pain. No, no that doesn't make sense. I used condoms all weekend with Romeo. I know I would've used them with . . . the other two.

And holy fucking shit. I had sex with Santorini *and* a stranger in the same weekend.

Oh my god. My pulse beats wildly inside my veins as I fucking panic-spiral closer and closer into the abyss.

I take a deep breath through my nose, trying to calm myself down. The panic soaks up the walls around me, growing larger with every erratic beat of my heart.

I'm incredibly stressed too, and I know that's a big one. Stress can take its toll on a woman's body, messing up all kinds of things.

I nod to myself, a frantic tipping of my chin as my speed increases. Yes, that sounds right. It's just stress, I'm sure that's it.

There's a beep and a moment later, the hotel door swings open. My sister barges into the room, a white plastic bag swinging from her hand.

I rush her, snatching the bag from her hands and running to the bathroom. I don't even bother closing the door before I try to gather the skirt up high enough to pee on a fucking stick.

I huff, my chest pinkening with my increasing panic. Sweat coats my entire body like some disgusting onesie, and I want it off.

"Maeve?"

Panic wraps around my throat like a boa constrictor, coiling tighter and tighter. I gasp for air, ignoring my sister's voice. I can't think. I can't focus with this fucking dress on.

I drop the plastic bag to the floor, the contents spilling all over the heated marble tile. I don't care though. I don't care that my sister bought four different tests from four different brands because she's fucking thorough and knew I'd want a second and third opinion.

The only thing I can focus on is getting air into my lungs. Black spots dance in my vision as I claw at the back of the dress. My fingers search for the hidden zipper behind the row of fake buttons, but it's too low. I can't reach the pull tab.

I grasp the buttons and start pulling until I hear the unmistakable sound of fabric ripping.

My sister's in front of me in an instant, her hands on my shoulders. She shakes me a little, and it snaps my gaze to her. Some of the haze eases from my senses enough to hear her.

Her eyebrows are drawn together to form a little vee above her eyes. "Hey, hey, hey. I'll get you out of the dress, okay? Just stop for a second."

"Hurry, Keira, I can't breathe in this thing," I rasp.

She spins me around and a moment later, cool air greets my overheated skin. I wiggle the dress down my hips and let it pool on the floor. I stand in the middle of it in my black lace panties and matching strapless bra, my favorite thin blade strapped to my thigh. I tip my head back, gulping in air like I've been underwater for too long.

Keira's hand rubs soothing circles on my back. And the touch is so comforting, tears prick my eyes.

"I'm all sweaty," I murmur. It's a half-hearted protest to her affection.

"You're my sister."

345

She's so matter of fact, like those three words are the explanation for everything. My sinuses burn, and I press my hand to my mouth to keep the tears inside.

"What if I'm pregnant, Keira?" It's barely louder than a whisper. I'm not usually superstitious, but this feels different. Like maybe if I don't say it loud enough, it won't be real.

She widens her comforting circles on my back. "Then we'll figure it out. Whatever you want to do, we'll do it together. But we won't know until you take a test."

My lower lip trembles, and I whisper, "I'm scared."

She wraps her arms around me, resting her chin on the space between my neck and arm. "Maeve King is scared of nothing and no man. You're just nervous, but you don't have to be. I'll be with you the whole time."

I sniff and nod a few times. "You're right. I am a total badass."

She chuckles. "Want my help?"

I shake my head. "I'll be alright. But don't go too far, yeah?"

She squeezes me in a half-hug before she lets go. "I'll be right outside. Just holler if you need anything, okay?"

I wait until I hear the snick of the door closing to turn around. I step out of the pool of fabric and scoop up all of the tests from the ground.

A SOFT KNOCK on the door startles me out of my stupor.

"Maeve? Everything okay in there?" Keira calls.

I clear my dry throat. "I'm fine."

"It's been fifteen minutes. Can I come in?"

"Aye." I scoop up the plastic bag from the ground and gather all the packaging and instructions and stuff them into the bag.

"Well?" She approaches me with an open expression, her steps hesitant.

I tip my chin toward the counter without saying anything, placing the plastic bag on the shelf next to the bathtub.

Keira stares at the four little sticks of plastic in a neat row. "Holy shit," she says on a quiet gasp.

I step back into the heap of satin and tulle and start the tedious process of shimmying it up my legs and over my hips. "Can you help me zip this up? I need to get to the bridal suite soon."

"Hey," she says, reaching out to grasp my arm. Her eyes are wide and bright, a smile playing along the corners of her mouth. "You're pregnant."

"Aye, I know."

Her gaze scans my face, her lips tilting into a frown. "Is this— is this not a good thing?"

I bite the inside of my cheek between my molars, letting my gaze drift away. I—I don't know how to feel about it. It's unexpected, not unwelcome, but the timing couldn't have been worse. All I know is that my plan is no longer an option.

I've always run our little flock like a democracy. No, more than a democracy—a collaborative committee of badass women righting the many, many wrongs of the world one day, one move at a time.

But not this time. I can't.

Guilt and shame curdle the latte I had for breakfast, sloshing my insides around like a busted pinball machine. Never in all my years since we started this have I withheld any information from them. And I'm about to ask Keira to break that same unspoken vow for me.

Because I can't tell them. Not yet.

One of them will try to intervene somehow or throw a Hail Mary and swap places with me.

And I can't let that happen either.

I only see one way to get through it. And I'm going to need Keira's help.

I spin to face my sister, clutching the wrinkled remains of my wedding dress around my waist. She leans against the counter, tentative joy lightening her features.

My own joy yearns to break out and join her, like two sunflowers searching for the sun. But I can't allow myself to feel such hope, not until I'm free of this mess.

"I slept with three men in the last six weeks, Keira. Three verifiable strangers. And I'm supposed to be walking down the aisle to a man I've never even seen before in an hour. So I really don't know how to answer that." I pause, and then rush to say, "It's not a bad thing though."

Keira whistles under her breath. "Damn, sis, you really took the *live your life* speech I gave you to heart, huh?"

A smile cracks through my pursed lips.

Keira shifts from one foot to the other. "What? Rosie's not here to break the tension and make you smile, so I had to."

"I'm the worst for asking this of you, but I need your help."

"Anything," she says quickly.

"And you can't tell anyone. Not even our sisters."

She swallows and straightens up. "I trust you, Maeve."

I clasp my hand over hers and squeeze it. "Thank you, Keira."

She flips her hand around and squeezes mine right back. "What do you need?"

"First, I need your help getting back in this dress. I have a small sewing kit somewhere in the room. It doesn't need to be perfect, just passable. And then I need you to raid the maintenance shed for potassium nitrate."

Her lips part before they slowly curve into a grin. "You want me to make a bomb."

348

42

MAEVE

I ADJUST the long lace veil along my hair as I look at my reflection in the seven-foot rectangular mirror propped against one wall of the bridal suite. Keira was able to sew one seam shut and put a few buttons back on, enough that no one should notice.

My lipstick is a deep, bold red, not too different from the color I've left in dozens of homes over the last several years. I thought it was a fitting nod to who I was.

I'm not sure if I'll ever be her again. Too much has changed, too quickly and without warning.

I feel a little adrift, three of my four tethers to this world too far away to appreciate the tautness of our bonds. Intellectually, I know they're only a plane ride and a phone call away, but I'm feeling melancholy and anxious.

As I suppose I should, considering my sister is placing four smoke bombs in strategic areas around a church. The same church I'll be walking down the aisle in today. The very loose plan is to herd everyone toward the front while I slip out the back. I already scouted the church yesterday with one of the wedding coordinators since I wasn't allowed to see the groom before the wedding. Some bullshit Milano family tradition.

I'm glad for it now.

I hear the soft notch of the handle turning and the door opening before Keira's slipping into the suite. I rush to my feet.

"Did it go okay?"

She grins, a dirt smudge above her left brow. "Aye. Four smoke bombs—without color— around the nave and one baby bomb on a timer in the back." She hands me a burner phone. "Here. It's already programmed. All you have to do is hit one and the call button, once the call connects, it'll start the timer. So make sure you're long gone before then, yeah?"

I tuck the phone in my right pocket with a nod. "Aye, this isn't my first time with a bomb. I'm just not as familiar with them as you are."

We all learned the basics during childhood, something Mum wove into our games of spy. But I never enjoyed explosives, not like Keira does.

"You're lucky I know my way around a maintenance shed *and* how to improvise." She grins and rocks back on her heels.

"You're amazing, and I love you," I say, wrapping my arms around her.

She hugs me back and murmurs, "I can stay, you know. Wait for you around the block or something."

"No. I won't be able to concentrate knowing you could be in danger," I say, not letting her go yet. I squeeze my eyes closed and exhale, trying in vain to dislodge the weight on my shoulders.

"How did we get here?" I murmur, squeezing her to me tighter.

"I don't know." Her voice is quiet, contemplative.

"I was going to go through with it, ya know? Get married to the fucking Milano gun-running winemaker, let a few months go by, and then slip some thallium in his drink. He'd have a heart attack, I'd be a widow, and all of you would be safe."

"It's not your job to take the fall for us. We're all old enough to take care of ourselves and *each other*, Maeve. Lean on us."

Her words of comfort soothe me a little, but it doesn't just erase two decades' worth of feelings about looking after them and the responsibilities that followed. I glance at the ornate clock on the wall behind her. "I know. It's time for you to go."

She squeezes me once more and pulls away. "Call me the moment you're able."

"I will, I promise."

"Good. Then I want the full story about what really happened in New York City."

I laugh, just as she intended me to. "Maybe," I concede.

"Love you, bye," she sings with a wink before slipping out as quietly as she came in.

Five minutes later, there's a knock on the door. "They're ready for you, Miss King."

I recognize the wedding coordinator's voice. "Just a moment," I call out, giving myself one more cursory look. I exhale and drop my shoulders, lifting my head up high.

I open the door and step in the dim hallway. Soft candlelight illuminates the small room at the back of the church. The ivory wax drips down the sides and lands in a small puddle on the stone floor.

A sweeping bouquet of white roses and baby's breath lays on the small table beside the door, waiting for me.

The double set of wooden doors are closed, but it doesn't block out the murmuring of all the people on the other side.

"Wow, Miss King. You look phenomenal," the wedding coordinator gushes.

"Thank you." I offer her a tight-lipped smile.

"They're just about ready for you if you want to take this." She hands me the bouquet.

The music inside swells to a crescendo. I don't really recognize the song, since it's not the traditional wedding march. But I suppose when you're getting married under unconventional circumstance, you can play whatever song you want.

My fingers tremble as they wrap around the bouquet. It's surprisingly heavy, the arrangement almost as wide as I am. The fragrance tickles my nose, and I fight the urge to sneeze. My heart slams against my ribs, doing its best impression of a collegiate drumline.

"It's okay to be nervous, Miss King. Just keep your eyes straight ahead and don't lock your knees at the altar, okay?"

I nod and exhale. I can do this.

She smiles at me, a genuine grin. And for a moment, I feel bad for the trauma she'll undoubtedly face today. But if it's between me and my sisters and her? I pick them. I always pick them.

Except for today. It's the most selfish thing I've ever done, and yet, I can't make myself not do it.

Today, I'm picking me.

The music changes to something slower, and the crowd quiets. A moment later, the double doors open and all eyes are on me.

But I only have eyes for the person at the end of the aisle.

Dark hair, bewitching blue eyes, dressed in a gold-and-cream colored chasuble.

Romeo.

43

MAEVE

THE TIPS of my white Doc Martens peek through the layers of lace as I quickly walk down the aisle. I ignore the hushed words from the wedding coordinator to slow down. Shock quickens my steps and the possibility of betrayal strengthens them.

The bridal bouquet hangs limply from my hands, the blooms pointing toward the floor instead of the ceiling. I ignore the hundreds of eyes on me, doing my best to tune out their commentary.

I forget everything I'm supposed to be doing: how fast I should be walking, how I'm supposed to go slow so no one sees I swapped those awful heels for my favorite boots, how I should be looking at the groom and not the priest.

Confusion bleeds into anger. Every step I'm closer to him, the hotter my temper rises.

How did he find me? What is he doing here? Was this all part of some elaborate scheme?

What the fuck is going on?

I'm at the altar in a blink. My eyes weren't playing tricks on me. Romeo, my Romeo, is standing in front of me.

He winks one ocean-blue eye at me. "*Mon chéri.* Have I mentioned how stunning you look in white?"

"I thought you preferred red," I hiss, leaning toward him and lowering my voice.

"White, red, nothing—you're exquisite in everything you wear."

I step toward him. "What are you doing here, Romeo?"

"Wait a fucking minute, here. This is *my* bride and you're the fucking priest," the guy across from me says.

He's a few inches taller than me with thinning black hair slicked back with enough gel for an entire high school dance team. He's wearing a black peak lapel tuxedo that's two sizes too big—boxy in the shoulders and the sleeves too long. His clip-on black batwing bowtie is crooked, and his shoes look straight out of a Christmas movie with elves—pointed and curved upward at the end.

I cut him a glare, jerking my head so fast, my neck spasms. But apparently the infamous King glare isn't as effective on pampered little mama's boys who act like they're tough shit.

Do I sound bitter inside my own head?

Yeah, that tracks for my day.

Milo Milano clamps his hand around my arm, right above my elbow, in a punishing grip. He jerks me back a step, away from Romeo and closer to him.

"Now you listen to me, you little cunt. I don't give a fuck how you know the priest here. I paid a pretty penny to your daddy for a compliant little wife." He jerks me harder, my shoulder bumping into his chest. "Starting now, you keep your fucking mouth shut. I won't have you embarrassing me in front of the family. *Capisce?*"

I yank on my arm, jerking my body backward. After the third time, I rip free of his grip, gritting my teeth at the pain of his fingernails digging into my arm.

My fingers tremble with the overwhelming desire to grab my knife strapped to my thigh and embed it in his eye. Instead, I'm granted another boon from the universe.

Murmuring from the people behind us picks up, loud enough that Milano and I are forced to break our stare-off.

He looks over his shoulder first. "What the fuck is that?"

I barely have time to look when strong arms wrap around my middle.

"Time to go, Juliet," Romeo murmurs against the back of my hair.

"I'm not going anywhere with you. I don't fucking trust you," I snarl, twisting out of his grip.

His hands get tangled in the wide arms of his chasuble, and I'm able to slip free just as the second smoke bomb goes off.

"Are you trying to take my wife?" Milano roars before he launches himself at Romeo. The two of them end up in a tangled heap on the floor in what looks more like wrestling than fighting.

"I'm not your fucking wife," I snarl. I doubt he can hear me over the grunting and shitty punches he's throwing. But I didn't say it for his benefit, I said it for me.

Encouragement and a reminder rolled into one.

I need to get out of here.

The crowd of people leap to their feet and start yelling and pushing one another out of the pews. Cries and yelps harmonize in the space, the yelling bouncing off the acoustics in this old church.

The third and fourth smoke bombs go off one right after the other, and I feel my internal clock winding down again.

I drop my bouquet to the group, pick up my dress by the armful, and hop off of the altar. There aren't any windows to open to let any of the smoke out, so it's getting thicker by the moment. But it's doing its job: distracting and herding the people in the opposite direction from where I need to go.

Instead of heading toward the front steps, I round the corner and beeline for the bridal chamber. At the end of the other hall is my escape route.

The church shudders, debris falling from the walls and I skid to a stop in the middle of the hallway. I cock my head to the side and listen. A low groan, and another shudder. It sounds almost like thunder, but only if the storm was right above us.

What's happening? This isn't part of my plan. I don't even know what would cause an old brick church to shimmy like that.

Then I hear a noise that has the breath whooshing from my lungs: gunfire. The rapid pop, pop, pop splits the air, swiftly followed by screaming.

What the fuck is Romeo doing?

The staggering realization that I don't actually know anything about him hits me square in the chest. I don't even know his last name.

Another low boom sounds nearby, but it's impossible to tell if I'm running toward something or away from it?

I do the only thing I can. I *run*.

Sounds of an all-out war punctuate the smokey air, and I turn the corner too sharply. I lose my balance and slip on the train of my dress. I slam against the stone floor with a grunt, my hip taking most of the impact.

"Fucking hell that hurts," I murmur, panting.

Gathering my skirts in my arms, I take off running again. There, at the end of the hall, is my ticket to freedom. Hope springs to life on my tongue, tasting like fresh strawberries and cream.

My chest heaves with big, deep breaths. It feels like I can't get enough air in my lungs, but I don't have time to work through an anxiety episode right now.

My actual life is on the line.

A low groaning noise splits the air, and the building shakes. Dirt and debris fall from the ceiling and the top of the walls. For a half-second, I worry that it's Keira playing the white knight, but I dismiss the idea almost as quickly as it comes. She would never set off something this big with me still inside.

Besides, it sounds like there's an army outside. And while Keira thirsts for vengeance harder than the rest of us, she's not a fan of baseless violence.

I reach the door at the end of the hallway, sweat beading on my brow and chest heaving. I yank the wrought-iron handle and tug, but it doesn't budge.

"Fuck," I snap and then try shoving it open with my weight in my hip. It opens with a groan, and I breathe the smallest sigh of relief.

There's a large window on the upper half of the wall across from the door. I'm going to crawl out of that window and hope that whoever is shooting stays away from this side of the church.

I spin around the room, spotting a bronze metal folding chair in the corner. I drag it underneath the window and open it up.

I do my best to tune out the gunshots and low rumbles. But my adrenaline is pumping too hard, and my hands shake as I try to unlatch the window.

Seconds feel like an eternity, and all I keep thinking about is what would happen if I die in here. Would my sisters be safe? Who would look out for them if I'm not around?

And what about me? If I died today, I'd never get the opportunity to welcome this little bean into the world, I think as I briefly cradle my lower stomach with my hand.

Finally, I'm able to unlock it. I slide open the window and stick my head out to see how high up we are. Six or seven feet, if I had to guess. The sparse bushes don't look like they'd break my fall much, but it's not too high.

For a moment, everything stops. The rumbling, the gunfire, even the screams seem to go quiet. The hair on my arm stands on end, and my instincts are screaming at me to get the hell out of here right now.

My veil gets stuck in the window, and I blindly reach up to yank it free—of the window or my hair, I don't care. My hands are shaking so hard that it takes me three tries to find the clips to wrench it free.

I lean out of the window when I hear a different sort of groan. It's the kind of noise ships make when they brush up against rocks. A low, creaking, death rattle of a groan.

Nausea climbs up my throat, fear turning my veins into Pop Rocks, sparking over and over again.

I'm so close to freedom, I can taste it on the back of my tongue. Tangy and coppery and bittersweet.

I'm going to get the chance do all the things my own mum wasn't able to do. To make my own traditions with my own family.

I send a prayer up to a god I don't believe in, begging for Romeo's safety, and throw a leg over the windowsill.

And then the building explodes.

44

TOMMY

WHEN ROME SUGGESTED his grand plan earlier, I admit, I had my reservations. But I have no problem admitting when something works either. And our baby brother came fucking through with this plan.

Dozens and dozens of people have poured through the open doors of St. Anne's Catholic Church.

Nic and I have systematically taken out all the men, including the high-ranking officers of the Milano family.

It's exactly what Vito demanded of us, but Rome found a loophole, so at least the women and children are spared. My hands are eternally stained with blood, I have no desire to add the heavy weight of innocent blood to my soul, as black and tarnished as it is.

I notch my favorite gun against the open window of the old Ford truck we liberated from a grocery store parking lot earlier today. It's light to carry and easy to break down. Plus, I've never missed a target, not once, including today.

Vito gave us orders to wipe out the Camarillo family at some wedding, but I like Rome's plan better. We still take them out, but only the men. Only the ones in the family.

Plus, Rome's got a sweet little costume to wear today.

I have no idea what Rome did inside, other than play pretend as the priest. But whatever he did, it worked.

Smoke pours from the open doors, billowing out into the afternoon sun. I don't remember fire on the list, but maybe he blew something up inside.

Catholic churches are tinderboxes one match away from turning to ash.

Movement from the corner of my eye snags my attention away from the front of the church. Three guys in suits stop on the corner across the street, mouths open. The guy in the middle hits the other two in the stomach with the back of his hands, and I know they're going to run before they do it.

"I'll be right back," I murmur to Nic.

"What? You can't leave right now," he snaps.

"Relax, you'll be fine. Rome's in the doorway," I call over my shoulder. I slink through the parked cars, and just as I get a view of the guy in the middle, they turn and run.

That was Marco fucking Colombo.

I take off after him, following him around the back of the church. I knew this slimy fuck was involved in something shitty, but I have no idea how deep it goes. I can't let him escape.

I pump my arms, one hand still holding my rifle, and close the distance between us, breathing heavy.

A loud boom wrenches through the air, the church shuddering in protest. I sincerely hope Rome didn't rig the building with C4, because we are nowhere near far enough away for that. He's fucking lucky I'm a roll with the punches kind of guy, because this plan of his is falling apart at the seams.

Someone yelps, and flashing white to my left steals my attention from Colombo. My steps slow before I even contemplate what I'm doing.

Black hair, white veil tangled in the window frame? I'd bet my last dollar this is the Milano bride.

Indecision wars within me. Colombo might be able to help us with the laced coke but the Milano bride might be able to give us info that will end Vito.

"Fuck," I yell into the air as I change directions, running toward the struggling woman in the window.

She yanks her veil off and shoves her hair off her face, and I fucking trip over my own feet. Adrenaline surges inside my veins.

I hit the cracked concrete hard, my rifle clattering to the ground. The small pebbles shred my hands as I stare in shock at the woman halfway out of the window. I push to my feet, dusting my hands off on my jeans.

She's got one leg out and one inside when the building gives a long, low groan. A heartbeat later, it explodes into a fiery mass of bricks and sin. The blast sweeps my feet out from underneath me, and I slam into the concrete once more. My brain rattles inside my skull, and the last image I think I'll ever see is the one of her.

The dark haired bride fleeing her own wedding.

It's the same dark-haired goddess who rode my cock in my brother's office with a knife to my balls two months ago.

A NOTE TO READERS

I hope you're loving the first book in Maeve's duet!

I know I gave you some twists right up until the end, but never fear, book two, The Wild, is available on KU today!!

Read The Wild here!

This story has been on my mind for over a year, and I am so, so excited that you get to read it now. I hope you enjoyed reading it as much as I loved writing it. I know it's not my spiciest story, but I hope you enjoyed all the angsty tension!

And if you feel so compelled, slide into my DMs or my FB group, Penelope's Black Hearts and tell me your favorite scene or character! Those kinds of messages are like fuel to my little author heart. Plus, I love seeing people's favorites in the harem!

As always, my DMs are always open if you need to slide in there and chat—or proverbially throw your kindle at me! ;)

I would be honored if you had the time to leave a brief review of this book! Reviews are the lifeblood of a book, and I would appreciate it so much.

xoxo

—pen

Stay in the loop!
    Join my newsletter
    Join my Facebook group, Penelope's Black Hearts
    Follow me on Instagram @authorpenelopeblack

ACKNOWLEDGMENTS

Thank you to my readers! Thank you for hanging in there with me on all those cliffs on just about every book I write, sending all of you air hugs for that!

Thank you to my husband who's always the first one to champion me. And I love that you're always shouting, "My wife's a romance author!" with pride to anyone you pass on the street. You're the best, and I love you so much.

To my tiny humans: I love you both more than all the stars in the sky. And you have to wait until you're older to read Mommy's books.

To all the bookstagrammers and bloggers and readers that send me messages and create beautiful edits for my books—I'm still in awe. Thank you so, so much. On my most insecure days, I pull up your edits and kind words and never fails to reignite my spark.

To my wonderful family who's encouraged and supported me —thank you, thank you! And thank you to each and every one of you who read my books.

To my gals Erica + Jen! I'm so grateful to have you both on my team. Thank you for all your help and kindness!

To my beta besties: Tracey, Dorothy, Elaine—I'm so thankful for each of you. Your kindness and support mean the world to me.

To Christine for always being so incredibly kind and helpful.

Thank you to the amazing babes on my ARC team! I'm so grateful to have you in my corner!

To my Songbirds—I'm so lucky to have you all with me on this journey! Thank you for being a safe space!

And finally, I want to thank my author besties! I found y'all this past year, and trust me when I say, I'm never letting you go! I'm forever grateful for the ease in which you fix crowns, champion one another, and become a safe haven for me.

ALSO BY PENELOPE BLACK

THE BROTHERHOOD SERIES

Wolf

Rush

Sully

THE FIVE FAMILIES SERIES

Gilded Princess

Twisted Queen

Vicious Reign

Fractured Dynasty

STANDALONES

When It Ends:

A Dark Apocalyptic Romance

THE KING SISTERS WORLD

The Wren

The Wild

Made in the USA
Coppell, TX
03 October 2023

22329946R00222